Index

5

KAZUMA KAMACHI

ILLUSTRATION BY
KIYOTAKA HAIMURA

"Eh? What on earth—
wait, what the hell?"

Academy City's strongest esper **Accelerator**

"Um, err,
were you serious?"

Mysterious vagrant girl **Last Order**

"Did you wait for meee? Are you even listening to me?! Don't ignore me, damn it!"

Academy City Tokiwadai Middle School student **Mikoto Misaka**

"I can't take Mikoto Misaka away when I know she'll cry. If she's not happy, then there wouldn't be any point."

Tokiwadai Middle School board chairman's grandson **Mitsuki Unabara**

"You're probably scared to die alone. I'd be honored if you chose me to go with you."

Level Six Shift experiment scientist **Kikyou Yoshikawa**

"Kindness really doesn't suit you."

Level Six Shift scientist **Ao Amai**

"What the hell
are you thinking?"

Academy City High School
student **Touma Kamijou**

"I'm finishing this quickly. I haven't the time to fool around with children."

Sorcerer **Ouma Yamisaka**

"…Touma!"

Nun managing the Index of Prohibited Books **Index**

contents

PROLOGUE   *THE NIGHT IT BEGAN*   Good_Bye_Yesterday   *1*

CHAPTER 1   *A CERTAIN SCIENTIFIC ACCELERATOR*   Last_Order   *9*

CHAPTER 2   *A CERTAIN UNSOPHISTICATED RAILGUN*   Doubt_Lovers   *47*

CHAPTER 3   *A CERTAIN MISAKA'S LAST ORDER*   Tender_or_Sugary   *105*

CHAPTER 4   *A CERTAIN FREELOADING INDEX*   Arrow_Made_of_AZUSA   *171*

EPILOGUE   *THE NIGHT IT ENDED*   Welcome_to_Tomorrow   *215*

VOLUME 5

KAZUMA KAMACHI

ILLUSTRATION BY: KIYOTAKA HAIMURA

NEW YORK

A CERTAIN MAGICAL INDEX, Volume 5
KAZUMA KAMACHI

Translation by Andrew Prowse

TOARU MAJYUTSU NO INDEX
©KAZUMA KAMACHI 2005
All rights reserved.
Edited by ASCII MEDIA WORKS
First published in Japan in 2005 by KADOKAWA CORPORATION, Tokyo.
English translation rights arranged with KADOKAWA CORPORATION, Tokyo,
through Tuttle-Mori Agency, Inc., Tokyo.

English translation © 2015 Hachette Book Group, Inc.

Yen On
Hachette Book Group ·
1290 Avenue of the Americas
New York, NY 10104

www.hachettebookgroup.com
www.yenpress.com

Yen On is an imprint of Hachette Book Group, Inc.
The Yen On name and logo are trademarks of Hachette Book Group, Inc.

First Yen On edition: November 2015

ISBN: 978-0-316-34059-5

10 9 8 7 6 5 4 3 2 1

RRD-C

Printed in the United States of America

PROLOGUE

The Night It Began

Good_Bye_Yesterday.

1 (Aug31_AM00:00)

He had a nosebleed.

It was the middle of the night, and Touma was rolled up in his emptied-out, wiped-down bathtub, holding his nose. The bleeding was probably because he ate too many of the peanuts in that mixed snack bag earlier. He'd been fiddling with his cell phone, but he decided that it was in its best interest to evacuate it to the edge of the tub.

This bathroom was Kamijou's bedroom. He lived in a student dormitory, but one other person—a girl calling herself Index—was living with him.

Being a healthy high school student, this caused him no end to his worries. He'd been locking himself in the bathroom until dawn broke every night so that he wouldn't commit any blunders involving the entirely defenseless girl staying there.

(Incidentally, he didn't know why he was living with her. He was an amnesiac. One day he'd woken up, and there she was, already beside him.)

Normally the girl would be the one to use a locking door, but Index wasn't any girl. She would just get up, still half-asleep, then unlock the door and go to where he was anyway. There wouldn't be a point in doing things that way.

Urgh, where're the tissues?

His fingers still gripping his nose, Kamijou unlocked the bathroom door. The lights were all out, and Index had probably fallen asleep by now. Only the dim moonlight allowed him to discern the faint outlines of objects.

He thought briefly that he could hear people fighting somewhere far away—likely outside the dorm—but he couldn't make it out from where he was. His attention was directed out the window only for a moment, and then he reentered his room.

It was a disaster. Unfinished magazines and manga were scattered all about the floor. His books were all stuffed into his bookcase out of order. A handful of video game consoles were all attached to his television with another handful of extension cables. An unfinished plastic bottle of juice lay on its side, enshrined on his laptop on the table.

My bed is by the window, so the tissue box should be on the floor nearby, he recalled in sequence, making his way across the dark room. When he reached the bed, his foot came down on something and squashed it. It felt suspiciously like a paper box. He picked it up; upon closer inspection, it was, indeed, the now-flattened tissue box.

"...Rotten luck to the twentieth power. I guess if they still work... right?"

He hesitated for a moment at the thought of stuffing his nose with something he'd stepped on, but it wasn't like he had any other ones. He sighed, pulled one out of the box, balled it up, and stuck it in.

All of a sudden, a light shone in through the window.

Only about two meters separated Kamijou's dorm building from the one next door. When the light came on in the room right across the way, it would flood into his room.

The other room's curtains were drawn, but it only blocked so much.

The artificial glow blanketed his whole room in a weak light. Objects he could only see the contours of before now took on a myriad of colors and textures in the darkness.

Urgh. The brightness startled him for a moment.

Then came the sound of soft snoring.

Following it led his eyes to the girl sleeping on his bed.

She had long silver hair and pale skin and was fourteen or fifteen years old. She was short and light, but her body temperature might have been warmer than that of the average person. An ever-so-slight sweet scent wafted from her, even though she never wore any perfume—it was one of her unique traits.

The girl asleep in a single rumpled button-down shirt was named Index.

Her blanket had been knocked off the bed; it didn't look like she took well to the heat. She was flopped on her side with her arms and legs curled up, making her resemble a baby in a mother's womb.

The bed wasn't that wide, and yet for some reason, she slept at the edge of it.

It left an odd sort of space—the kind one would think had been prepared for another person.

Urgh...I'm no barbarian. I know I shouldn't even ask who that "other person" is.

Kamijou's face flushed a bit in the dim light of the room, but he shook his head. He got the feeling that her consecutive displays of defenselessness were because she trusted him—not quite because she liked him. It felt more like she was just being honest as a small child might. He didn't sense anything adult about it.

Besides, her trust wasn't in the person here right now.

Touma Kamijou was an amnesiac, and Index didn't know that. In other words, the old Touma Kamijou was the one she placed her confidence in, not this one.

So he wouldn't let himself misunderstand anything—not her defenseless slumber, not her attempt to use the bed with him, not the little movements of her lips every time he heard her quiet snores, not the rise and fall of her petite chest with her long breaths, not the white color of the thighs poking dangerously out of her shirt...

...Well, hmm...what I mean is, well, you know. Right.

Kamijou tightened up as he began to break out in a questionable sweat. Then, Index's breathing ceased to be consistent. She stirred restlessly on the bed, then began to breathe consciously. Finally, she opened her closed eyelids wide and groaned.

."...Touma?" she addressed him, rubbing hard at her eyes.

"Oh, sorry. Did I wake you up?"

"No, it's kinda bright, so I might have woken up on my own." She grunted. "The neighbors have their lights on, don't they? Goodness, and at a time like this! Have they no decenc—" She broke off mid-sentence.

I wonder what's wrong? Kamijou thought as, for some reason, Index began to look over various parts of her body and check her rumpled shirt. When she was finished, she hugged her own shoulders and glared up at him with the most reproachful eyes he'd ever seen.

"Umm, Touma. Just making sure...What are you trying to do here exactly?"

"What am I...? Hey, I just had a nosebleed—"

He was the one to break off this time as the situation hit him like a ton of bricks.

The sleeping Index, her single piece of clothing, her thighs poking boldly from it—and he was basically staring right at her face. Depending on how one looked at it, he was practically hanging over her. And he happened to have a tissue in his nose. And that meant he had a nosebleed.

Question one: If you were the girl who'd just woken up in bed, how would this look?

An unnatural sweat burst out on Kamijou's palms. He got an intensely bad feeling about the situation, and as if to lend support to his premonition, Index's eyes were rapidly shifting into all-out rage mode. Yes—he mustn't let himself misunderstand anything. Her unguarded appearance was out of trust toward him, but not because she would just allow him to do anything. Slipping into someone's futon while they're half-asleep and letting someone in are two totally different things.

"Hey, whoa, wait a minute now, Miss Index, don't get me wrong, noses don't only bleed because people get excited, I mean, this isn't some cliché manga or anything, and seriously, it would never happen anyway, it's only symbolic, a metaphor, get it—"

"Touma?" She cut him off flatly.

He couldn't tell from her expression if she was mad, or about to cry, or what—it was a supremely dangerous face she was making. She asked him, "Did you really feel nothing when you looked at me while sleeping? Can you swear it with God as our witness?"

She spoke to him with such straightforward, direct eyes that he was taken aback.

He grunted and shuffled in place.

The truth—the real, actual truth—was that when he saw her asleep, he did shake a bit. At the very least, he thought her face was cute, and when he really tried, he thought he could remember gulping to himself at the sight of her pale white thighs.

Obviously, he couldn't confess any of this to her. She was a bomb on the verge of exploding.

She had a certain vice, this girl, and it involved biting. On a good day she would just playfully nibble on his upper arm, and on a bad one, she'd go straight for his head. He'd never seen her doing any of this to anyone but him, of course, but this habit had him at a loss. A handful of his clothes had already begun to wear out, and he was a little young to be worrying seriously about skin damage.

"So do you swear?" Index asked again in confirmation.

Kamijou, who was ethically against biting habits, put on a facade of composure and retorted, "Hah! Don't be such a prude. Yeah, I saw you, but I felt nothing—"

He hadn't even finished the thought before Index had kicked him over and started chomping down on his head. If this were a fighting game, she would have just used all three gauges.

She demanded, "Nothing? What do you mean nothing?! I am a girl, you know, so it wouldn't shock me if you did feel that way!!"

Her teary eyes were filled with rage. It hurt more than necessary because she was speaking while biting him.

"Oh, you meant that? I misunderstood you! I'm sorry, Miss Index, the truth is that I, the lowly Touma Kamijou, did feel my heart skip a beat when I looked at you sleeping!"

"You can't just take it back at this point!"

"Hey, wait, so you're gonna bite me no matter what I choose?! Damn, not even that Railgun, Mikoto, gets this violent!"

One of Index's eyebrows twitched.

"…Touma, who is this Railgun Mikoto?"

"Ah…" His bad feeling swelled to unprecedented proportions. "Well, you know, she's related to Izanagi-no-Mikoto. The Japanese god who created all the islands."

"You're lying! You're definitely lying! I don't know what in the world a Railgun is, but the word clearly isn't Japanese!"

"No, actually, I have this faint recollection of who Izanagi is. Come on, there can be a Railgun-firing legend in Japanese mythology if we want—ow, oww!"

Kamijou desired nothing more than to be free of this berserk girl's straddle as soon as possible. Unfortunately, though, she had managed to pinpoint his center of gravity. The power sleeping in his right hand, the Imagine Breaker, could cancel out any abnormal power just by touching it, but in this situation, he was a totally useless Level Zero. His neck was the only thing that he could still move. When he flapped it around, the tissue stuck in his nose tumbled out.

Drip. The red fluid came out of his nose.

Index, after all this time, regained her calm at the sight of his blood. Her eyebrows came up with worry.

"T-Touma, that's a really bad nosebleed. How did that happen?"

"Huh? Oh, well, I think I just ate too many peanuts in that snack mix."

"…So I lost to a bag of peanuts, huh…?"

The silver-haired, green-eyed sister dropped her head sullenly, still on top of him. Now that he was more composed, he realized that a girl being on top of a man like this while wearing a single button-down shirt wasn't anywhere near what one could call a common occurrence. There was actually a strangely soft sensation around Kamijou's stomach, but it seemed like she was too downtrodden to notice anything.

She groaned. "I can't believe Touma's the sort of person who gets turned on by peanuts enough to make his nose start bleeding. But it's okay—I'll accept you anyway and prove that I've grown up that much more!"

"You know, it's almost funny how much you've managed to twist the conversation." He sighed. "Anyway, I'd like to stop this bleeding, so get out of the way. Or just give me a new tissue. It would be kinda gross to stuff a used, wet one into my nose again."

"Tissues, tissues...Wait, Touma, where are they?"

Index, still straddling him, bobbed her head to glance around, but she must have overlooked the box—it should have been right there. She tilted her head skeptically. Then, as if struck by lightning, she burst out, "Touma, Touma! There's some paper over here if you need it."

"Don't be dumb. If I stuck a piece of gritty printer paper in my nose it would totally wreck the mucous membrane. Man, just move it, Index. I'll get one myself—"

Suddenly, his mouth stopped working in the middle of his declaration.

He stared dumbfounded at the letters written on the scrap of paper Index was holding out to him.

"Uh, what? Hey, wait up, what does this say...?"

"Huh? Umm...it says 'Summer Vacation Homework: Math Problems.' Touma, I know there are some illiterate people in this country, but I didn't think you were one of them."

Kamijou's thoughts came to a complete halt.

That's right—his homework. His summer assignments. He'd spent his break in such a dramatic, fantastic, acrobatic way, but now that she mentioned it, none of those times involved the most binding shackles of all: his...summer......homework.

Still beneath Index, he twisted his head to look sideways at the clock and calendar. He then confirmed the time and date.

It was August 31, twelve fifteen AM.

There were approximately twenty-four hours remaining until the end of summer vacation.

"*...Heh-heh-heh. You thought I'd say what rotten luck, didn't you? But you know, when someone is having really, really bad luck, they don't even have time to do that. Heh-heh, heh-heh-heh-heh-heh.*"

"Touma, why'd you change your voice like that? And who are you explaining this to?"

CHAPTER 1

A Certain Scientific Accelerator

Last_Order.

1 (Aug.31_AM00:00)

——It was the middle of the night, and the sounds of shrieks, screams, and things breaking pierced the air.

It was a straight, narrow area, fenced in on both sides by concrete. Both were probably student dormitories. About seven enraged young men were there, and casting one's gaze lower would reveal three more lying on the ground, floating in pools of blood.

The seven were holding such weapons as jackknives, truncheons, and tear sprays. They were all powerful, to be sure, but the men didn't appear to be familiar with their usage. They looked more like brand-new purchases, just taken out of their plastic packaging. Nevertheless, any one of them could be used by a killer, and in reality, the novices' ignorance of the force of their own weapons presented its own sort of danger.

They surrounded a single person.

Their eyes were all bloodshot.

And yet the one person they surrounded didn't move.

In fact, he wasn't even thinking about the seven armed men. He stared up at the night sky, narrowly cropped by the tops of the buildings, seeming deep in thought. A store-branded plastic bag dangled from his hands—he might have been just returning from a trip to the convenience store. Its contents appeared to be cans of coffee. There were more than ten of them bulging from the bag.

Anyone who looked at him would see nothing but white.

And they would know. Oh, they would know that he was the strongest Level Five in Academy City.

He had a sudden thought. *What did this battle with these Level Zeroes mean? Did it mean anything?*

This person known as Accelerator pondered this, bored.

"Graah!" came a yell from behind him.

One of the encircling ruffians dove at his back with a knife in his hand. Accelerator didn't turn around, though. He wasn't even paying attention. The ruffian lunged at him, putting all of his body weight into the tip of his knife, about to stab his defenseless, even delicate-looking back.

The experiment that used twenty thousand of the Sisters to evolve him into a Level Six, an Absolute—it had ended.

Had his defeat changed the world? If it did, then how?

There was the *criiick* of bones breaking behind Accelerator.

Of course, they didn't belong to him. They belonged to the scoundrel who tried to stab him in the back with his knife. His wrist was broken. The force vector of all his body weight behind the knife had been reflected…and his slender wrist couldn't endure the strength of the rest of his body.

"Gyaaahhh!!" came a new shout from the thug.

He fell to the filthy ground and rolled around, holding his wrist. It was a comical sight.

It seemed that after the experiment…he was no longer Academy City's strongest.

Nothing had even changed, though—he was still one of only seven

Level Fives in the city, and he could still freely alter the vector of any force that came into contact with his skin, whether kinetic, heat, or electric.

Spurred on by their comrade's mad shrieking, the remaining six young men came at him all at once.

But how many of them believed that they could win, in the true meaning of the word?

Their eyes were certainly bloodshot.

But that also seemed like the result of hyper-anxiety, or unease, or terror, or exhaustion.

A great number of people had begun to attack him regularly at all hours of the day after that battle.

Unfortunately for them, they really did think that his wall—the title of Academy City's strongest—had been torn down.

They shouted and brandished their blades and nightsticks, but Accelerator couldn't have cared less. He left his hands hanging lazily at his sides. They would defeat themselves without him doing a thing. The vectors of their attacks would all be reflected and concentrated back into their complex and frail wristbones.

But every single one of those people, without exception, immediately knew as soon as their first shot had failed.

The strongest esper in Academy City was indeed alive and well.

He heard the biting crunches of thug bones breaking, one after the other. They screamed and they writhed, and yet Accelerator simply ignored them. Finally, someone attempted to use an ability against him—either they had reached the conclusion that physical attacks were too dangerous, or they had been displaying what incredibly little goodwill they had from the start.

And yet the attempts wouldn't stop.

It didn't matter how many he crushed, or how many he defeated, or how much he proved himself. Not one of the idiots could seem to tear off the mark of a Level Zero.

Accelerator couldn't tell what sort of esper this particular one was. He didn't quite catch what kind of power was coming at him. He just reflected it. The esper's eyes ballooned as his confidently loosed attack whipped back toward him and knocked him to the ground. Seeing as he was still alive, he couldn't have been any more than a Level Two, an Adept.

Now, then, he mused.
The battle with the Sisters and Railgun was over. Could he say that he had changed for it?
Had he grown weaker? Had he grown stronger?
Or was it that nameless Level Zero? Had he grown stronger? Had he grown weaker?

"Huh?"
Suddenly, he realized that the clamor around him had quieted. At last, he tore his gaze from his view of the sky, demarcated by the ground, and glanced around. The punks who had surrounded him of their own accord were now sprawled out on the filthy ground of their own accord. Perhaps a relaxed expression like *sprawled out* wasn't enough to convey how much blood was in the scene, but at least nobody was dead.

They had exchanged blows with none other than Accelerator fair and square—it was a miraculous outcome considering they were still all breathing.

As he turned around, he saw ten of the rats knocked out on the pavement, but he hadn't done anything. This hadn't even felt like a battle to him. For him, he just happened on his way home with some coffee after a late-night run to the store.

He didn't consider finishing any of them off, either. Anyone who could be killed today could be killed tomorrow, and anyone he

could kill tomorrow he could kill at any time next year. Letting it get to him would be stupid. He could get as excited as he wanted, but he had no goal, unlike the experiment did. And an eternity without a goal was equivalent to drowning.

"Ah, somethin's wrong. It ain't like me to let idiots like these snap at me and get away with it. Something's definitely changed. But what? What's up? Whaaat iiisss thiiisss?"

Accelerator cocked his head to the side, perplexed. He had discovered firsthand a kind of battle where it was possible for him to lose. Was he now caught up in the glorified idea that he couldn't be satisfied with anything less than an overwhelming, one-sided victory in such a fight? After all, if a person were to look back on a time where they had been beaten to a pulp and smile about it, then that person would surely be a masochist.

He groaned and folded his arms. The coffee inside the bag clattered around. There were more than ten cans, all of the same brand. He was trapped in this cycle—whenever he found a brand he took a fancy to, he'd drink it for days on end. Then, within a week, he'd just get bored of it and go looking for a new kind.

Man, what the hell? I don't feel like doin' shit.

He gazed up into the night sky once more, his view of it enclosed by the tops of the buildings, far up high—and then he heard what seemed like a girl's voice.

"Nothing? What do——nothing?! You know——a girl———— shock me——feel that way!!"

It was midnight, so her voice was oddly shrill.

Just some arguing couple, he dismissed, reflecting on the meaningless voice floating down toward him—more precisely, all air vibrations. If he had been a few seconds later in doing so, he would have heard the cry of a certain Level Zero he knew quite well.

He could reflect things unconsciously and doing this only required some simple measurements. First, he would calculate the minimum amount of force that he needed (gravity, pressure, radiation, oxygen, heat, voices), then he would formulate an equation that would let him reflect all other forces aside from that. If he did actually reflect everything, gravity would lose its grip on him and he'd soar out of the atmosphere.

Accelerator again added a reflection setting for the sounds descending upon him, then crossed through the alley and exited onto the street. He walked along, looking up at the sky for no reason in particular. He wasn't looking ahead of himself, but then, he really didn't need to pay attention to obstacles anyway.

His reflection kept his body impervious to pain.

But that's why he had realized it so late:

Somebody had gotten right up behind him and was moving their throat hoarsely, desperately trying to shout something.

"Eh?" He turned his head to look over his shoulder, still walking.

The person he saw was…rather odd. First of all, they were dressed strangely. All he saw was a dirty blanket draped over their head. The makeshift mantle, made of a sky-blue cloth that almost looked like part of a secret-society uniform or cultist garb, entirely covered their face and body. He couldn't even tell their gender, nor what type of clothing they were wearing underneath it.

On top of that, they were extremely short. Accelerator wasn't very big himself, of course, but they only stood up to his stomach. *Must be a little kid. Like ten years old maybe.* They were clearly too young for the average homeless person. Though given that 80 percent of the population of Academy City was comprised of students, there were still a few similar instances he could think of.

The little monster blanket was shouting something at him.

"———!!……, ————……………?!"

Unfortunately, it didn't reach his ears, since he was reflecting the sound. He looked up, relaxed, and stopped the reflection just for a moment as a test.

What he heard was a piercing, yet somehow plain and clear, female voice.

"———and, well, how should I put this—the fact that you're so utterly and completely ignoring me is actually kinda refreshing in a way, and you're walking too slowly to be angry at me or anything, so maybe you're just the world's ultimate airhead, hmm? says Misaka says Misaka, all confused and stuff."

The girl was standing not ten centimeters away from him. If anyone who knew who he was were to witness this, they'd stop at nothing to pry the girl away from him. Or maybe they would just give up, assuming that it was already too late.

He could kill someone just by touching them with one finger. The girl might as well have been peering into the mouth of a yawning lion.

However, the bloody tragedy never came to pass.

She just stood there, looking carefree.

Accelerator grimaced a bit. His ability was that he could change any vector he pleased. That meant that no matter how close she got, as long as she didn't lunge at him, she wouldn't get hurt.

His reflection was a defensive ability—he only directed its fangs at those who meant him harm.

He would never injure someone who bore him no ill will in the first place, at least.

"...What a friggin' joke."

"You keep walking away while muttering under your breath, can't you see me, or are you just treating me like a fairy, hey, Misaka's right here, you know! says Misaka says Misaka fervently, like, appealing to her own existence, and yet you're totally denying it?"

Accelerator cracked the muscles in his neck and continued walking back home. Then, as if the girl had gotten a little flustered at being left behind, she called out, "Hey, I said, Misaka is Misaka is right here—or wait, are you pretending that this isn't happening right now? says Misaka says Misaka, tilting Misaka's head in confusion in a very Misaka-like way...huh? Wait, how many times did I just say Misaka, wonders Misaka wonders Misaka as her thoughts get all muddy and stuff."

"Wait...Misaka?"

His feet came to an abrupt halt. *What's she so happy about, any-*

way? That was all it took for the blanket girl to come jogging up to him. He didn't know for sure, though, since her face wasn't visible.

"Oh, you finally admitted that Misaka exists, yay! cheers Misaka cheers Misaka, delighting in self-praise and stuff. That whole 'I think, therefore I am' sounds like total lies, huh, since you can't really have a self just by yourself, you need someone else there to acknowledge that you exist, I guess, says Misaka says Misaka, like, rejecting the *cogito, ergo sum* philosophy with mistaken knowledge that she's only pretending to know, and stuff."

"Hold on, wait, shut up for a second! Take that damn blanket off your head and show me your face."

"Uh, huh? Um, err, ummm, wow I can't believe you're asking a girl to take off her clothes after just meeting her, that's being a little bit too forward, don't you think, and I mean, there's a line for what you can ask someone to do and what— Hey, excuse me! asks Misaka asks Misaka. Were you serious?"

"…"

"Ack, he went quiet. His eyes say he's serious, they say he's for real, but please, you, don't pull on my blanket! There's no telling what you may find underneath, says Misaka says Misaka, and yet—gyaaahhh…?!"

Her clear and unaffected voice trailed off near the end, but that wasn't going to help, as the blanket on her head was already falling down, down, down to the ground.

——The first thing he saw was her face.

It was the exact same face as all those mass-produced electric users, the Sisters, also known as Radio Noise, who he knew well. While the Sisters' age was set to fourteen, however, this girl didn't look more than ten or so. Her eyes widened, surprised at something. That motion wasn't very much like the Sisters, either.

——The next things he saw were her shoulders.

Perhaps she was wearing clothes that exposed her skin. Her build was certainly that of a ten-year-old, her shoulders looking like they would snap if someone were to even touch one, betraying her delicacy.

————In addition, he saw her bare chest.

————On top of that, he saw her naked waist.

————The last things he saw were her unclothed feet.

"Eh? What on earth— Wait, what the hell?"

Accelerator's face drew back, his hand still on the blanket. If anyone who understood his personality had seen this, then (aside from getting a chill of fear) they would have started laughing uncontrollably.

The conclusion that needs to be stated here is that she wasn't wearing anything under the blanket.

She stood there vacantly, as if forgetting to react, her mind not having caught up to the situation yet.

When all was said and done, there was a completely and utterly naked girl in front of him.

2 (Aug.31_AM00:25)

The girl started demanding that he "give back give back the blanket the blanket" with tears in her eyes, so he hurled the filthy rag back onto her head. She took it, then squirmed around, wrapping herself in it again. Then she launched into an explanation he didn't really ask for.

"Misaka's serial number is 20001. I was created as part of the final lot of Sisters, says Misaka says Misaka, beginning her explanation and stuff. My code name was left as Last Order, for being the last one, and I was supposed to be used in the experiment, says Misaka says Misaka, like, complaining about it and stuff."

"Uh-huh," muttered Accelerator inattentively as he trudged down the road.

Last Order frantically caught back up to him and went on. "By the way, hey wait a minute, as you know, the experiment ended prematurely, so Misaka's body hasn't been adjusted all the way, says Misaka says Misaka, giving even more explanation. I got kicked out

of my incubator when I wasn't finished yet, so I'm all compact and stuff, says Misaka says Misaka...Are you listening to me?"

"And whaddaya want me to do about it?" Accelerator asked, still walking.

He'd heard that all of the remaining Sisters had been entrusted to different organizations after the experiment ended. There were almost ten thousand of them, though, so it was more than possible they couldn't get a handle on all of them. Maybe that's why one slipped away from their oversight and started wandering around the city without a guardian.

The seemingly ten-year-old homeless girl pulled on her blanket. "You were the whole point of the experiment, so you can probably get in touch with the scientists, right? If you can, it would be great if you did, wonders Misaka wonders Misaka. Misaka's body and mind right now are in an incomplete, unstable state, so if you tell them you want it, they can put me back in the incubator and get me completed, suggests Misaka suggests Misaka, like, putting her hands together and tilting her head in a cute way."

"Ask someone else."

"Wowie! An immediate answer—a swift and utter denial! cries Misaka cries Misaka in despair. But I don't have anywhere else to go, so Misaka won't Misaka won't give up!"

"..." *What the hell is with her?* Accelerator sighed.

He was a murderer. He'd already killed more than ten thousand of the Sisters, those somatic cell clones of Mikoto Misaka. All of them shared memories via a brain-wave connection, so Last Order should be well aware of that fact, too.

Or could the incomplete Last Order not possess the functionality to hook up to that connection yet? Her personality data, which should have been input from a Testament, did seem different than the normal Sisters' personality, too. Although in this case, it was a little blurry as to which one was more "incomplete"...

He was fed up with how familiar this girl was getting with him, but when he thought about it, he figured that her lack of a danger sense was pretty much the same as all the other ones.

3 (Aug.31_AM00:51)

They veered off the main road onto a side one, then passed through a handful of narrow streets. A five-story dormitory building rose up to meet them. All the buildings around it stood at a proud ten stories tall, so it seemed enveloped in a pensive, humid darkness. It was as if melancholy itself permeated the concrete walls to their very core.

"Whoa! You sure do live in an amazing place, says Misaka says Misaka, all impressed and stuff."

"The hell? Was that sarcasm?"

"It's a wonderful thing to have your own room and a space all to yourself, says Misaka says Misaka, her eyes all glittery as she explains."

Last Order was still trying to patter up behind him in her bare feet. She harbored no ill will. Accelerator ignored her, entered the building, and started up the unfaced concrete staircase.

He could still hear the sound of her blanket dragging across the floor behind him.

He turned around as he climbed the stairs and spoke up. "Hey, how long are ya gonna follow—"

"Thanks for letting me stay with you, says Misaka says Misaka, striking preemptively."

"..."

"Thanks for letting me eat with you, says Misaka says Misaka, hoping for three meals a day, naps, and snacks."

I think she wants me to make sure she's got shelter until I can get in touch with the researchers in charge of that experiment. What a pain, sighed Accelerator, shaking his head. "Listen here. Either you walk back down these stairs or you go flying off the railing, got it?"

"Wowzers! Looks like I was wrong to think you'd gotten any friendlier, says Misaka says Misaka, knocking herself in the head. But if we split up here, I don't think I'll be able to get in touch with anyone. More importantly, it's way too dangerous for a girl to be living on the streets, so I can't back down, says Misaka says Misaka, like, clearly stating her intentions."

Accelerator reached the third-floor hallway, and there Last Order passed by him. He watched as she spun around to face him. She spread her arms, evidently in an attempt to block his passage.

"Where's your room? asks Misaka asks Misaka."

"I'm ignoring you."

"What number is it? C'mon, you can tell me, what number? insists Misaka insists Misaka, like, trying repeatedly to deliver a message to you, who has no communication ability whatsoever."

"Do I need to kill you for you to shut up or what?" Accelerator retorted needlessly. Last Order, however, didn't respond. She wasn't at a loss as to what she should say—it was more like she was creating a distance between them with her quietude. An odd, heavy silence fell upon them.

At last, she spoke—quietly and slowly, while narrowing her eyes.

"Activating EM sonar. Oscillating at a frequency of 3,200 megahertz. A group of five people who have acquired suspicious items has been confirmed to be present on this floor, reports Misaka reports Misaka. That could be your room, adds Misaka adds Misaka."

"…What?" Accelerator thinned his eyes slightly. He'd been under constant attack by thugs, as could be seen by the happening in that alley. Getting ambushed here wasn't out of the question.

"C'mon, let's go, tell me, okay? What number's your room? presses Misaka presses Misaka."

Hmm. He thought for a moment. "Room 304."

"Oh, I think that's right here, says Misaka says Misaka, pointing out the door. Let's see…thank you for letting me in! says Misaka says Misaka, deeming politeness necessary."

Last Order approached the door to room 304 as she spoke. For someone going on about intruders, she sure didn't have much caution.

She grabbed the doorknob and opened it. She must have used her ability in order to undo the electric lock. Satisfied at her own skill, she flung the door open and went in. Accelerator watched out of the corner of his eye, then put her out of his mind and began walking briskly toward his actual room.

Directly after, from out of the opened door behind him, he heard both the yell of the room's occupant—who was apparently watching late-night television—and Last Order's shouted, yet somehow quiet, apology.

Then, he heard the door fly back closed with a *bang* and her frantic footsteps came toward him.

"That was a completely different person's room, you know, says Misaka says Misaka, kind of indignant. I didn't know you had this kind of mean streak, protests Misaka protests Misaka, her eyes welling up with tears, but you're not listening to me anyway."

"Put a sock in it, will you? Tryin' some stupid bluff on me like that…And what are you talking about anyway? Three thousand two hundred megahertz is microwaves!"

"Urk. Your point is moot because microwaves are used in radar and super-multiplexing communication anyway, contends Misaka contends Misaka stubbornly."

She didn't deny that she'd lied about detecting people. Accelerator clicked his tongue, uninterested. "Besides, 304 can't be my room. All you had to do was look at the nameplate on the door, idiot."

"I don't know your real name, argues Misaka argues Misaka."

"I don't know yours, either."

"It's a miracle! Houston, we have conversation! says Misaka says Misaka, not letting this chance out of her grasp. O-okay, so this time for real: Which room is yours? asks Misaka asks Misaka."

"Three-oh-seven."

"Got it!" she replied in a somewhat quiet voice. Ten seconds after she threw open the door, she realized it was someone else's room again and walked back after Accelerator, positively crestfallen.

"Why are you being so mean to meee? asks Misaka asks Misaka, her shoulders drooping. Misaka doesn't mind even if your room is a mess, offers Misaka offers Misaka."

Accelerator settled on ignoring her outright and came to his room, 311. There he stopped.

Something was…a little odd.

"Hey, wait, what the hell?"

First off, there wasn't a door.

And beyond the gaping entrance, there was nothing that could properly be called furniture or belongings.

Only a handful of muddy footprints remained on the floor—everything else was destroyed. The wallpaper and the floorboards were both torn up, his shoe box was broken, there were traces of a fire in the kitchen, the television was in two pieces, his bed was flipped over, and the cotton that was once in the sofa was now all over the place.

He really had been raided while he was out at the store. The sad state of his room was doubtlessly the raiders' revenge after finding him absent.

"Whoa, it really is a big mess in here, says Misaka says Misaka, at a loss for words and stuff."

The corners of Accelerator's lips turned down at the understatement. "Looks like your bluff was actually on the spot."

For a moment, for the slightest split second, he caught his breath at the sight.

This, in the end, was his essence.

His power could thoroughly defend himself, but it couldn't protect a single thing besides.

"…What a damn pain."

Accelerator stepped into his apartment without bothering to take his shoes off. He heard a *crack* as his heel crushed something plastic. No particularly strong feelings came to him as he looked at his utterly devastated room. He flopped down on the cottonless sofa, ready to sleep.

"Um, err, ummmm. Shouldn't you report this to Anti-Skills or Judgment or something? says Misaka says Misaka, poking her nose in someone else's business and stuff."

"What good would that do?" sighed Accelerator. They might catch the criminals responsible, but it wouldn't stop the constant attacks he was going through. Tomorrow a different person would come to strike and a different one still the day after that.

"So, what're you doin'? If you wanna stay over, then that's your business, but you'll end up the same as that smashed TV. Seriously, you might be better off laying in the middle of a slum to go to sleep," he told her, offering a dispassionate evaluation of his own living space. "And there's all sorts of glass and whatnot all over the floor. Kinda makes walking barefoot a challenge in itself, eh? Hah. You'd be safer sleeping out in the hallway than you would in here."

"Hmmm. Misaka thinks she'll still stay in here anyway, Misaka requests Misaka requests."

"Eh? What for?"

"Because I want to be with someone, answers Misaka answers Misaka immediately."

"..." Accelerator fell silent, still on the couch.

He stared dumbly at the ceiling.

"Okay, then if you don't mind...Oh, it must be a miracle! That table looks safe, says Misaka says Misaka, pointing it out. Misaka will try to sleep on the table, then...Wait, I'm warning you, don't you dare do anything to me while I'm asleep, says Misaka says Misa—"

"Go to sleep."

"Wowie! I've made sure it's safe, but it's a little bit unbearable, says Misaka says Misaka."

He shut his eyes. From the darkness he heard Last Order squirming around. He also heard her coughing repeatedly, like she wasn't used to dusty places.

He felt his entire body's pent-up exhaustion wash over him.

He thought about why and finally came up with one answer.

What the hell...

Embraced in his gentle, dark slumber, like a small, sleepy child, he may have thought,...*Now that I think of it, how long's it been since I talked to someone who didn't have it in for me?*

4 (Aug.31_AM11:35)

The strength of the sunlight shining into the room woke Accelerator.

This dorm was surrounded by many taller buildings in the neighborhood, so light only got into the room during a certain time of day. He hazily realized that morning was nearly past—and then noticed the person hovering over him, looking at him.

It was Last Order, brimming with curiosity.

"Wow! Ya really have a meek face when you're sleeping, don'cha, says Misaka says Misaka, trying out a fake Kyoto accent. Yes! You've got that mean old look on your face the rest of the time. Your sleepy face is totally different, and that's okay! says Misaka says Misa—"

"…" Accelerator, on the other hand, his face looking none too pretty, was completely reflecting Last Order's entire voice.

"—ike, smil**ing and stuff whoaah?! Misaka's voice Misaka's voice got really loud?!!**"

Last Order nearly toppled over. Her own voice struck her like a megaphone right next to her ear. She shook her tiny head back and forth, but then, without hesitation, addressed Accelerator again.

"…"

Slowly and without haste, Accelerator rubbed under his eyes. It wasn't so much that he was moving slowly than it was that he didn't have any energy. He stared blankly at Last Order, who was peering at his face.

"Blanket…"

"Huh? Are you still half-asleep? asks Misaka asks Misa—gyaah?! Stop, wait, don't pull on Misaka's blanket, it's my treasure, I'm telling you…!"

"…So tired."

Blanket in hand, he rolled himself up in it like a moth in a cocoon and gave himself over to sleep again.

5 (Aug.31_PM02:05)

Accelerator awoke to an empty stomach.

He looked at the clock—just barely hanging on the wall—and saw that it was past two o'clock, meaning it was already past lunchtime. As he figured he should probably get up and eat something, Accelerator suddenly noticed the dirty blanket covering him.

"What, what's this…wait, why are you still here?…You look kinda grumpy. Why d'you have a tablecloth hanging from you?"

"…I yelled at you and I hit you and you didn't respond at all and you're really sleepy, could that be your weak point? says Misaka says Misaka, all stricken by her own powerlessness and stuff."

Her body mostly wrapped in a torn tablecloth, she dropped to the floor, as if she'd used all her savings on lottery tickets and lost every single one of them.

His reflection worked while he slept, too. And to be even more undisturbed, he made it impossible to be woken up from outside stimulation by reflecting sounds as well.

She sniffled. "Give back give back my blanket my blanket, demands Misaka demands Misaka. That blue blanket has been with me sharing my joys and sorrows all throughout life, so it can't be replaced, says Misaka says Misaka, trying out a bluff to make you cry."

Accelerator didn't really need the filthy rag anymore, so he tossed it on her head. Then he stared toward the kitchen, still slightly dazed.

He never cooked anything. There should have still been some food in reserve in the fridge, but when he looked into the kitchen from his position, he sullenly dropped back onto the sofa again. The fridge was on its side. The food had been flung out of it, and the vinyl packaging was torn and strewn about the floor.

Last Order, after her equipment swap from tablecloth to blanket, seemed to have regained her upbeat mood. "Good morning, even though it's pretty late already, says Misaka says Misaka, like, bowing. I'm hungry so if you would make me some food some food Misaka's happiness level will go up by about thirty points—"

"Go to sleep."

"Holy cow, both your hospitality and calorie intake are perfectly zero, cheers Misaka cheers Misaka. Also, that was not an expression of happiness, but a gesture of surrender, so please take it as such, says Misaka says Misaka, like, giving a polite and succinct explanation. Anyway, it's morning! Morning, morning, morning, morning—"

"...Shit, it's two already?!"

That was enough to open even Accelerator's eyes, terrible at waking up though he may have been. He was, in fact, hungry, but his sleep being disturbed was mostly Last Order's fault. He could have just reflected her voice, but that would be like covering one's eyes when there were bugs flying around their face. It wouldn't feel very good. He decided to throw the brat away somewhere and lifted himself off the sofa. *I'll grab a bite to eat on the way,* he thought, making his way toward the door.

"Huh? That's not the way to the kitchen, Misaka says Misaka says, pointing in the correct direction."

"Why do I gotta make food? Do I look like I cook?"

"Aww, I wanted to see Accelerator making home cooking in an apron for the surprise factor, complains Misaka complains Misaka. Huh? Wait, wait! You didn't even bother with a comeback! You just ignore me by default, don't you? cries Misaka cries Misaka, but you're still ignoring me, huh?!"

Accelerator silently left the apartment. Last Order went after him, mumbling away.

6 (Aug.31_PM02:35)

There was nobody to be found on the streets on August 31.

Given that 80 percent of the residents here were students, most of the population must have been holed up in their rooms finishing their homework. That didn't have anything to do with Accelerator or Last Order, though.

He walked through the near-deserted city, the young girl in tow.

She pulled along her blue blanket and tried to walk up next to the boy of white.

"Is that hair natural? asks Misaka asks Misaka," asked Misaka as they neared a family restaurant chain.

"Eh?"

"Your hair! says Misaka says Misaka. White hair isn't normal, points out Misaka and stuff. And how do you biologically even have red eyes, too? asks Misaka asks Misaka, all confused."

He should have ignored her, but if he did, she would probably start to get noisy again, so he decided to give a noncommittal answer. He'd grab a late lunch, and then it didn't matter to him if he gave her to the researchers or if he left her on the side of the road. Thinking of this as the last time, he was able to put up with the slight annoyance.

"This isn't natural. It's a side effect of my power or somethin'. I don't know. The pigments in your skin and hair and eyes protect your body from UV rays, but I always just reflect all the extra shit anyway, so my body doesn't need color. Somethin' like that."

Unexpectedly, he found himself feeling rather loquacious. He was always arguing needlessly during the experiment too. Maybe he liked to talk more than he thought.

"Wow, that's, like, kinda logical and stuff, says Misaka says Misaka, surprised. It's like, you're Accelerator, so anything goes, says Misaka says Misaka, giving up."

"Why the hell you sayin' you're givin' up? It's just that my power's too strong. My hormones are out of balance or somethin' because there's barely any outside influence, so now I've got this body that you can't even tell if it's a girl's or a guy's."

"Wait, then which are you? says Misaka says Misaka, straight up asking."

"What, can't ya tell by lookin'?" he responded, a bit confused at his own words.

His normal thought processes didn't seem to be aligned properly with this thread of conversation. He, too, lived in a society of humans...but he didn't kill everyone he laid eyes on or anything. Yet the fact that he could make conversation with a mass-produced Sister, of all things, was something that had never happened before.

The conversation he'd had with the one of them during the experiment...

"Yes, Misaka's serial number is 10032, responds Misaka. But would it not be proper to first confirm the password just to be sure you are a participant in the experiment? suggests Misaka.

"I am having difficulty understanding the vague word stuff, *answers Misaka. There are three minutes and twenty seconds remaining before the start of the experiment. Have you completed your preparations? confirms Misaka."*

…That, of course, didn't feel at all like a conversation between two people. It was just an exchange with a machine built to immediately answer any of his questions. From Accelerator's point of view anyway.

"Seriously, after doing this ten thousand times a guy gets bored, so I was just thinkin' we could kill a little time or somethin', but I guess not. You're impossible to talk to, you know that?"

He never thought they were actually talking to each other from the start, and they never actually had a conversation at all.

And yet…

Then did somethin' about me really change? he thought.

If something did change, then what?

What in the world was the reason for it?

And what in the universe had changed?

"Hello? Hello hello hello hello hello, says Misaka says Misaka, making sure you heard her. Are you thinking about something? asks Misaka asks Misaka, looking at your face."

"What? Uh, I was just thinking, are you seriously gonna walk into a store with just a blanket on?"

"…Waah. Are you asking what Misaka will do if she's refused service? asks Misaka asks Misaka, slowly and nervously."

"Go to sleep."

"Yahoo, that's turning into your favorite phrase, says Misaka says Misaka, getting kinda desperate."

Last Order, face completely straight, started waving around her arms. Accelerator looked away from her and into the afternoon sky.

They were making conversation.

Somewhere he couldn't see, something was changing.

7 (Aug.31_PM03:15)

"Welcome! Will it be the two guests, then?"

It ended up that the waitress smiled at the girl in the blanket and allowed her entrance. But her face was a little strained. She must have been a part-timer, so she probably didn't know how to deal with incidents that weren't in the customer service manual.

Accelerator and Last Order took a seat by the window. Eighty percent of Academy City's population was in school, so August 31 seemed like the day everyone stayed inside to finish their remaining homework. If it were actually lunchtime, there would have been many more people here, but it was off-hours at the moment.

As he stared out the window vacantly, he caught sight of a hunched man in white clothing walking down the road.

"Huh?"

When the man noticed his gaze, he scrambled into a parked sports car and left as if he were being chased by a stampede.

"Was that...Ao Amai?" muttered Accelerator.

Last Order made a "Huh?" noise and looked up from her menu.

Ao Amai. A researcher in his twenties, and one of those who pushed ahead with the Level Six shift experiment until the very end. It was planned around the predictive calculations of a supercomputer, but the results of those calculations had been found incorrect, so the entire experiment was frozen semipermanently. The faction that wanted to continue it would have been searching night and day for the bugs in the mountains of data they possessed, but...

"Him?...What the hell is he doing around here...?"

"What do you see what are you thinking what are you saying? asks Misaka asks Misaka."

"Would you be quiet? Don't you remember what you set out to do in the first place?"

"It was to eat lunch, right? replies Misaka replies Misaka instantly. Oh! Wait, is this the plot development where you say I can ask for anything I want, just for today? hopes Misaka hopes Misaka."

He sighed. "No, forget it. I don't care anymore."

What happened to her original objective to contact the scientists? He watched Amai's car disappear down the road as he contemplated that. Last Order didn't notice. She rubbed her eyes and started wobbling left and right.

"Umm. Lately no matter how much I sleep I don't get less tired, says Misaka says Misaka, kinda confused."

"That so."

The waitress came to give them glasses of water. Accelerator ordered something at random off the menu. Suddenly, he noticed Last Order giving him a strange look from across the table.

"Oh! Also, begins Misaka begins Misaka, choosing her words carefully. Well, I guess you can order food and pay like a normal person, huh? says Misaka says Misaka in admiration."

"Eh?"

"Yes. I imagined you as someone who would just kick down the front door, eat all the food, then leap out of the window and calmly run away without paying, answers Misaka answers Misaka frankly, even though she's trembling."

"Oh, right," nodded Accelerator, yawning. "I mean, I could do that, too, but...the experiment is frozen—there's no organization backing it at this point, is there? If I make a show of myself, shit'll probably hit the fan."

"But that's already weird, interrupts Misaka interrupts Misaka. I don't think anyone can stand up to you, whether it's Anti-Skills or Judgment, says Misaka says Misaka, offering her candid opinion. And if we go that far, it's strange that you went along with the scientists in the first place, says Misaka says Misaka, confused."

"I'm telling you..." Accelerator sighed. "It ain't worth thinkin' about. Let's say I caused some trouble here in this shop. Then we just ran away without paying. Who'd come after me first?"

"Umm, I guess the employees and stuff, answers Misaka answers Misaka."

"Yeah. I'd kill them in no time flat. Like, seriously, you wouldn't be able to blink. Then who would come next? The manager? Another blink and down he goes. Anti-Skills next? Judgment? Those ones are actually easier. The stronger their weapons, the more potent my reflection becomes. After that...I mean, if Academy City couldn't rein me in, then the outside would get involved, right? But so what? Police forces, riot squads, the SDF...Not even the military, or special forces, or assassination groups would be able to do anything. Would they start to drop bombs on me? It could all just end in a torrent of nukes.

"But what would that accomplish?" he declared.

If nuclear warheads did start flying around, he'd win the full-scale, international war against him. The only thing left after humanity was destroyed would be life in a cave, like primal humans lived. In order to live with the minimum requirements to be human, he ultimately needed to live within a society.

This was actually only a problem for those who had the power to destroy. He vaguely wondered if a president holding the firing code for nuclear missiles felt the same way.

"Oogh…Do you always talk in such a ridiculous, crazy way? asks Misaka asks Misaka."

"You're one to talk."

"Hmm. The information installed in my mind states that there is a thing called school, says Misaka says Misaka, wondering. How do you mesh with your class with zero communication ability? asks Misaka asks Misaka again."

"Oh, that's not a problem. I don't got any classmates."

"?"

"I'm in a special class. Though I'm not sure if it's good-special or bad-special," said Accelerator casually.

After his powers had been awakened via a Curriculum, he was moved into a special class. He was the only student. He had no classmates. He didn't participate in any athletic meets or culture festivals. He just sat there at his desk, by himself, in a cramped classroom. In a school with two thousand students.

It wasn't like he'd ever felt dissatisfied by it.

But long ago, the scientists had told him it was because he was the strongest Level Five. The class was to have him shift to Level Six. He remembered thinking about what would happen if he was no longer the strongest, if he evolved into something invincible. What would change?

"Are you lonely? asks Misaka asks Misaka."

"Eh?"

"Power comes with isolation, but Misaka probably wouldn't understand that feeling and neither would anyone else, I think, predicts Misaka predicts Misaka. So—"

"I don't even understand what you just asked. What? If I said yes, you gonna come over here and pat me on the head to console me or somethin'?" he said in a low voice. Only a cold silence followed.

No matter what anyone else said, Accelerator was a cold-blooded butcher responsible for the deaths of more than ten thousand. It would be pointless, meaningless, for someone to comfort him with all the dark solitude within him that nobody could understand. And to think—he might have been driven into the experiment in the first place just because he needed a place to vent all that.

"_____"

Was that it?

Is that really the case? He frowned.

Vaguely, he decided that if it was true, then something else was wrong. Yeah, something was certainly strange. But he couldn't figure out what he was so hung up on. Accelerator thought back one more time to the experiment…and then realized what it was.

"Seriously, after doing this ten thousand times a guy gets bored, so I was just thinkin' we could kill a little time or somethin', but I guess not. You're impossible to talk to, you know that?"

That was strange.

If everything really was just him venting, if he had just been killing the Sisters like they were no more than stuffed animals made to be beaten, then why did he even consider talking to them?

The only one acting irregularly during the experiment had been him.

Maybe they didn't make any actual conversation, but that just meant that the Sisters were performing to specifications. They were being practical. They were obeying all the supercomputer's predictions, calculations, plans, and programs for the sake of the experiment.

If he limited his scope to just the experiment, then he was the irregular one—he had broken the rules and talked to one of the Sisters. In actuality, none of the scientists nor the Sisters had tried to talk to him at all.

Then what had spurred him to such irrational actions?

That was the strange part. If he had approached the Sisters just to kill them or blow off stress, then the idea of talking to one should have never even crossed his mind.

People generally talked to other people because they wanted to get along and to make friends with them, right? He felt like that wasn't the case, either. He was the one disparaging, maiming, and killing all the Sisters, after all.

"Ah, she's here she's here finally! says Misaka says Misaka, pointing to the waitress. Yay! Misaka's food came first!"

The waitress placed Last Order's food in front of her. It seemed like Accelerator's would take a little longer.

"Wow, this is the first time I've had a hot meal, like, ever! exclaims Misaka exclaims Misaka. Some really hot steam is coming off the plate and stuff, says Misaka says Misaka, eyeing the food carefully."

A few days had passed since the experiment was suspended. If she had been chased out of the lab right after that, then she'd have been wandering around for…

"…What a damn pain," he muttered under his breath.

He turned his gaze from the girl back to the window. He waited a moment but didn't hear her start eating. Thinking it odd, he looked back to see her politely sitting behind her piping-hot plate of food, looking at him. She wasn't even trying to eat or anything. Anyone looking at her would have seen through her facade, though. She was just itching to dive into the food.

"? What are you doin'? This is the first hot meal you've eaten, 'like, ever,' right?"

"But this is also the first time I'm eating with somebody else, answers Misaka answers Misaka. I've heard that people give thanks for their food before eating it, recalls Misaka recalls Misaka. I wanna do that! says Misaka says Misaka, ever hopeful."

"…"

It took fifteen minutes for Accelerator's food to be brought out.

Her food was no longer steaming in the slightest.

She was still smiling, though.

Grinning happily.

8 (Aug.31_PM03:43)

After quite some time had passed since entering the restaurant, Accelerator and Last Order began eating their meals.

Last Order didn't seem used to utensils—forks and knives were one thing, but she didn't even seem to know how to use spoons or chopsticks. For some reason, she stuck a fork into her white rice, looking confused.

Accelerator's meal was mostly meat. It was tough, though. The wooden palette and small hot plate under his dish weren't quite the right size, so everything kept shaking around, making the meat difficult to cut. He stopped for just a second, then firmly held the burning-hot hot plate steady. A waitress walking past looked extremely surprised, but Accelerator reflected all unnecessary heat anyway, so he wouldn't get burned by it.

The scene of them eating would have stood out enormously.

"This is good! This is great! praises Misaka praises Misaka."

"This is a freakin' parade of freeze-dried microwavable meals. We don't even know how many weeks these ingredients have been stuffed in a warehouse for!"

"But what's good is good! says Misaka says Misaka, satisfied. And it feels different when you eat with someone else, says Misaka says Misaka, offering a psychological explanation."

"...You know what?" Accelerator removed his hand from the heated hot plate. "I shoulda probably asked yesterday, but you've got nerves of steel, you know that? Don't you know what I did to all of you? Wasn't it painful? Distressing? Brutal? Humiliating?"

Just before the experiment ended, after the Level Zero had intervened in the fight at the switchyard, he thought he could feel the one Sister (whom he seemed to be calling Little Misaka) glaring at him with hostility.

Did they not acquire actual human fear and emotion at that time? Or was that limited only to Little Misaka herself?

"Weeelll, Misaka has Misaka has a brain-wave link with all 9,969 other Misakas, so she's mentally connected with them."

"Yeah? And?"

"There's this mental network that creates those brain-wave links, explains Misaka explains Misaka."

"You mean like a collective unconsciousness or whatever?"

"Well, it's a little different, corrects Misaka corrects Misaka. The link and individual Misaka's relationship is like that of synapses and brain cells, Misaka says Misaka says, offering an example. It would be correct to say that there is a giant brain called the Misaka network and that it controls all of the Misakas, says Misaka says Misaka."

Accelerator fell silent.

Last Order, however, continued on with her explanation.

"When an individual Misaka dies, the Misaka network itself doesn't disappear, explains Misaka explains Misaka. Going with the brain analogy, Misakas are the cells, and the brain-wave links are like the synapses that convey information between cells. If a cell is destroyed, then the memories experienced go away, so it does hurt, but the Misaka network can't be completely destroyed until the very last Misaka goes away—"

Accelerator was overcome with a sense of hatred, like the kind one would get if a giant spider was looking at them. Not because this person was scary, of course. He could kill her instantly. Right at this moment. He'd killed ten thousand of them, after all. Given time, he could hunt the rest down.

But that wasn't it.

There was something more fundamentally different. This girl, wrestling with the food on her plate—it was like she was built entirely differently from humans, like an alien...

"—thought Misaka thought Misaka, but I think I changed my mind."

"?"

"Misaka taught me—Misaka taught Misaka of her worth, she declares. She said that there is value in each individual Misaka's life and not the whole Misaka, and she told me that if I, the Misaka here right now, were to die, then there would be people who would cry for me, asserts Misaka asserts Misaka proudly. So Misaka won't die anymore. Not even one more can die, thinks Misaka thinks Misaka."

So she said, in a human way, looking into Accelerator's eyes with human directness.

She had declared one thing: that she would never forgive what Accelerator did.

It was a proclamation of hatred. An announcement that Last Order would never forget about that time as long as she lived.

"Haah..."

Accelerator unconsciously slumped deep down into the back of his chair and, looking up at the ceiling, breathed a sigh.

He didn't know.

He had known that they had emotions this whole time, but...no one had ever come face-to-face with him and denounced him on the spot. That's why Accelerator didn't understand their pain. And those Sisters, whom he'd treated as puppets until now, were humans. They could feel that sort of pain—and he hadn't realized that until everything was over.

"_____"

Accelerator opened his mouth. He moved his mouth. But no words came out of his mouth.

He had none to say.

"But Misaka is grateful to you, says Misaka says Misaka. If you weren't around, the experiment would have never formed and the declining Radio Noise project wouldn't have been picked up again by someone else, explains Misaka explains Misaka. You were savior and killer, Eros and Thanatos, life and death—I have no doubt that you're the one to thank for the lifeless Misakas gaining souls, says Misaka says Misaka, all grateful and stuff."

So she said.

Her voice was soft, as if welcoming him.

That irritated him.

For some reason, it really ticked him off.

"The hell?" began Accelerator in a low voice. "That makes absolutely no logical sense. You'd need a shit-ton of apathy to accept that life is just a zero-sum game where people are born and people die, and that's it. Either way, it doesn't change that I was killing all of you. I had fun. I was happy about it. I wanted to do it!"

"That's a lie, denies Misaka denies Misaka. I don't think you wanted to be in the experiment at all, surmises Misaka surmises Misaka."

That messed with his thoughts even more.

He'd understand it if she started crying and hitting him and telling him off. Last Order shouldn't have had any reason whatsoever to defend him at this point.

The inexplicable situation began to put him on edge.

"Wait a second. You've gotta be modifying your memories so it's more convenient or somethin'. You can't say stuff like that without glorifying some part of it somewhere. Besides, did it look like they were making me do anything against my will? Your life meant shit to me as long as I could keep going on with the experiment. End of story," he finished in an almost admonishing tone of voice.

Meanwhile, he was confused about why he seemed to want to look down upon himself like that.

"That isn't true, argues Misaka argues Misaka. If it was, why'd you start talking to the Misakas during the experiment? asks Misaka asks Misaka."

Last Order was not to be dismayed. Her words continued coming at him.

She was like a sweet older sister giving him a talk.

"Think back and remember what happened, pleads Misaka pleads Misaka. You talked to Misaka a whole bunch of times, but why? asks Misaka asks Misaka, even though she already knows."

Accelerator didn't have anything to say for a moment.

The reason he talked to the Sisters...He didn't know it, either.

"Hah-hah! Why ya runnin' away? You tryin' to seduce me by shakin' your ass all happy like that?!"

"Whatever. I don't got the right to say anything to someone tagging along, since this whole 'experiment' is to make me stronger. But you

sure do seem calm. Don't you think about stuff in this kinda situation or anythin'?"

"Seriously, after doing this ten thousand times a guy gets bored, so I was just thinkin' we could kill a little time or somethin', but I guess not. You're impossible to talk to, you know that?"

"Hah! Why're ya walkin' around like it's nothin'? No plan? If you wanna feel the pain that bad, then I'll make you cry! Maybe suck on a cough drop or somethin'!"

"Okay, then! Got a question for ya. How many freakin' times have you died already?!"

"If you think about it calmly, all of it sounded strange, analyzes Misaka analyzes Misaka. The reason people want to talk to others is because they want to understand them or to be understood—basically you want to connect with them, and if you just wanted to kill us so that the experiment worked out, then you wouldn't have decided to talk to us, deduces Misaka deduces Misaka."

"…Eh? What part of what I said sounds at all like I wanted to connect with anyone?!"

"Yes, that's the second strange part, says Misaka says Misaka, putting up a second finger. Every single thing you said was completely abusive toward Misaka, so it ends up being far away from wanting to connect with them, continues Misaka continues Misaka.

"But…," she said.

"…What if you said those words in the hope that she'd deny them?"

"What?" Accelerator stopped.

"You always asserted yourself before the experiments…before battle, recalls Misaka recalls Misaka. Almost like you were trying to scare Misaka **and almost like you wanted to make her say she didn't want to fight anymore,** suggests Misaka suggests Misaka."

"Huh?" He caught his breath.

"The Misakas didn't catch on to those signs—they didn't notice them even one time, says Misaka says Misaka regretfully. But what if, hypothetically, **Misaka had said she didn't want to fight?** says Misaka says Misaka, talking about a choice for something that's already over."

"…" His heart felt like it would stop.

Yes, what if…

What if that day, at that time, the Sister had said she didn't want to be a part of the experiment anymore? That she didn't want to die? Would Accelerator have been helpless then?

Of course not.

There's no way. The experiment itself was to get him to shift to Level Six, and its core was Accelerator himself. If he had refused to cooperate, it would have ended. They couldn't just get another esper and use them instead. And even if the scientists had wanted to restrain him, there's no way they would have been able to.

Because he was the strongest esper in Academy City.

Of course he was the strongest.

What if…

What if, at the very beginning, when the experiment was just starting…

At the very beginning of everything, before a single one of the Sisters was sacrificed…

What if all twenty thousand Sisters had come to beg, with fear in their eyes, that none of them wanted a part of this?

What would he have done then?

He probably wanted that all along.

That's why he questioned them. Over and over. And they never gave an answer, so his questions steadily escalated, eventually turning into an unbearable whirlwind of cruelty and abuse.

He wanted someone who would stop him.

He wanted something that would make him stand up to it.

Accelerator thought back. Ever since the experiment, ever since that one battle in the switchyard, after his fight with the Level Zero, what about him had changed? It was the first question he asked. The answer was right there.

He remembered that battle in the switchyard and the Level Zero who stood up over and over again. He knew he was glorifying his own memories to the extreme. And yet, despite that, he thought…

That one moment, at the very end, where a totally normal fist took him down…

What was he thinking at that moment?

What?

"…Fuckin' hell," he cursed, closing his eyes and turning his head toward the ceiling.

That was all he had to say.

He could whitewash it all he wanted—he was by no means a good person. He just had to think over what happened at the switchyard. The Sister saved by that Level Zero would have refused to die for the experiment, but Accelerator tried to kill her anyway. He couldn't deny that. Nobody could.

There was nothing from Last Order. He wondered what sort of face she was making right now. His eyes remained closed, still closed, still closed…and he realized something was off.

No matter how long he waited, Last Order didn't say anything.

The moment he opened his eyes in doubt, he heard a dull *tonk*. Last Order had collapsed onto the table in front of them. Not on her food or anything, but her spoon was stuck between her forehead and the table.

He could tell at a glance it wasn't just because she was sleepy or tired. The strength in her body seemed like it was all gone. Her muted breath sounded to his ears like the panting of a stray dog. It was as though she'd come down with a fever.

"Hey?"

"Ah-ha-ha…," laughed Last Order in a voice that sounded exhausted. "Well, I wanted to get in contact with the scientists before I got to this point, says Misaka says Misaka, forcing a dizzy smile."

"…"

"Misaka's serial number is 20001, the last one, explains Misaka explains Misaka. Misaka's body is still in an incomplete state, so I really shouldn't have been let out of the incubator, sighs Misaka sighs Misaka."

"…"

"But somehow, some way, I'm using every trick in the book to get through it, so I think I'm okay, thinks Misaka thinks Misaka. I wonder why?" she said in an extremely unhurried tone, seeming to be on the verge of fainting.

It almost looked like if she lost consciousness like this, she wouldn't ever open her eyes again.

"Hey!"

"————Hm? What, what, what is it? asks Misaka asks Misaka."

There were three seconds before she gave her response.

She just kept smiling.

She started to sweat profusely like she was sick, but she was still smiling at him.

Accelerator's face began to lose its expression, his emotion steadily draining away.

Despite their encounter, it wasn't as if he could do anything. He had the strongest power in Academy City, but that's all it was. He couldn't protect anyone with it. Even if someone begged him for help, all he could do with his power was shut himself in, alone, trembling miserably, in what amounted to a nuclear shelter. He couldn't protect. He couldn't save. He'd always survive alone at the end. He could only watch as everything around him was destroyed. Just like when his room was ravaged. Just like how this girl was now collapsed before him.

"…"

Accelerator stood up from his seat without a word. Last Order looked at him without moving.

"Huh? Where are you going? asks Misaka asks Misaka. We still have food left."

"Yeah, I think I lost my appetite."

"Okay…I wanted to thank them for the food, though, sighs Misaka sighs Misaka."

"Yeah? That's too bad."

Accelerator grabbed the bill, his expression cold as ice, and walked toward the register.

Leaving Last Order behind him.

9 (Aug.31_PM04:11)

Accelerator walked down the road alone.

Last Order's face as he left her in the restaurant came to mind for a moment, but there wasn't anything he could do back there. He wasn't some hero who could do anything anyone needed him to. He wasn't some famous detective from a mystery novel. He didn't immediately analyze every possibility in a certain situation with a few seconds' thought.

There was nothing he could do.

So he left without doing anything.

That's it, he thought vaguely as he walked. *Besides, doing that kind of thing doesn't really suit me. It's like a totally different world. Not mine.* It was a job better suited for someone like that Level Zero who stood in his way at the switchyard.

"Wow, this is the first time I've had a hot meal, like, ever! exclaims Misaka exclaims Misaka. Some really hot steam is coming off the plate and stuff, says Misaka says Misaka, eyeing the food carefully."

Besides, what could he do at this point? Did he even have the right to do anything? It was his fault the Sisters got dragged into the experiment. It was also his fault that Last Order got chased out of the laboratory mid-development when the experiment got frozen. Whichever way the cookie crumbled, it would be weird to even think about wanting to save someone at this point.

"But this is also the first time I've eaten with somebody else, answers Misaka answers Misaka. I've heard that people give thanks for their

food before eating it, recalls Misaka recalls Misaka. I wanna do that! says Misaka says Misaka, ever hopeful."

He walked down the street, crossed a bridge, went past a convenience store, walked by a department store, went into a dark alley, passed by a dormitory, and walked, walked, walked, walked, walked...

"Okay...I wanted to thank them for the food, though, sighs Misaka sighs Misaka."

There, his feet stopped.
He lifted his gaze.
"What in the hell did I come here for?"
A single laboratory stood towering over him.
It was the one that planned the experiment and produced all those Sisters. He wondered if there were still any incubators left for creating Radio Noise. He wondered if he could make the necessary adjustments to finish Last Order's physical development if he used one.

There was nothing he could do, so he'd left.
He came here in search of something he could do.
Accelerator set foot into the building lot.
He knew that any of his wishes being granted was pure fantasy.
But he did it anyway—in order to save her.
Aug.31_PM05:15 End

CHAPTER 2

A Certain Unsophisticated Railgun

Doubt_Lovers.

1 (Aug.31_AM08:00)

Academy City was a giant institution in which 2.3 million people resided for the development of supernatural abilities. Tokiwadai Middle School was an elite all-girls school said to be one of the top five in the city. Currently, it had less than two hundred students, including two Level Five "Superpowers" and forty-seven Level Four "Masters." A person needed to be at least a Level Three "Expert" to enroll at the school—and that was just one of the requirements.

The lifestyle rhythm of mornings at Tokiwadai never changed, even during summer vacation. Students woke up at seven AM and had thirty minutes to get their appearance to the point where they didn't look like a disgrace, and then assemble in the cafeteria at seven thirty AM. After roll call, they would finish their breakfast by eight.

Incidentally, the reason breakfast ended at eight AM is because the school encouraged the use of school buses.

The school's gates closed at 8:20, so if one didn't take the bus, they'd have to run through town as fast as they could.

Today was August 31—still summer vacation—so aside from din-nertime, the curfew, and lights-out, students were free to do as they pleased. Apparently the rest of the world used this time to romp around trying to finish homework, but there was none of that hurried tension in the air here.

Sitting in the exceedingly, needlessly large and majestic cafeteria was one of those Level Fives, Mikoto Misaka, stretching her arms out wide. Despite the time of year, she wore her school uniform. Tokiwadai's rules consider the dormitories and the school to be a single establishment, so personal clothing was forbidden. Mikoto's shoulder-length brown hair, her indomitable eyes, and the fact that she would talk for twenty minutes if a person asked her one thing—everything about her was exactly what one wouldn't expect from a proper young lady.

But that wasn't all there was to her. Around her, the students in the cafeteria were sticking around after breakfast to talk to one another, and most of them gave the same impression. Wherever they happened to be, they were Japanese middle school students, after all. The prim and proper young ladies in manga and novels, normally symbolized by horseback-riding hobbies and piano-playing skills, were extremely rare (though they did exist).

Manga, manga…Oh, that's right, today's Monday, isn't it?

Mikoto rose from her seat as she realized it. She went to the convenience store and stood there reading manga magazines every Monday and Wednesday. However, she was ignorant of the plight of the unfortunate high school students forced to endure the tattered page edges of the resulting magazine every single time she got one into her hands.

Normally she'd leave her reading session until after school, but summer vacation meant she could start right from the morning. She had to know who the criminal in the detective manga with all the hidden rooms was, and she wanted to get there right away, so she got her stuff together. As she was about to leave for the store, the waitress in maid clothing who was cleaning up the dishes noticed her. She was a middle school student from a different school—a housekeeping one—and she worked in girls' dormitories as part of her "training." This training seemed to be quite multifaceted, but the fact that she came all the way to Tokiwadai's dorms belied her standing as one of a handful of top students.

"Misaka, Misaka! Are you going to the convenience store? Or the bookstore?"

"Today isn't the tenth and it's Monday, so I'm going to the convenience store. Also, Tsuchimikado, you're training to be a maid, aren't you? Isn't it bad to be talking so casually?"

"Misaka, Misaka! If you're going to the convenience store, then can you buy me some questionable manga? You know, that kind, the ones that are meant for girls and kinda sexy, but not adults only!"

"Uh, were you one of those BL-reading types? Also, Tsuchimikado, you're training to be a maid, so you can't ask your guests to run errands for you."

"Misaka, Misaka! I'm not the one with those hobbies—it's our head chef, Genzou! I like those other ones, you know, those ones where the big brother and the little sister get all dirty!"

"Those are meant for young adult men, not girls, aren't they? Also, Tsuchimikado, you're training to be a maid, so you shouldn't be mentioning your love for your brother right in front of your guests."

Mikoto heaved a sigh and left the cafeteria, then headed for the lobby via an awfully long hallway. She didn't run into anyone on the way. The majority of the students were staying in the cafeteria to chat after finishing breakfast.

She reached the entrance hall and threw open its big doors.

In contrast to the dormitory's antique, western mansion feel, outside was near-futuristic cityscape as far as the eye could see. Wind-generating propellers sticking out of the ground instead of power lines, oil drum–shaped police robots automatically patrolling the streets, a blimp in the sky with a huge display screen across its side—it was a little different from normal cities, but those who lived here were so accustomed to the place that they didn't know how different it really was.

Right across from the stone-walled dorm, there was a twenty-four-hour convenience store. Mikoto smirked at the marked difference.

She stepped out toward the road…and suddenly a man's voice addressed her from nearby.

"Ah, if it isn't Miss Misaka. Good morning to you. Where are you going? Oh, did you start going to a school club? If you'll allow it, may I accompany you midway there?"

Mikoto groaned and stiffened up for a moment. Then, desperately suppressing a rankled grimace from crossing her face, she turned toward the voice's owner.

He was a tall man, one year older than her, standing there. He was slim but with an athletic build, had silky hair and whiter skin than most Japanese—he was the sort of person who would approach sports from a logical angle. His looks just weren't fair. He'd look good no matter what—whether he was holding a tennis racket or typing on a laptop. He had this impression that made you think he'd begin to glitter with reflected light when he sweat and that he'd be smiling happily and peacefully no matter where he was or what was happening…That was the sort of person he was.

Mitsuki Unabara.

He was one of the people Mikoto found hard to deal with. He was the grandson of Tokiwadai's principal or something. For Academy City, whose main objective was supernatural ability development, his level of influence was, in essence, that of the family of a very large corporation's CEO. The school was girls only, so he wouldn't actually come into the school or the dormitories, but he didn't hesitate to put himself anywhere else.

The thing she found most difficult about him, however, was not that he flaunted his authority.

"Well, it's good to be absorbed in your hobbies if you're not in a club. Miss Misaka, do you play any sports? I can teach you a lot of them if you're interested, like tennis, or equestrianism, or squash, or golf—things like that—so feel free to ask me…hmm? What's wrong? Are you not feeling well?"

"Uhh…no, it's nothing."

Mikoto exhaled a little at Unabara's genuinely worried tone.

Mitsuki Unabara was certainly aware of just how vast and total the effects of his authority could be, but he never tried to flaunt it. He would always purposely match the level of Mikoto's gaze, and he would speak to her as if she were an equal. If anybody asked her, that measured, distant, adultlike part of him didn't match with the rest, but as long as he approached her as an adult, she would hesitate to just start flinging lightning at him to solve the problem (unlike a certain other high school student). It would make her look extremely childish.

Mikoto had trouble dealing with him because she always had to mind every action she made and every word she spoke, no matter what. She wasn't talking to a friend—it was more like trying to keep an upperclassman at a school club happy.

That's still strange, though. He wasn't all over me like this a week ago. Lately he's doing it every single day...Ergh, has the summer changed the man? What a bad way to change.

Thinking back, he'd only ever talk to her if he ran into her in town. They'd stand and talk for a minute, but he didn't interfere with her schedule. This was different, though. It was almost like he was following her actions, and from a certain, more aggressive perspective, he was—

"Miss Misaka?"

Yikes, she thought, flinching back. Unabara had suddenly closed the distance between them while she was lost in thought. To make matters worse, he was peering into her face from above.

"Um, please don't worry like that. Where are you going from here?"

"Uh, umm...(frankly, you're the kind of person who would mercilessly burst out laughing if I said I was gonna stand in a store and read manga or something, and so if possible I don't want anyone I know standing next to me while I'm doing that, and I mean, well, if it were Kuroko Shirai or that moron, there wouldn't be a problem, but...)"

"What?"

"N-nothing! Nothing at all! My thoughts aren't escaping through my mouth or anything!"

"??? Do you not have any pressing errands to run? Ah, then how about this. There's a place with the most delicious seafood nearby, so if you're free, then…"

Is this guy seriously inviting me to eat somewhere right after break-fast?! thought Misaka, not letting it show on her face.

"Ah, but, well, I'm happy you invited me, but I sort of do have something to do…"

"Then shall we go now? I'll accompany you."

"Uhh, err, I do have something to do, but how do I put this…?"

"…?" Unabara frowned a little. "Could it be somewhere it would be difficult for me to go with you?"

"Uh, yeah, that's it!" Mikoto pounded her hand with a fist. "I-I'm going to…(ummm)…right, I was just about to head to the department store to look at underwear. See, that's not somewhere a guy would want to go, right?"

"I'll accompany you." His answer came immediately. He didn't seem insane. His smile glistened.

He slipped right by it?! Mikoto thought, mentally holding her head in her hands.

Ugh, what do I do, what do I do? Oh yeah, I'll pretend I'm waiting for another guy. Then he definitely couldn't come with me. All right, it'll be pretty corny, but let's just latch on to some guy and say, "Sor-ryyy, did you wait for meee?" and then ad-lib it from there! It'll bother the person who gets involved, but I'll just treat them to some juice from the vending machine or something

Mikoto looked from right to left, looking for the male who would play the part of her boyfriend. Unfortunately, it was August 31.

For Academy City, where 80 percent of its population consisted of students, today was a day for shutting oneself up in their house and wrestling with their remaining homework.

Meaning there was nobody around, as far as she could tell.

Jeez, this is hopeless! she wailed internally, when at that very moment, as if she had received a gift from the gods, three young men turned a nearby corner.

2 (Aug.31_AM08:25)

Motoharu Tsuchimikado and Aogami Pierce.

Touma Kamijou had run into them in town early this morning. Apparently they were classmates—*apparently*, since he had amnesia and had essentially never seen a classroom environment before.

Kamijou didn't actually have the time right now to be walking the streets. He hadn't even touched his homework at all for the entirety of summer vacation until today, August 31. He was embroiled in a race against time.

Now in a standstill with his homework, he concluded that it was going to be an all-night job and had gone to buy some coffee at the store. Unfortunately, the shelf normally containing the brand he always drank was conspicuously empty. As he wondered to himself who was hoarding all of those mail-in prize tickets, he was accosted by Aogami and Tsuchimikado. His classmates had long since finished their own homework and wanted to do something memorable to fully enjoy the last day of summer break. But still—

"Aahhh, can you believe it's the last day of summer break already, Kami? Man, bro, I didn't meet a girl falling out of the sky, or find a cat-eared girl in a cardboard box on a rainy day, or open the front door to find a cute freeloader who ended up at my place at some point, or anything like that this year, either! I mean, seriously, what the hell? Not one event triggered this summer. If this were a novel, the author would just outright ignore me and say, 'The student passed his time during the break,' wouldn't he?!"

Such were the words of Aogami, in his fake Kansai accent, looking toward the past…

"Ah, I want a romantic comedy already! Our school is coed and everything, dang it. There's gotta be some kind of rom-com waiting for me this semester! An unrealistic one, too, where for some reason every female, from upperclassmen to underclassmen to teachers to classmates to class presidents to childhood friends to the dorm managers, every single one, has zero experience with men, see?"

…And such were the words of Motoharu Tsuchimikado, in his odd way of speaking, looking toward the future.

Kamijou put a hand to his forehead at their entirely infeasible opinions.

"Earth to idiots. Are you really doing this even though you know that I, the humble Touma Kamijou, am currently swamped with homework? Just stay out of my way, at least for today! Actually, I'd like it if you used your friendship power to help me out or something!"

"It's fine, Kami, bro! If you haven't done your homework, then you get to have private lessons all alone with Miss Komoe! Ah, why did I have to go and do my homework, dude? I probably wanted her to praise me or something. Looks like I've got a lot to learn from you about calculated work, bro!"

"And I mean, helping you with your homework doesn't have anything to do with my love comedy. But if a girl falls out of the sky drawn to your math problems, then I'll gladly assist ya, nya!"

The two of them were clearly reveling in his misfortune; Kamijou grinned darkly.

"How should I put this…There's really no point in being friends with either of you. Wait, what the hell? Girls falling from the sky? Does that mean you're into air force ladies?"

In response to his yell, Tsuchimikado answered absentmindedly that these days, girls who fell from the sky would get caught on people's balconies anyway. Kamijou didn't understand what he was talking about.

He was an amnesiac.

On the other hand, Aogami responded, in classic Aogami fashion:

"Hah! Kami, what're ya sayin'? I don't only go for descended heroines; I'm open-minded enough to welcome any girl, including but not limited to stepsisters (older or younger), stepmothers, stepdaughters, twins, widows, upperclassmen, underclassmen, classmates, female teachers, childhood friends, preppies; girls with blond hair, black hair, brown hair, silver hair, short hair, bobbed hair, ringlets, straight hair, twin tails, ponytails, braids, pigtails, wavy hair, frizzy hair, cowlicks; girls in sailor uniforms, blazers, gym clothes, judo clothes, archery clothes; kindergarten teachers, nurses, maids, policewomen, shrine maidens, nuns, soldiers, secretaries, lolis, shotas, tsunderes, cheerleaders, stewardesses, waitresses, goths in white, goths in black, girls in china dresses, girls with weak constitutions, albinos, girls with crazy fantasies, deluded girls, split personality girls, queens, princesses; girls wearing knee-high socks, garter belts, men's clothes, glasses, hair over their eyes, eye patches, bandages, school swimsuits, one-piece swimsuits, bikinis, sling swimsuits, ridiculous swimsuits; nonhumans, ghosts, and animal girls, okay?"

"One of those was definitely not even female!"

Kamijou found himself exhausted after that one. Tsuchimikado gave a smirk.

"But hey, Kami, what girls fall within your strike zone, eh?"

"...Ladies managing dormitories. Proxies are fine, too."

"We're in a male dorm! Our manager is an old dude!"

"Shut up! I know full well it's realistically impossible! It's like an only child wishing for an older sister! Why didn't you ignore that?!"

"Urk. I see, though, administrative ladies, eh? But aren't ya into little sister characters, nya? No matter what you meant to say, it's basically still great," nodded Tsuchimikado, who had a younger stepsister in real life.

Kamijou and Aogami, though, looked at him painfully. Kamijou spoke as the representative of his friends.

"Hey, as your friend, there's something I need to warn you about so that your relationship with your stepsister goes well."

"Wh-what is it?"

"Your stepsister? She's one of those girls who calls everyone 'big brother.'"

"What did you just say, you bastard?!" screamed Tsuchimikado, infuriated, swinging his hands around. "That can't possibly be true!

She would never call anyone but me big brother, no matter where, when, why, or who it was, dang it!"

"He's right, bro. I treated her to lunch yesterday at the department store underground in front of the station and she totally said, 'Thanks, big brother!'"

"Yeah, and yesterday when I ran into her on that main street over there, she said, 'Hi, big brother.'"

Scriiich. He thought he heard the sound of Tsuchimikado biting something deep in his mouth.

"I'll kill you...Wait, what the hell are you doing taking my sister out to lunch without asking?!"

With that, the raging fist of an older brother came upon Kamijou and Aogami.

3 (Aug.31_AM08:35)

Mikoto Misaka froze in place for ten full minutes as soon as she saw the three of them. During that time, they all did what seemed like a reenactment of the final battle of the last fifteen minutes of some Hollywood blockbuster. Every once in a while, Unabara would hesitantly wave a hand in front of her face and say, "Hello?" but she didn't notice. She just watched them, her mouth still forming the *s* in "Sooorryyy, did you wait for meee?"

Wait, just wait, wait a second, that's who's gonna be pretending to be my boyfriend? Unabara doesn't know anything, so he'll think he actually caught a glimpse of my boyfriend, but...Oh, God, that one is talking about his little stepsister...!

That was enough to finally thaw out Mikoto's iced-over mind; she buried her face in her hands.

"Are you not feeling very well?" came Unabara. She faked a smile and took another look around. *Nope, there's not a soul around save for those three.* On top of that, even they were getting farther and farther away from her. If she didn't act fast, she could quickly be stuck spending the entire day with Mr. Smooth here.

There's no other way. They're showing me the most intense battle scene I'll see all day, and I have a feeling they actually mean it, but I'll have to choose one of them, she thought, making up her mind.

Who would she pick?

Let's start with him. He's got kinda blue hair and earrings...No, not that one! He's spouting crazy lingo not even the manga-loving Miss Mikoto understands, so he would probably feel like a three-dimensional girl was intruding on his two-dimensional thoughts.

Mikoto shook her head from side to side.

Next is that one. He's got kinda blond hair and sunglasses...not him, either! From what he's saying, he seems like a dangerous person who would lay a hand on his sister even if she was blood related!

Mikoto wagged her head so much she felt her brain rattle.

Okay, so the third...Wait a minute, is that...? Aah, crap! No, anything but that! Er, but still, leaving him aside, only the blue-haired guy and the one in sunglasses are left, so, umm, aaahhhhhhhhhh!!

"Ah, wait, Miss Misaka, where are you going?!"

Mikoto shut her eyes and dashed. She heard the voice of Mitsuki Unabara behind her, but she paid it no mind. There were about twenty meters to her target. The battling boys caught up in their final battle had yet to notice the enemy approaching fast.

4 (Aug.31_AM08:40)

"Sooorryyy! Did you wait for meee?"

When they heard the girl's voice from behind them, Kamijou and the others, having just launched into the thrilling climax of their fistfight, stopped and made sour faces. They looked like someone had just dumped water all over them. Obviously, none of them had been waiting to meet up with a girl, and each one of them was grinding their teeth, thinking, *Shit, there must be some hot guy nearby and that's got nothing to do with me!*

However, when they calmed down a little, they realized that today was August 31—there shouldn't be many people around.

"?" Kamijou looked confused, and just then—

"Did you wait for meee? Are you even listening to me?! Don't ignore me, damn it!"

A girl tackled into Kamijou's waist from behind. There was a magnificent *thud* as he and the girl crashed down onto the sidewalk.

Now crushed underneath her, he managed to twist his body and get a good look at the identity of the person now attached to his body.

"Sh-shit, who the hell…? Wait, what?! Misaka?! Of all the people!"

"…(What the heck is that supposed to mean?! Oh, never mind, just please, please play along!)"

Kamijou gave a "Huh?" to Mikoto's whispering and his eyes shrunk to pinpoints. Aogami and Tsuchimikado reacted quite differently.

"Hahh?! K-Kami's being hugged by a middle schooler from Tokiwadai! He's already had that shrine maiden and that nun and Miss Komoe! Is the curtain about to rise on an all-new Legend of Kamijou?!"

"Wait, Kami, how many digits was the number of flags you had to trigger for this?"

Mikoto shook with rage at their voices. But that was all. It was a far cry from her usual attitude—she was a Level Five electricity user and had the habit of flinging lightning every which way no matter where someone happened to make her angry.

"Uh, Miss Mikoto? What on earth is going on here?"

"…(Shh! Quiet…argh, this is bad. I can't talk to him from this long a distance…Wait, how were you all messing around again? Okay…)"

Mikoto unsteadily held a fist aloft, looking somewhere far off into the distance. Kamijou followed her gaze with a "?" A little ways off on the sidewalk, there was one of those real smooth dudes a person sees from time to time, standing there by himself. It looked like he was frozen, at a loss as to how to deal with Mikoto's sudden odd behavior.

Move it! said Kamijou, irritated, his heart beating a little faster.

At this, Mikoto took a deep breath. "A-ha-ha! I'm so sorry I'm late! Did you wait? Did you wait for meee? I'll treat you to something later, so please forgive me, okay?"

"..What?"

Her voice echoed. He didn't know what to say. Aogami and Tsuchimikado were frozen in time. The smooth dude was looking away awkwardly.

And then, all of a sudden, *bam!* The windows in the Tokiwadai Middle School Girl's Dormitory flew open all at once.

"Uhh..."

Mikoto's face stopped moving, locked into its smile. The female students looking out the windows were all talking among one another in hushed tones. The twin-tailed girl, Kuroko Shirai, was making a truly amazing face, and her mouth was moving as if she were devouring something. A little ways off through one of the windows, an adult female appeared, looking like the person in charge of everything.

The adult female said something. She said it quietly, and she was far away, so the sound of her voice didn't reach Kamijou and Mikoto. Despite that, her magnificent words clearly pounded themselves into their brains.

"How interesting. You have guts, Misaka, for arranging your rendezvous in plain sight of the entire dormitory."

"Ah-aha-ha..." Mikoto's facial muscles stiffened quite strangely. "Aha-ha-ha-haaa! Uwaahh!"

Mikoto, retaining her completely fake smile, grabbed Kamijou's hand and launched into an explosive sprint. Without a scrap of understanding, he was dragged away.

5 (Aug.31_AM09:45)

And such it was that Kamijou and Mikoto ran around the city for a whole hour.

"W-wait! I don't think time passes like that! Why have we been running around nonstop for an hour now?!"

"Shut up! Be quiet, just be quiet! Please, just let me get my feelings in order!"

Mikoto, for her part, had been shaking her head from side to side for a while now, groaning.

Kamijou checked around them. They must have entered a back road somewhere. Tall buildings surrounded them on all sides, though one of them, shorter than the rest, seemed to be a dormitory.

Mikoto took a deep breath, then finally calmed down.

"Whew. Sorry, it seems like I lost my head there a bit. I'll explain everything, so let's go somewhere we can sit down, all right?"

"The hell? Explain? Are you going to get us into even more trouble?"

"Huh, it's already ten? Places to eat should be open at this time. I just ate, though, so maybe we should just go for some lighter food. A hot dog stand might be good…"

"Wait, hey, don't ignore me! I'm asking if you're gonna get us into even more trouble! I've got homework to do, you know! And wait, you got a buttload of people involved in your nonsense! You can't excuse yourself with just one cheap hot dog!"

"Hmm?" Mikoto put an index finger to her cheek. "Okay, let's do that."

"Huh?"

"I'm saying, we're gonna get the most expensive hot dogs in the world. You'd be okay with that, right?"

"Well, that wasn't the issue…Ah, forget it, she's not even listening to me!"

He wasn't given time to worry about it as Mikoto dragged him forcibly down the road.

6 (Aug.31_AM10:15)

One for two thousand yen.

Kamijou stared at the prices, mouth agape. The guy doing the selling inside his modern-looking stall—probably a renovated motor home—gave him a strained smile. He probably got that a lot.

"Two…thousand…How is it that much? What ingredients could they possibly be using?"

"If they told people that, they'd go out of business. Oh, can I get two hot dogs?" requested Mikoto, making an order on her own in the meantime. Kamijou watched the clerk as he worked. Neither the bun nor the dog was especially large or anything. There also weren't any strange ingredients in it. He didn't want to say it, but it looked to him that if a person put one of these hot dogs next to one from another place, they'd barely be able to tell the difference. And from its small size, it felt more like a snack than a meal.

She's gonna pay two thousand for that? Kamijou slumped as Mikoto indeed handed over the money in exchange for the two hot dogs.

"H-hey, that money—"

"What are you so confused about? There're all sorts of different hot dogs, just like anything else. Stands in LA are basically shops where movie stars pull up in a limousine to order. You sure you're not just unfamiliar with how these things are priced?"

"No, I didn't mean that. I mean I'll pay for mine with my own money."

"Hah? No, don't worry about this little thing. No point in getting out your wallet for it, right?" she answered plainly, causing a dry smile to cross the face of Kamijou, living as a poor student. No matter what he might say, Mikoto Misaka was one of the elites—a proper lady who attended Tokiwadai Middle School.

There were benches right nearby—maybe the hot dog guy had opened up here because there was a place to sit and eat. The sunlight overhead was blocked by the roof of street-side trees, so it looked nice and cool...but it was probably actually hot. The sweltering Kanto heat was real, and it had no mercy. To make it worse, there was a shrill sound, possibly from some building construction, floating to them from far away.

"Here's your hot dog."

Mikoto handed over his hot dog. He stared at it. Then he ate it. He didn't want to admit it, but it was good. More than that, though, he hated not knowing the difference between this hot dog and other ones.

Mikoto bit into hers, battling to keep the mustard from getting on her nose. As she continued, she began her explanation—about how she was being followed around by a real "smooth" customer named Mitsuki Unabara, how it was kind of hard for her to just turn him down, how she was fed up from him constantly asking her out for the last week, how she was trying to pry him from her side by using a false boyfriend, how Kamijou was the only candidate in sight, etc.

Kamijou took a quick look around. Expectedly, Unabara wasn't there. *Well, I don't think he'd be keeping his distance and watching closely from the shadows of the trees around the clock, but...*

"But, I mean, you got away from him for now, didn't you? So we don't need to pretend anymore. There's no point in putting on an act where he can't see us, right?"

He had a mountain of homework left to do. He really wanted to put himself first for once.

"Hmm. Well, I mean, I did only get away from him for now. Next time we meet, he's definitely gonna start following me again. Since I have this chance, I kind of want to make sure he won't ever do it again."

"...Wait."

"I'll stick with you for the rest of the day. I want to show it to as many people as possible. If we run into Unabara a few times in town, it might leave a stronger impression on him. What I mean is, anything goes if that makes Unabara leave me alone, but, well...What's wrong with you? Why are you holding your head like that?"

Kamijou, head in his hands, replied that it was nothing and sighed.

This all meant that Mikoto was asking him to pretend to be her boyfriend for the entirety of the day. Kamijou thought, though, that even if her plan worked spectacularly, him ending up as a crazy person who started something with a middle school student would be fait accompli. He was already living with Index, after all—but he didn't know how old she was. He had a female teacher who looked twelve, so he could never be too careful about the topic.

And more importantly, he had his summer homework. He obviously wanted to refuse, but then he saw Mikoto's eyes suddenly growing steadily more irate. *This is bad. If she seriously gets mad at me, homework will be the least of my problems. She'll probably drag me into a twenty-four-hour endurance battle (though that would be needlessly drawing it out, and somehow I don't think I'd lose anyway).*

Seeming vexed at his prolonged silence, she asked, "So, you got questions? Thoughts? Anything?"

"Not one. Could you just wipe that mustard off your nose?"

Mikoto squeaked and went red. She wrapped her half-eaten hot dog in a paper napkin and set it down on the bench. Then, turning away from him, she frantically tried to wipe it off of her face with a handkerchief, but...

"Eeesh??!"

This time she held her nose and kicked her feet around. It seemed like in her hurry to wipe off the mustard, she'd accidentally gotten it up her nose.

"Uh...are you okay?"

Kamijou followed her lead, wrapped his hot dog up and put it down on the bench, and searched his pocket with his other hand for a tissue or handkerchief. Seeing that, Mikoto forced a smile and said, "I-I'm fine. I mean, nothing happened in the first place anyway."

She wanted to treat her clumsy mustard self-destruct as if it never happened. When he looked again, her face wore an expression of calm. But that was just on the surface—a lot of mustard must have gotten up her nose, because her cheeks flushed pink and she pursed her lips, desperately holding back the tears about to form at the corners of her eyes. Her shoulders trembled.

"S-so, don't you have any questions, or thoughts, or something?"

"Seriously, are you okay? Anyway, maybe it's just like you to tear up and turn your eyes up like that for such a silly reason. Could you actually be one of those people who cries really eas—"

"Shut up! I told you already, nothing happened! Jeez! Quit it with that weird, nice face! Don't bring that tissue near me!"

Her words bit into him; he hastily drew his hand back.

Well, if she wants to forget about it, then I guess I will, too.

He sighed. Then, as he reached for the hot dog he'd placed on the bench, he blurted out, "Huh?"

There were two hot dogs nicely wrapped in paper napkins there in the small space between the two of them. They obviously belonged to them, but he couldn't tell which one of them he had been eating.

Mikoto came to the same realization and asked, "Umm…Do you remember which was yours?"

"Not really…but it was probably the one on the right."

Without thinking about it too hard, he reached for the hot dog on the right. Before he could do anything with it, Mikoto grabbed his wrist with amazing speed.

He looked at her, surprised.

"W-wait a minute. Let me make sure."

"What?" he responded dubiously.

She took the hot dog from his hand and compared the two side by side. Then, she unwrapped them both and looked closely at the eaten portions.

But as far as he could tell, there was no way to know the difference. They had both eaten about half, so they were still about the same length, and they had all the same toppings on them—he just didn't know.

They were both the same exact thing anyway, so he didn't really care.

"So did you figure it out?"

"…"

"Did you figure it out?"

"…"

"Did you—"

"Ah, jeez, be quiet! I don't know! Whatever. Just take the right one, and I'll take the left one, like you said! Pay more attention next time, stupid!"

Kamijou took the hot dog from her, confused at the inexplicable nonsense she was jabbering.

"What in the world are you making a big deal out of this for? You ordered the same thing for both of us anyway," he said, casually taking a bite. As he expected, there wasn't any difference at all.

Then, Mikoto's complaints suddenly stopped. She wasn't moving at all, in fact, like she had frozen in shock.

"What's the matter with you?"

"Nothing at all," she replied.

She grabbed her hot dog with both hands, stared at it for a moment, and then finally put it into her mouth like a small, nervous animal. She blushed a little.

"...Anyway, getting back to the subject. I want you to pretend so that I can fool Unabara. Do you have any thoughts or questions?"

"Um, seriously, what's the matter? You're suddenly acting like a fish out of water. Was the mustard in your nose really that ba—"

"Be quiet! That wasn't what...No, wait! Forget it! I'm just asking you if you have any damn questions or thoughts about this!!" she yelled as her face turned bright red, leaning toward him. Their faces were almost touching, so Kamijou quickly pulled his back.

"Whoa?! Um, er...My thoughts are, 'What the shit?' and my question is, 'What the heck am I supposed to be doing exactly?' I guess."

"Huh? What you're supposed to...?"

"Yeah, like, what the heck should I do to come off as your boyfriend?"

"..."

"..."

What to do? They both stopped.

How young they both still were—they hadn't actually started dating because of anything, and neither of them knew what would make them appear as such.

7 (Aug.31_AM10:45)

They eventually agreed to chat idly while sitting on the bench.

Though since all the students in the city were probably hard at work finishing up their summer assignments, the streets were dead silent. The only one who heard them was the guy selling hot dogs. Kamijou quickly began to realize that this was a problem—the point of their facade was to let as many people see them as possible.

"So after that whole experiment, there aren't even ten Sisters left in Academy City anymore. Apparently most of them got sent to places on the outside for physical adjustments," said Mikoto.

"Wait, they went to outside places? I thought they were espers. If they really examine their bodies, won't they figure out the Curriculum secrets and stuff?"

"I mean, there're corporations and laboratories in cahoots with Academy City on the outside, too. The city can't stand on its own, you know. It might be hard to see, but there're connections all over the place for raising funds, controlling information, legal services..."

"Huh. So I guess that means they're all up and at 'em. That's good to hear."

Mikoto quieted a little at that. Her expression implied that she wasn't convinced of something or that she was somehow irritated. Whatever it was, Kamijou didn't know, so he stopped for a moment as well.

"Hmm, you think this is a little deep for a conversation between boyfriend and girlfriend?"

"Well, I dunno. With all our talk of research facilities, Academy City collaborators, and physical adjustments...probably."

"...(Yeah, right. You're getting worked up because we're talking about other girls, isn't it?)"

"What?"

Kamijou didn't quite make out what she had said, but Mikoto flatly insisted it wasn't important.

She shot a sidelong glance at him that went unnoticed. He took a piece of folded paper out of his pants pocket—it was a packet with classical Japanese or something printed on it. He then took out a mechanical pencil and got to work on the questions.

"...Are you actually understanding what I'm telling you? What part about this makes us look like we're dating?! Ignoring the lady and burying your nose in your studies is as patriarchal as Europe in the Middle Ages!"

"Oh, ah, right. Wow anthropomorphic Mikoto-tan is so moé..."

"Anthropomorphic? I don't even get to be human first?!"

"Oh, but oh my, a heart-pounding study group event! I wrote a poem for you about our school lives! What I mean is, I haven't done a single scrap of my summer homework, Sarge, so these last twenty-four hours look like they're gonna be hell!"

"??? Whaddaya mean summer homework?"

"…Umm, Miss Mikoto, would you happen to not know about summer homework?"

"Well, hmm. You know, I have heard of it. Those are the assignments they give you so that you don't get lazy or dumber during long breaks from school, isn't it? But it's not like you have to actually do any of it. People don't get lazy or dumber like that, right?"

Words escaped Kamijou. Surprisingly enough, it seemed that Tokiwadai Middle School had no such concept.

"Grr, that's not fair…Why do they let you run wild over there?"

"How should I know?" she snapped. "So what kind of homework are you doing, then?"

"Huh? I guess I can show you, but they're high school–level problems, so a middle school kid like you probably wouldn't know them."

"Just lemme see already."

She peered at the pile of papers in his hands.

Kamijou was about to inadvertently look at her, but then he pulled back in surprise. She had leaned in pretty far to look at his papers, so she'd come so close their cheeks were almost touching.

"Hmm, Classical Japanese, is it? Wait, this is all just simple review stuff."

As if she didn't notice anything, she took Kamijou's pencil from his hand and, almost like she was snuggling up against him, began smoothly writing down the answers. Her hair got in her way when she looked down, so her other hand came up and tucked a lock of hair behind her ear. He could smell the faintly sweet scent of her hair conditioner.

Yipes…! Th-this is bad. I don't know why but this is really bad!

If he moved any part of his body, it would end up touching her. His body locked up for a moment, but then he suddenly came to his senses.

"…Umm, how can you answer these?"

"How can't you?" she countered with a straight face without any sort of nastiness behind it. Kamijou very nearly ran away, but Mikoto held his shoulders and smiled as if to calm him.

"Well, I mean, see…Everyone's got strong and weak subjects. Oh, right. Should I tell you the answer to this question to pay you back for my request?"

"A middle school student is admonishing a high schooler about his studies…"

"Ah-ha-ha…wow, you're really taking this hard. Let's get a drink for a change of pace. I'll go buy one for you, but you have to finish your homework or whatever once you're done with it, okay?"

"Huh? No, I'll buy it. Getting up and walking around would be a good enough change of pace for me, and I still owe you two thousand yen."

"I said I'll do it, and I will. It's more embarrassing if you refused something like this."

Mikoto grinned wryly, stood from the bench, and left to go. A glance revealed no vending machines nearby. He wondered if she was planning on going to the convenience store a little bit away.

Wait, all we're doing is drinking and eating.

Kamijou, left on the bench, stared after her for a moment, but finally lowered his gaze back to his Classical Japanese homework packet. He honestly didn't know if it could even be considered Japanese. It might as well have been Advanced English for all he knew.

"…Blech."

Kamijou shook his head and pried his eyes away from the paper.

A small dog ran past him. It was dragging a leash behind it from its neck, so it must have run away from its owner.

Kamijou watched in vague surprise as it ran away, and then a smooth-looking man passed right by him as well in pursuit. That had to be Mitsuki Unabara. He caught up with the puppy in no time and grabbed hold of its leash.

A little while after that, a boy who looked to be in elementary school came up behind Unabara. He must have been the dog's owner. Unabara handed it over in the same sort of way you might hand over a balloon that was stuck in a tree, and he said a few things to the boy, who now had the leash in his hand.

How smooth. How totally cool. I wasn't sure people like that even existed. In terms of rarity, let's see…he's about the same level as a runaway girl sitting on the swings in the park at night, nearly in tears, he thought, half in admiration and half in disgust. He figured, though, that he was also about as rare as a boy fighter saving a girl being hassled by punks in an alley.

Then their eyes met.

Unabara looked a little taken aback, as if he remembered him, and then gave a half smile. He didn't seem to want to leave, though. After getting his mental state in order, he came over to Kamijou on the bench.

"Nice to meet you, umm…what should I call you?"

"Huh? It's Touma Kamijou. Mitsuki Unabara, right?"

"What? I mean, yes, my name is Mitsuki Unabara, but how do you know it?"

Unabara looked confused, but Kamijou had heard all about him from Mikoto. In fact, he was the one responsible for Mikoto dragging him all over the place when he had so much else to do today.

"So what does Mr. Mitsuki Unabara need from Mr. Touma Kamijou?"

"Er, I mean, nothing in particular…," replied Unabara, a little flustered. "Umm, I would like to ask, if you don't mind, but are you a friend of Misaka's?"

"You wanna know?"

"…Yes. You're sitting next to the person I love, so of course."

Wow, thought Kamijou, reappraising him.

He suddenly started to like him. He didn't think he'd just come out and declare it like that. Kamijou really liked idiots like him.

Hmm.

He thought for a moment. Mikoto had asked him to play along so that he'd give up, after all.

"Hey, which answer do you want to hear? **The one you expect or the one you don't?**"

"Whatever this case is, my own answer won't change," he asserted without skipping a beat.

He had the resolve to raise himself to a higher position rather than achieve it by climbing atop others. Maybe he looked like a stubborn, annoying person from a certain point of view, but strangely enough, Kamijou didn't feel any insidious intent—probably because he didn't view Kamijou as an enemy, nor did he resent Mikoto in return.

8 (Aug.31_AM11:02)

When he talked to him, Mitsuki Unabara turned out to be a pretty nice guy.

Kamijou knew he was the rich grandson of Tokiwadai Middle School's board chairman…but his initial assumption that Unabara was surely some disagreeable, high-class person was way off.

"So I think Misaka should be clearer about whether she likes or dislikes people. By the way, the answer to that question is three, because the word *hi-doru* means 'roast,' and it's a ru-verb with an irregular conjugation."

"Three, huh? All right, three. You think so? She seems more the type who is pretty honest with her emotions. She flung all that sparky nonsense at me that one time when all I did was forget her name."

"I sort of feel like when she is being honest, there's embarrassment or acting in there. To be frank, I'm not confident I've ever heard what she's actually thinking. Not even once. Um, that answer there is four. I think two is a trick."

"Hey, thanks. Hmm…you might be right about that."

"It's true! She doesn't make anything clear, so somebody like me just ends up chasing after her all day, every day. I'm being serious about this, so I think she should give me a serious answer, too. Oh, that one is one."

"Ack, it's not four? You've really made up your mind, huh? It's like you're just pulling the trigger during a game of Russian roulette without even knowing how many bullets are in the gun. There may be two possible answers she can give you, but it's not a fifty-fifty chance."

"I understand that. I'm scared, you know? I don't know what'll happen to me if she outright says no to me. But even still—"

"Even still?"

"—I can't. I can't take her away when I know she'll cry. If she's not happy, then there wouldn't be any point."

Tsk. Kamijou cursed mentally.

He'd really wanted to start cheering this guy on, but it looked like the results were already in.

Man, that's youth for you.

He sighed. Problems like this were honestly out of his comfort zone, and on top of that, after Unabara's frank discussion, he didn't even know if he wanted to keep going through with this act at all.

Then, he suddenly heard footsteps beside him.

He looked to find Mikoto holding two juice bottles, standing there looking quite startled.

"Eh? What's wrong with you—"

Before he could fully voice his question, Mikoto strode over to the bench and gestured with her chin for him to stand, as if to tell him to get away from Unabara.

"Come with me, you."

"H-hey!"

Kamijou looked at Unabara. He had a forced expression, like he was in shock but still trying to maintain a smile.

Mikoto looked at him and said, "Sorry. I have something I need to do with this person."

"Oh, I see."

"I'm sorry. See you."

Mikoto smiled, but for Kamijou, who knew a little bit about her, it was an unnatural act of politeness toward another person. Unabara might have realized it, too, because he didn't seem willing to persist. Meanwhile, Mikoto turned her back to them and started walking.

As he was worrying about what to do, Unabara smiled and told him to go.

9 (Aug.31_AM11:20)

They walked for a while in silence before reaching a back alley, where Mikoto finally stopped. Kamijou, following behind her, almost bumped into her.

She turned around and said, utterly exasperated, "Jeez, I can't believe you! Why did I even bother asking you to put on this whole act? There's no point if you start getting friendly with Unabara!"

"..."

"Understand? Right now, you're...my b-boyfriend, okay? We're trying to make Mitsuki Unabara give up on following me around! Please don't forget about this crucial point!"

"..."

"Why aren't you saying anything?"

"I can't do it," he replied straightforwardly. "He's totally serious! He's completely prepared to get hurt as much as he needs to, and he wouldn't even hate you if you did hurt him, and he still says he likes you. I can't trick a person like that. I don't want to."

"Oh, come on..."

Mikoto seemed somewhat surprised as she looked at him.

Kamijou didn't notice Mikoto's subtle trembling.

"I'll ask you instead—why do you instinctively dislike him so much? Does he really have some kind of huge shortcoming? Well, I mean, it's probably wrong to force yourself to go out with him when you don't like him, but...is there some other reason?"

"..."

Mikoto glared at him like she really wanted to say something. Her mouth was zipped shut—he couldn't even hear her breathing, much less speaking.

The two of them were silent.

Finally, she blurted out, "You know, you're..."

"?"

"...I see. Never mind." She cut herself off like she was correcting herself. She grinned like it was nothing, but he thought he saw a hint of loneliness swimming in her eyes.

10 (Aug.31_AM11:45)

Mikoto and the boy were the only ones in the alley.

The words that had come out of his mouth shook her more than she let on. But what rocked her very core—that she did not realize. Nevertheless, she unconsciously understood that she'd be better off not letting it show. Or rather, she possessed a compelling force telling her that she mustn't do so.

However, without care, it would erupt within her. She was desperately holding it back, like a raging vortex of steam trying to escape her body.

It was strange.

She didn't want to let it show on the surface, but she felt pained trying to hold it back. Would that not mean that deep down she wanted to let it show? But that wasn't the case. Just thinking about letting it show nearly made her red in the face.

And she didn't even know what the essential thing was.

She held everything in her throat, not understanding why.

One way or another, she'd realized it.

Mikoto had always kind of thought she was a unique existence. She had thought that even her distance to this boy had shrunken just a little bit compared to everyone else. Like if he was browsing a list of a thousand names and saw the name Misaka, he'd at least stop for a moment.

But no—she'd been wrong.

And that fact by itself had a big effect on her. She didn't even understand why something as insignificant as this had caused her so much damage, so she of course couldn't think of a way to deal with it. She wanted to run away right now if she could—from this unidentified pain.

But she couldn't.

She didn't want to turn tail and run away from him.

It would hurt him.

The pain would be much more than what she was feeling now.

...Man, I really am an idiot, if I do say so myself, she sighed.

He didn't seem like he caught on at all. He said in wonder, "???
What are you smiling about?"

11 (Aug.31_PM00:00)

As Kamijou and Mikoto left the smaller back roads for the main one,
they decided to discuss what to do from here on out about Unabara.

"So what are we gonna do now? Keep putting on the act or quit it
already?"

Mikoto sighed. "What do you think we should do?"

"Well, I'd rather we just gave up. There's no point in continuing.
Besides, Unabara doesn't seem like the kind of person you think he
is. I don't think he'd resent you for turning him down or anything."

"That may be true, but it's kind of scary. He's been so aggressive
with his advances lately he seems like a different person...Hey, you
sure are sticking up for him. Did something happen?"

"I guess. He really just helped me out with my homework."

Mikoto gave a "?" face, and Kamijou showed her his Classical Japanese homework packet. The correct answers Unabara had told him
were written in.

But when she saw that, her expression suddenly clouded over.

"They're...all correct and everything, but..."

"But? But what?"

"Was he a good student? I didn't think he was actually all that smart."

"But he answered my homework correctly, didn't he?"

"Well...His grades do put him at the top of his class, but...he's got
that Level Four ability—telekinesis. It's the power to move things far
away with an invisible force."

"How does that have anything to do with how smart he is?"

"It does." Mikoto folded her hands. "Kuroko Shirai jumped the gun and looked into it. What he's doing is cheating. He sticks his power like a plastic film on the monitor, and then when the light and heat from the monitor pushes back onto it, he calculates backward to the image being displayed on it…Well, it's like a listening device. His good grades have nothing to do with how smart he is."

"Whoa…," Kamijou grunted. He did know about special kinds of devices that could calculate electrical signals by measuring subtle changes in the magnetic fields that monitors and transmission codes emit. What surprised him was the fact that a normal person could do the same thing without even using any tools.

"Wait, you managed to explain all that pretty calmly."

"Don't patronize me. Is that weird? I'm an electric user anyway, so I can do something similar. Like steal your credit card information from the magnetic field coming from the magnetic tape on it," she explained, far too calmly, leaving the Level Zero Touma Kamijou speechless.

12 (Aug.31_PM00:12)

It was lunchtime.

Kamijou wasn't feeling too hungry because of the hot dogs they ate earlier, but it reminded him that Index was left by herself in the dormitory. He'd left things like bread in the kitchen, edible things that she wouldn't have to cook, so he didn't think she'd have a problem. He got the feeling, though, that her personality dictated that she would wait patiently until he got back.

"All right, then let's stop the boyfriend-girlfriend thing. I'll treat you to one last thing as a tip. Want anything to eat?"

"We're gonna eat more?! It's fine, I'm not hungry!"

"I'm trying to thank you here, so be quiet and accept it. Oh, I heard that if you can eat an entire jumbo-size bowl of super-spicy fried rice, you get it for free. Want to try?"

"Now you're just doing it out of spite!"

It being midday, the students who were all in a race against time to finish their homework were overflowing into the now-lively city streets in search of food.

Mikoto was walking ahead of Kamijou, so as he made sure not to lose her in the crowd, he asked, "Hey, we're done with the whole acting thing, right? What are you gonna end up doing about Unabara?"

"I'll settle the score myself. The school board chairman will probably give me hell for it...but that's my own problem, too, so," said Mikoto as if she'd gotten past something. Kamijou didn't get another word in.

They looked around for someplace to eat, but everywhere was full. In the end they just went to buy a cheap hamburger or something and eat outside. Despite this compromise, though, there were giant lines in front of the fast-food joint's counters.

"I'll go line up. You can just take it easy here. You don't have any complaints to me deciding our order, right?"

Kamijou grunted in confusion. "Why don't we just line up together?"

"It's fine, okay? I'm the one who put you through all this. I have to at least pay you back this much."

Right after she said that, she went into the line. The restaurant seemed pretty popular—as soon as she got in, others lined up behind her, and she disappeared into the mountain of people.

Pushing his way through said mountain to get to Mikoto would probably bother everyone else, so he gave up and decided to wait by himself outside the store.

Ugh...With this direct summer sunlight, waiting in line inside would have been less painful. Ack, but what should I do about my homework?

He glanced up toward the sun, looking like a wilted decorative plant left on the windowsill in the sunlight for too long. Then, a familiar face appeared.

It was Mitsuki Unabara.

"Hm? Fancy seeing you here. Are you alone? Is that errand of yours finished?"

"Eh? Oh, actually, Misaka's battling her way through that pile of people," he said, pointing toward the store counter. "You want to go talk to her? She's calmed down now, so you might be able to."

"No. I don't think I could. She seemed really angry a little while ago," he replied with a slightly troubled look.

13 (Aug.31_PM00:15)

If the phrase *packed in like sardines* ever applied to a situation, it was the crowd at the counter of the fast-food place.

She looked up at the ceiling tiredly, swallowed by the waves of people.

It's summer, and it's crowded, and it's so hot…Ugh, why is it so hot even though the air conditioners are going?

She began to consider going somewhere else when she saw the line not moving at all. But when she turned around, there was yet another human wall. She'd bother everyone else by trying to push through them.

Ahh, aha-ha…this is hell.

She smiled dryly when suddenly the crowd near the entrance began to churn. Someone seemed to be forcing their way through the congestion. Stifled complaints and dissatisfaction spread through the store like a wave.

Then, the crowd in front of Mikoto parted to either side.

The one who fell toward her was someone she knew well.

"Huh? Hey, just what do you think you're—"

"…——ease, run…," he said, cutting her off.

His body was soaked with sweat, and for some reason, his right arm was wrapped in white bandages.

The boy cried out, his eyes bloodshot.

14 (Aug.31_PM00:15, at the same time)

"Oh, hey, thanks for your help with my homework," said Kamijou, standing under the burning-hot sun waiting for Mikoto.

In contrast, Mitsuki Unabara, in the middle of the scorching-hot road, gave an incredibly cool smile and replied, "Not at all. I just did what I was able."

"What I was able," huh...

That struck Kamijou as a little off. Then Unabara, as if sensing the oddness of the conversation, asked, "Is something the matter?"

"Mm. I'd like to ask you something, if that's all right."

"Go ahead."

"Are you...a smart guy?"

"Huh?" Mitsuki froze for a moment in confusion. "Um, well, rather, I'm sorry—were my answers wrong?"

"No, that's not what I meant..."

He obviously couldn't just straight up ask if he cheated in school. He hurriedly tried to change the subject...but something else happened before he got his words out.

"What is it?" asked Unabara, seeming a little surprised. Kamijou didn't answer. Actually, the problem wasn't Unabara himself. He was staring at something—someone—behind him.

Behind Unabara, a big crowd of people was gathered in the fast-food joint where Mikoto was lined up, since it was lunchtime and everything. Students walking along nearby were steadily joining the mess.

And there, among those people...was another Mitsuki Unabara.

His face, his height and weight, and even his clothes—everything about him was the same as Unabara. He was dripping with sweat from every pore on his body, and he was diving into the restaurant with bloodshot eyes.

Mitsuki Unabara finally seemed to realize where he was staring. He turned around to look at the building, but the man had already disappeared entirely into the throng.

Kamijou bent his head in bewilderment. Was it a case of accidental resemblance? They looked so alike, though. The air that they gave off may have been slightly different, but they looked exactly the same—just like Mikoto and Little Misaka.

"Hey, do you have a brother or something?"

"No, I'm an only child. Why do you ask?"

"Well...A second ago, a guy who looked just like you went in there," he explained, pointing toward the restaurant. Unabara, somewhat startled, turned around again.

"I-I see. I would have liked to have seen him myself, but you only got a short look at him, right? Couldn't his hairstyle or clothing just have been similar? Regardless, I don't have any siblings."

Kamijou got that feeling as well. He'd only gotten a cursory glance at him, so he didn't remember any details. Then, Unabara, with a somewhat nervous expression, looked back and forth between Kamijou and the restaurant. "Did that person really look that much like me?"

"Huh? Uh, well, it was more than just looking alike—it was almost like he was an identical twin. But it was probably just a coincidence. This sort of thing happens sometimes. It's nothing to get into a fuss over, is it?"

"That person went into the shop where Miss Misaka is currently in, right? Doesn't that seem creepy to you?"

Worried, Unabara looked toward the restaurant entrance.

"There are espers who have metamorphosis abilities in this city. Just as the name implies, they can change their face and body into that of somebody else. I don't think it's possible to change their own genetic information, but still...," went on Unabara, seeming a bit anxious.

Kamijou thought that maybe he was worrying about this an awful lot, but perhaps this much was natural for someone who was in love with her.

"Well, coincidental or not, you can just go in and see for yourself. I don't really think it's worth worrying about, but imaginary fears are best cleared up quickly."

Kamijou immediately began to walk forward, but Unabara took a step back instead.

"Oh, I couldn't...Miss Misaka got awfully mad at me earlier. If I really am overthinking this, then it could end up with her getting angry at me again. The thought scares me."

"Don't give me such a lonely looking smile. You're only worrying about her, that's all."

"There's a thin line between helping somebody out and being

nosy. If you would be so kind, could you go in and see if anything is out of the ordinary for me?"

"Jeez, fine. But look here. I don't really have any place to say this, but I don't think you need to get all spineless at this point. She's been refusing your invitations all week long and you haven't given up yet, have you?"

"Refusing my what?"

"Huh? I said—"

"I've been out this whole week at a training camp for my school club. I could figure out that she'd been avoiding me, so I thought I'd cool off for a while and regroup. This is the last day of summer vacation, so I just wanted to see Miss Misaka again."

Kamijou gave a start. Mikoto had said that a person—Mitsuki Unabara—had been following her around every day. But if the real one had been away at summer camp, then who was the one with her this whole time?

Unabara didn't know about it. Kamijou hid all this to not cause him needless worry. He swept past the young man and headed for the fast-food place.

Then, suddenly, he remembered something. Unabara had been keeping up his good marks by cheating, and he had also easily helped him with his homework—what was going on?

As he was thinking about it, he suddenly heard Mitsuki Unabara's voice behind him.

"I tell you, tricking people never goes well, does it?"

Slam!! A powerful impact landed in the middle of Kamijou's back. It took him a few seconds to realize it had been a punch. The air in his lungs rushed out of him like he was a blown-up plastic bag that someone had stepped on. He couldn't breathe, much less cry out in pain.

He looked back over his shoulder to see Mitsuki Unabara standing there with freezing-cold eyes.

What was going on? His breath caught in his throat, but while he stopped thinking entirely for a moment, Unabara took his other hand, brought it behind him, and took out a bladed object.

He came down with it at the same time that Kamijou took a step forward in panic.

He felt a sharp, cold sensation as it lightly scraped across his lower back, but he forced himself to get his breathing in order. He had been attacked after Unabara had driven the air from his lungs and prevented him from screaming. So many people were around that they were blind to anything below their chests, so the attack had been far more difficult to see than if he had covered his mouth and stabbed him. Even if Unabara had used this tactic to kill him outright, he could have just joined into the crowd nonchalantly and no one would be the wiser.

It hadn't been a bullet—that would have assured his own destruction. It had been an assassination, which would have let him go home alive.

An act of murder committed in broad daylight with dozens of people around.

But he didn't scream, so it didn't cause panic. That fact directly confirmed Unabara's high level of skill.

Could he be...?

Kamijou, still dizzy from the assault, tried desperately to bring his body back around, but he couldn't stop his staggering legs. It brought him around in an arc, with Unabara precisely at the center.

Was this one the fake all along...?!

The corners of Mitsuki Unabara's lips twisted upward as if he had realized from Kamijou's eyes what he'd been thinking.

He glanced at the object in Mitsuki Unabara's hands—it was like a knife made out of a black rock. The rock didn't look like it had been filed down. It looked more like it had been broken to create its sharp edge.

It was wholly unlike a weapon, so perhaps that was why people nearby didn't stop to think about it when they saw it.

Blinded with pain, Kamijou thought desperately about what to do and uttered, "...Damn...it! Why...are you...?!"

"Why, you ask? This was supposed to have been my very important latent period...but you wouldn't understand how vital it was if I told you, would you? Still, for the real one to have escaped...I suppose I should have just killed him outright instead of going for the milder option of confining him. Oh, and by the way, I'm neither his brother nor a stranger who happens to look just like him. I believe there is a way to do this called metamorphosis on your science side of things, but there are other ways to achieve the same effect, you know."

Mitsuki Unabara waved around the black stone knife as he spoke. This time, he didn't cut him, but rather raised it toward the sky...

Zoom!!
Something invisible shot past his face.

An unseen laser-like thing had come out of the tip of his knife and collided with an illegally parked car behind him. As if it were a branding iron, a complex sigil appeared on the car's door. Then, with a *gzzzzt*, something else invisible erupted from the indentation it had created. Something he couldn't see but could certainly feel, like a malicious gaze upon him. It was hard to explain with science, and at the same time, it seemed to be representing itself as something outside of science.

In other words—sorcery.

After the one second of silence...

With a series of metallic noises, every part of the car, from its doors to its glass windows to its chassis to its tires, split apart into a thousand pieces. It wasn't like somebody had broadly cut and sliced it up. The screws, the bolts, the welding—everything holding each part of the car together just neatly fell apart, almost like converting an already-built plastic model kit into its component pieces.

Kamijou saw it and went white.

He had realized, one way or another, what would happen to a person hit by it—what would become of their parts.

A stir began to spread in the crowd, but there was no screaming or panic. To the people there, it was a mysterious occurrence. Their thoughts hadn't quite caught up to the point where they had figured out it had been a clear attack.

Mitsuki Unabara didn't look around.

He continued swinging his knife.

"?!" Kamijou's back broke into a cold sweat.

Unabara's attacks were scary, to be certain. Kamijou's right hand could nullify any abnormal powers, but sensing an invisible attack before it happened? It was like trying to dodge a bullet once a person saw it heading for them.

The sparky attacks Mikoto shot at him were similar, but those were all limited by having electrical properties. In other words, all he needed to do was stick his right hand out in front of him, and the spears of thunder would all be naturally attracted to it like a lightning rod.

However, Unabara's unknown attack didn't follow those rules.

But the most terrifying thing of all was **that his aim was all over the place**. He had missed the utterly unprepared Kamijou from a distance of just five meters. And then the attack's power ended up destroying a car in an instant.

A lot of people were around. They were surprised at how the car had broken apart before their eyes, but they hadn't realized it had been an attack. And Unabara didn't seem to care about collateral damage at all anyway. If a sorcerer let loose here, the stray bullets would surely hurt people.

"Shit!"

Kamijou turned his back to Unabara, completely aware of the danger of doing so. He darted from the main road onto a side road, trying at least to get away from people. Then, he turned onto a back alley.

The enemy, equipped with an invisible weapon, followed him in steady pursuit.

15 (Aug.31_PM00:24)

Damn it, what the hell is going on?! Why's a sorcerer just hanging around in a place like this? What the hell does he want?!

Cursing to himself, Kamijou ran through the alleys.

First of all, he needed to know what kind of attack his enemy was using.

As he ran, he grabbed his cell phone. Fortunately, the enemy didn't seem able to fire rapidly, nor accurately. Nevertheless, the fact that someone was chasing him from behind with a ranged weapon was enough to put immense pressure on him. As his fingers flew across the buttons, he realized they were trembling erratically.

The ringtone sounded once, twice, three times, four times, five times, six times, seven times, eight times, nine times—

"H-hello! Hello, this is the Kamijou residence, hello!"

"What took you so long?!" shouted Kamijou angrily for no reason.

The girl on the other end got mad, too. "Mgh. Is that you, Touma?! You're the one who's taking too long! When are we gonna have lunch? Or should I evacuate to Komoe's house again? You need to be clearer about these things, for my sake!"

"Sorry, Index, we'll talk about food later! There's something I gotta ask you, okay?!"

"Later?! Why are you so—"

"Damn it, are you listening?! There's a sorcerer or something in the city. I don't know what he's after, but it might be you! Tsuchimi-kado...might be back at his dorm right now. Index, I want you to go next door, all right?! He's an ally!"

"Touma...Are you being chased?" Index's voice changed to a quiet tone. She must have guessed the situation he was in.

"Yeah, I'm in full escape mode right now! I could really use a hint to turn this around on him!"

"...Anything unique? Like his clothes, or his weapon, or the way he talks or acts."

Kamijou told her everything strange he knew about Mitsuki Unabara, like the fact that he had transformed into somebody else and the properties of the stone knife he held. Index was silent for three seconds, then immediately came back with a reply.

"The black knife might be…obsidian? A lance of reflected starlight from a mirror…that's probably the Spear of Tlahuizcalpantecuhtli."

"Tola-what?"

"The Spear of Tlahuizcalpantecuhtli. It comes from the name of an Aztec god. He was the god of Venus and calamity. It's said that the spear **will kill anyone and everyone exposed to the light of Venus.**"

Kamijou gave up. That was just an embellished legend. If it was true, everyone in the world would have died a long time ago.

"Venus…? You know, Index, enough with the backstory. I need to know what to do here as soon as possible—ack?!"

A loud *zoom!!* cut off his needless retort.

The mysterious attack had lunged right past him, barely missing. It dismantled an outdoor air conditioner. Still bathed in a cold sweat, he whipped around another corner.

"Touma, if you don't listen carefully, you'll be the one who gets hurt!"

"Yes, I'm sorry, Miss Index! I will never nitpick at a specialist's words again! So please, just give me a hint as soon as you can!"

"Okay. For now, just remember that the spear itself is made from the light of Venus."

Kamijou immediately looked up. In the slender sky, bordered by buildings on either side…Venus was not. That didn't mean that Venus wasn't up there, but that he just couldn't see it because of the bright sunlight.

"But I don't get it. Everyone in the world is exposed to Venus's light. If the spear has that kind of power, then you couldn't avoid it no matter where you were. Wouldn't mankind already be wiped out?"

"That's right—it's a godlike power. But it's a double-edged sword. There's no way that humans can completely control the same kind of techniques a god can handle."

"I don't get it."

"To put it simply, the spear that people use is a replica. If you used the real spear, everyone in the world would die. Hmm, I think the replica is probably using the obsidian knife as a mirror. It reflects the light from Venus coming from the sky with the mirror, exposing something to the light to attack. In other words, as long as you don't get exposed to that light, it's more than possible to evade his attacks. You could probably block it with your right hand, Touma, but figuring out the trajectory of something invisible is the important part."

"An invisible light ray…So it's basically like a portable laser!"

"Lay-ser?"

He could almost see Index making her confused face from here.

As he ran, he tripped over a parked bicycle on the street, probably because his focus had waned. He pitched forward but managed to keep himself from falling and ran farther.

Behind him an eerie *zoom!* rang out.

He looked back at the bicycle he'd stumbled over. It had been dismantled into its wheels and frame by the unseen strike. It didn't seem like the sorcerer was very precise with the spear. He saw the sorcerer swing the knife around behind him again and rushed around another corner.

"God, he's firing that thing all over the damn city. Think about your surroundings, stupid!"

"Hmm. Without knowing the blueprint of the technique, they can witness the magic's outcome without causing a problem for the sorcerer. Even if an unknowing person saw what it caused, they wouldn't be able to calculate backward to the technique's construction!"

"I mean, well…that's not really what I wanted to say."

Kamijou sighed and swerved into an even narrower street.

He was in a race against time, but there was still something he needed to ask.

"Gah. Then is Aztec magic or whatever responsible for him disguising himself as Unabara, too?"

"Probably. There's an art where Aztec priests tear off the skin of human sacrifices and wear it, so I think it's being applied here."

He caught his breath.

He knew this wasn't the time for it. If he didn't concentrate, his feet would stop moving.

"Do what with their skin?"

"They wear it. They slice it off with a knife. But I don't know if he needs to go that far if he just wants to disguise himself. He could imitate someone's form just by cutting off a piece of skin around fifteen centimeters long from the arm and making a talisman out of it."

A vile sensation rose gradually from his fingertips. His pursuer suddenly got a lot creepier.

"What the hell? Cutting people's skin off and wearing it to disguise themselves? Are all sorcerers this messed up in the head?!"

"Mgh. Touma, that sounded an awful lot like occupational discrimination to me—"

He didn't have any more time to listen, so he hung up the phone.

This particular alleyway was shorter than he'd thought, and Kamijou ended up coming right back out onto a main street. He hurried across it and dove into another alley. Behind him, he heard the strange sounds of things being dismantled by the invisible spear.

Should I flee into a building? No, he could just dismantle the whole building from the outside, and I'd be buried alive! It's hard not knowing how extensive his attacks can be. I could even be buried in the underground mall.

As he ran, he tried to make sense of the situation. Was the sorcerer's aim related somehow to Index? She was a library of grimoires who had 103,000 of them memorized, so he couldn't discard the possibility that sorcerers from around the world would come and try to take her.

But that didn't really add up, either. Why would he have changed into Mitsuki Unabara in that case? Unabara was acquainted with Mikoto, and he didn't have any direct link to either Kamijou or

Index. He'd think that if Unabara was trying to kill him, he'd have changed himself into someone closer to Kamijou…

Kamijou shot around another street corner.

"Damn it!" he swore. It was a dead end, with an in-construction building blocking it. Shovels, cement bags, and other construction tools were taking up the narrow path, and it didn't look like there was a way past them. There was a giant arm overhead from a crane or something that had been set up on the roof of the incomplete building.

Kamijou ran for the construction site anyway and shot a glance over his shoulder. The footfalls of his enemy were surely and steadily getting closer. He couldn't run away.

What now? What now?!

The instant he scanned his surroundings, Mitsuki Unabara came running around the corner. As soon as he spotted Kamijou, he brandished the black stone knife in his hand.

There were only five meters between them.

However, Kamijou didn't go to punch him. Instead, he grabbed a nearby shovel. During that time, Mitsuki Unabara began to change his knife's angle, trying to get it to shine light at him. Kamijou, all too aware of the sweat dripping from his palms, swung down the shovel with all his might.

Not at Unabara, but at the bag of cement close by.

The shovel stabbed into the bag with a sharp *zzzkkk* noise, but he didn't stop there. The gray powder inside flew all over the place.

Unabara's vision, his surroundings, and the sky—all of it had been blanketed in gray.

He still swung the knife, but then he realized it.

The spear wasn't activating.

The cement powder had severed the space linking Venus and the spear. He couldn't fire the weapon because it needed to use the light from Venus.

Thwop! A heavy object flew right past Mitsuki Unabara's face.

As soon as he realized it was the shovel and readied himself—

"Wooohhh-aaahhhh!!"

Kamijou's fist came from directly in front, stabbing through the gray curtain. Unabara reflexively bent over to dodge it. There was no sense behind the action—only instinct. As a sweat now broke out on him, he took the obsidian knife, which had become just a blunt object at this point, and tried to bash it against the side of Kamijou's face. But because of his unstable stance, there was no strength behind it. Kamijou gave a roar and drove his toes straight into Unabara's gut.

Unabara attempted to leap backward to lighten the damage as much as possible.

He might have also realized the disadvantage of this cement curtain, as well, because he soon switched into a retreat.

He took two steps back, then a third, but Kamijou immediately closed the distance, moving many times faster than him. It was only natural—human feet are made for running forward much faster than backward. He clenched his fist again and went to throw another punch. Unabara instantly readied his obsidian knife.

Then, a *whooosh*.

In that moment, an entirely uninvited gale blew through the back road.

It drove away the curtain of gray covering their surroundings all at once. The sky, enclosed by the buildings, reappeared. And the light of Venus, its grace, showered down upon Unabara.

He brandished the knife and angled it.

Right before his eyes was a surprised Kamijou.

"Hah. You should prepare yourself!!"

He fixed the angle. Venus, the mirror, and his target were all in alignment. He concentrated mana into it, weaved his spell, transformed the starlight into an invisible spear, and sent it flying straight toward his enemy!!

The symbol of Venus and calamity: the Spear of Tlahuizcalpantecuhtli.

Kamijou...

…thrust out his right hand, but he couldn't figure out where the invisible attack was coming from…

…and as if slipping through the cracks in the divine protection of his right hand, the attack was set straight on his heart to pierce it…

…but nothing happened.

"Wha…?"

Mitsuki Unabara couldn't help but grunt in confusion. There were many necessary conditions to fire one of his powerful spears, and he thought he had satisfied them all. Therefore, there was no possibility of it having backfired. The loosed spear had flown straight at Kamijou's heart, and his body should have been beautifully disassembled like a cow at a butcher.

He looked at the obsidian knife in his hand as if it were a flashlight whose batteries had gone dead.

He was astonished at what he saw.

The rough gray powder had stuck all over its surface, just like chalk powder on a blackboard eraser. He couldn't even tell what color it was anymore.

Its function was to be a mirror—to reflect and control the shining light from Venus.

The mirror had been clouded, and he was thus unable to connect the light from Venus with his target.

Kamijou's feet came marching in.

He had already gotten up close to Mitsuki Unabara.

"?!"

If Unabara had abandoned his obsidian knife and rethought his strategy, he might still have had a chance. Unfortunately, he decided he would wipe the dirt off of it. Of course—given the choice between a fifty-fifty bare-handed brawl and sorcery that would let one win for sure, anyone would choose the latter. He only needed to wipe it off a little bit—but that was the temptation, which defeated him.

It delayed his reaction to Kamijou, who was right next to him.

A dull sound ripped through the air. The obsidian knife, with which he had persisted until the end, flew from his hands as he fell backward.

16 (Aug.31_PM00:36)

Kamijou looked down at Mitsuki Unabara, lying on the road.

With a glass-breaking noise, the skin on the part of his face where he had been punched shattered to pieces. The face of the sorcerer beneath looked even younger than Unabara, and his complexion seemed darker. It was almost like someone had forcefully torn off a sunburn—fragments of his face still stuck. It was uncanny.

"All right, then. Answer me this," began Kamijou, breathing heavily. "Why did you decide to change into Mitsuki Unabara, of all people?"

"Hah. Must I really spell it out for you to understand?"

"Of course you do, damn it! You wouldn't get anything out of Unabara attacking me, so why did you go for him?! To get close to Misaka? Just because she happens to know me?!"

"…"

"Answer me. You tore off a piece of Unabara's skin and disguised yourself as him. Were you going to do the same to Misaka? She's got nothing to do with this magic world! Why are you trying to get her involved?!"

Kamijou's rage was met by Unabara's quiet tone.

His words were level and without feeling, like they were dripping out of his mouth.

"In all actuality, I should have just killed Unabara."

His voice was not cold as ice, but rather like lukewarm water, neither rising nor falling with emotion.

"It seems like when he was on the verge of death, he used his power—telekinesis, was it?—to harden his own body's movements at an atomic level. He basically put himself into a cold sleep. I tried stabbing him through the heart, but it was like sticking a knife into frozen meat. My spears couldn't disassemble him, either. I had no choice, so I tied his hands and feet and threw him into that room, but..."

It appeared that this sorcerer had done his research before coming to Academy City. He was dropping scientific terms like *telekinesis* and *cold sleep* all over the place.

But Unabara's quiet voice got to Kamijou the most. It felt like he was forcing an old, stretched-out cassette tape to replay.

When Unabara saw his expression, he seemed just the slightest bit satisfied. Emotion returned to his voice.

"And why did I come here? Is that seriously the first question you thought to ask me after all this?" he sneered. "You really don't understand what a dangerous thing you've done, do you?"

"What?"

"To make all this worse, you have sole possession of the Index of Forbidden Books—all 103,000 grimoires. On top of that, you've won over sorcerers from the English Puritan Church, a Level Five from Tokiwadai, and a trump card against vampires to your side, haven't you?"

Then, his tone turning to one of self-ridicule, he continued. "The world of sorcery and the world of science aren't naturally able to mix. And yet you've gotten familiar with both organizations. You're essentially creating a new body all its own—the Kamijou faction. Organizations like the one I belong to are terribly afraid of such a new faction upsetting the world's power balance."

His organization.

Did that refer to Academy City, the world of the Church, a sorcerer's society, or some economic power?

"That's why I was sent over here. Though it's not like I was originally aiming to become Mitsuki Unabara or trying to cause harm to anyone. I only came here one month ago, and I only changed bodies last week. I was just here to observe. If we found that your Kamijou faction didn't have an effect on the power balance, I would have just reported back that there was no problem."

The sorcerer gritted his teeth.

His glare shot straight into Kamijou's face.

"But you were too dangerous! Speculating purely from the shards of information I've received, you've destroyed numerous organizations during just this summer vacation! On top of that, your power doesn't use money or influence, so we can't control, restrict, or negotiate. It's arbitrary, dictatorial, and self-righteous, fueled by your emotions alone! Do you seriously think the higher-ups wouldn't think such an enormously unstable power dangerous?!"

"Wait…so then you're…"

"Yes. My goal is not just Touma Kamijou, but the entire Kamijou faction. Even if you died by yourself, the members of this faction are too close for it to just disappear."

That was probably why he would shape-shift into an acquaintance.

He would take on the face of somebody Kamijou knew well, be as terrible a person as he could toward him, and cause him to lose trust in the person. Once that was over with, he'd switch to some other acquaintance of his. He would cause this faction to steadily rot away from within.

Even if he got wise to the idea midway through, there would be no problem for this sorcerer. He could then tear apart his circle of friends by playing the "Which one is the fake?" card—and his doubts would beget yet more doubts.

Internal decay.

The same political maneuver had caused countless dynasties to crumble since days of yore. Behind such occurrences as seemingly steadfast rules rotting in no time at all and sagacious kings one day suddenly transforming into horrific tyrants were the invisible hands of secret agents. Such extremely vivid and cruel skill later came to be exemplified using beings like *kitsune* or demons, depending on the country.

"I was trying so hard to leave you until last, but there was no choice. You had already unveiled the truth. I suppose I will just have to take your face next!" he said, leaping toward the obsidian knife that he'd dropped on the ground. He wiped the dirt from its mirrored surface, then, still on the floor himself, twisted around and swung another spear at him.

Unfortunately, perhaps because he fired from such an unreasonable position, the spear seemed to fly in an entirely different direction. The sorcerer swore under his breath, stood up, and tried to ready the knife again.

Kamijou dove in close before he could.

"Shit!!"

The sorcerer tried to loose another spear, but Kamijou's fist was faster. His right hand punched the obsidian knife. With the sound of glass breaking, his Imagine Breaker caused the obsidian knife to shatter.

"I'm not gonna wait for you, you moron—"

Suddenly, his voice was cut off.

A loud, metallic *clatter-clatter* rang out from above Kamijou. He looked up to find the framework of the unfinished building about to come crashing down.

The spear that had missed its mark had hit the building right next to them.

The structure wasn't at the concrete phase yet, so it was more like a giant jungle gym made of steel beams. The spears caused objects to break up into their component parts. The thick girders, now without any screws or bolts attached, were raining down upon their heads.

"?!"

Kamijou and the sorcerer both leaped backward to get away from it. A steel beam weighing hundreds of kilograms stabbed like a holy sword into the spot where they had been.

It didn't take long before the building itself started to topple down like an avalanche. Common sense would dictate running away. But if he let this chance go, the sorcerer would get away. That would mean he would swap bodies with somebody again and cause harm to somebody close to him.

Their eyes met.

The sorcerer looked at him, grinning.

Damn it! My life is the unluckiest piece of shit I've ever...

Kamijou swore, glaring at the sorcerer, who also didn't seem to want to run.

"This may be a pretty clichéd line, but...we could have been friends."

He heard the shouts of construction workers running about, trying to escape. They were all aboveground, so there probably wasn't anyone inside the building. He didn't think anyone wouldn't run away at this point.

"I've never entertained that fleeting thought even once!"

His reply was immediate. A steel beam crashed into the ground right next to him, but his face didn't budge an inch.

"Seriously, it's a shame," Kamijou sighed. "All that stuff you said about Misaka—that was all faked, too, wasn't it? That's the biggest shame...because now I've got a reason to really beat your face in."

The air between them froze at those words.

The silence was colder than darkness and dominated the area.

"...Being a fake?" whispered the sorcerer to himself.

Before Kamijou could frown, he repeated it.

"What's wrong...with being a fake?" he growled at himself. "Can a fake not desire peace? Is a fake not even allowed to want to protect Misaka?"

"Eh...?"

He forgot about the building's ominous creaking and looked hard at the sorcerer.

"That's right, I never wanted to do any of this," he declared, not paying any mind to the collapse soon to come.

"I didn't even want to hurt Unabara, either. That would be the best solution. Everyone would be happy, and nobody would be hurt. I loved this city. Ever since I came here a month ago. Even if I could never be a resident here, I loved this world in which Misaka lived."

The sorcerer continued.

"But there was no other way. The results were in. The higher-ups decided that the Kamijou faction was dangerous. Do you understand what I felt like when I changed into Unabara? What I felt like when I knew I was harming this world she lives in?"

Extreme emotions twisted and turned his expression.

"You would never understand! You destroyed all of it! If you had just been a little more amicable, if you had let me tell them that there was no problem, then I would have left quietly! I wouldn't have had to attack Unabara or lie to Misaka! Yeah, we're enemies now, but whose fault is that?!"

An invisible, murderous aura hung in the air around his body.

As if in concert with his rage, the top of the building started its descent with a crash.

Kamijou looked into the sorcerer's eyes.

Then he asked, without looking at the falling building, "Do you really like Misaka?"

Even though he was a spy...even though he'd tried to use her...

...his response was yes.

The top of the building turned into countless steel girders and beams, and all came hurtling down at them.

"Did you want to protect this world Misaka lives in?"

Because he was a spy. Even if he had to use her.

His response was yes.

The metal framework collided with the lower parts of the building, causing even more parts to be dismantled.

"But I can't protect them any longer. I'm your enemy now. Her enemy now. I didn't want to be, but I had to. What else would you have me do? What else could I have done? Fought against an entire organization by myself, like some movie hero, and died? I can't. I'm not you. I can't be a hero like you," the sorcerer said with a strangely fleeting, weak smile.

Yes. Touma Kamijou understood.

These were his true feelings. The motives of a man who was forced to become his enemy even though he didn't want to. He was forced to have to lay a hand upon that which he wanted to protect more than anything else in the world. They were the words of a man whose heart had been twisted.

There was a man named Motoharu Tsuchimikado.

When he had identified himself as a spy, Kamijou had thought it was a pretty easy position to be in. That couldn't have been further from the truth. He'd gained his freedom in exchange for the immense risk of disobeying orders.

The sorcerer before him was unable to shoulder that kind of risk.

He knew his own weakness, too, and that's probably why he could never forgive Kamijou for tearing his dream apart…nor himself for being unable to protect it.

Those were his true feelings.

He vented all of the distorted words within his own heart and stood to block him with everything he had.

Kamijou decided that he wouldn't pull his punches, either.

Those were his true feelings as somebody who lived a life free from freedom, his actions uncontrolled by anyone, and able to remain an ally to those he wished to protect. For a sorcerer, there was likely no more painful reality. He was a light too brilliant for his eyes to handle.

"Hah. No future after this apart from laying a hand on her, you say?"

Nevertheless, he made up his mind to fight with everything he had.

Kamijou couldn't ignore someone who had bared all his motives and emotions to him.

"Then I've got no choice. I will kill…that illusion of yours!"

Because of the top section of the building crumbling, the entire thing came tumbling down like a giant hand trying to crush them.

The steel girders poured down like rain, one after the other, but neither he nor the sorcerer paid a glance above them. Nor did they flee backward. They simply clenched their fists and ran forward, each set on closing the distance between them to zero.

"Gah-aahhhhhh!!"

Kamijou's fist connected with the sorcerer's face. He didn't seem to have any intent to dodge it in the first place, though, and he seized Kamijou by the collar with both hands. He twisted his arms and flung Kamijou's back hard into the wall. There was a loud, dull sound. It forced all the air out of his lungs.

As he was leaning against the wall, the sorcerer grabbed his neck with both hands. Kamijou felt the disturbing sensation of the sorcerer's thumbs jabbing into his windpipe, but he whipped his foot into the sorcerer's stomach. It was enough to cause the sorcerer to bend over in pain—perhaps because he relied only on that strange technique, he had never trained his body.

Without worrying about the hands strangling him, Kamijou brought his fist down as hard as he could on the enemy's back, so straight he might have been bowing. The sorcerer's legs gave out. He delivered another downward punch, and the hands around his neck came off.

Clonk!! came the roar of a beam slamming into the ground right next to Kamijou. Then, to make it worse, another girder slammed right into the top of that one. A huge shock wave–like, ear-piercing sound like a church bell ringing right next to him flooded into his eardrums.

"Gh...uh...?!"

Then, suddenly, the similarly shaken sorcerer came at the staggering Kamijou...

"Aaaaaaaaaaaaahhhhhhhhhh!!"

...and tackled him at full force. Kamijou fell onto his back, but because the sound had rocked his brain, he couldn't move his body the way he needed to. On the other hand, the sorcerer, his movements faltering like he was drunk, still tried to get on top of him.

As Kamijou tried to somehow get away from the sorcerer about to fall on him...

"Oh."

...he saw it.

A huge swarm of iron beams was coming down from the sky, filling his vision. He saw one of them on a route that would skewer the both of them. They couldn't have been more than twenty meters away. They had, what, a couple seconds? The sorcerer was glaring at Kamijou underneath him, so he didn't realize what was happening.

"Get out of the way, moron!!"

He kicked the sorcerer in the gut before he could get on top of him, then delivered an openhanded slap to his cheek. His body fell to the left. He turned onto his back...and then finally got a grasp of the situation.

At that moment, their eyes met.

The rain of iron girders. He didn't try to avoid it. He smiled. It was a thin, lonely smile, like he had realized what would happen if he won this fight.

Kamijou had no responsibility to save this sorcerer.

Nobody would scorn his decision to leave him for dead.

But...

"Can a fake not desire peace?"

Even still...

"Is a fake not even allowed to want to protect Misaka?"

Kamijou bit down.

Aw, jeez! This is totally unfair, you asshole!!

He tried to grab the fallen sorcerer's arm. When he realized the latter was surprised at this, it riled him up even more. He knew it wouldn't be in time. He gritted his teeth—

—and the swarm of iron and steel crashed down, shaking the earth.

17 (Aug.31_PM00:47)

Huge clouds of dust swept up into the air and took away their vision.

He could hear an uproar from people nearby, but they didn't gather around like curious onlookers normally would. An onlooker would need to look at the dangerous place from a safe area, and the distinction between them wasn't clear in this case. They couldn't get close.

"...Ha-ha." Kamijou, at ground zero, chuckled weakly.

A steel girder had fallen into the ground right between his legs as he sat on his butt. That wasn't all. All around him, more of them were sticking out of the ground, covering them up, like a badly made hut with tons of holes in the roof. There was a precarious balance here that seemed so weak a breeze would cause the whole thing to come crashing down, but for now, at least, Kamijou hadn't been buried alive.

That was lucky...wait, that's impossible. I'm unlucky, after all. Which means...oh, I see. That Level Five can use the power of electricity to manipulate magnetism, too, can't she?

His luck had nothing to do with it. That one beam's trajectory had definitely led straight to him. Some kind of power must have been at work, and the beam's path had warped right before it hit him. That was the likely answer.

Still fearing further collapse of the unsteady iron framework, he looked around. He could see the sorcerer in the gaps between the steel pillars holding up the roof.

He seemed to have one hand caught between two fallen girders. But it hadn't been crushed by them. It was more like he'd stuck his hand in between a space that was already there. He was essentially bound by the world's heaviest handcuffs.

The sorcerer looked dazed, like he was mystified by the fact that he was still alive.

Finally, he spoke.

"Have I...lost?"

"Something like that. By the way, my hand didn't cause any of this, got it?" he insisted, scratching his head, but the sorcerer shook his head. Whatever the reason, he couldn't move. He couldn't make a comeback even if he wanted to continue the fight.

"So I've lost, then," said the sorcerer, smiling faintly. "That means I was stopped here, then, right? It means I don't have to kill Misaka or anyone else, right?"

"..."

Kamijou didn't answer. He looked at the sorcerer's face.

Thinking about it now, he was probably always lost as to what to do. Of course, he was probably trying to kill Kamijou with everything he had, but wasn't he worrying terribly and putting a limiter on his real power? After all, if he had won this battle, he would surely need to kill Mikoto with his own hands.

If he had used his spear as his first attack, Kamijou probably would have died, without any time to dodge it. And while he was running through the straight roads between buildings, now that he thought of it, there were plenty of chances for him to hit his back.

This sorcerer didn't want to hurt Mikoto Misaka.

He didn't want to destroy this world she lived in.

But his selfishness was not so easily granted. His own life would be in danger if he were to follow through with that. So he wanted a justifiable reason. An excuse, like "I used everything I had, but something got in the way and I failed."

Kamijou was a novice, but the enemy faction was seriously considering him and the group of people around him as a threat, after all. He was, so to speak, the boss of the bad guys. It felt rather terrible to be an opponent whose main way to fight was through lies and bluffs.

"You know...," the sorcerer began, "...the attacks won't end here. My superiors wouldn't let up just because a henchman like me failed one time. In fact, it might make them view you as even more dangerous. Others like me will come your and Misaka's way, and in the worst case, they might order me to do so again."

Kamijou listened silently.

"Will you protect her for me?" he asked. "No matter when, no matter where, no matter who it is, no matter how many times. Can you promise me that whenever something like this happens, you'll run to her side like a convenient hero and protect her for me?"

That was his wish that could never be granted.

That was the weight of surrendering the dream he really wanted to accomplish himself to somebody else.

And so...

...Kamijou said one thing...

...and nodded.

"That really was the worst answer you could have given," muttered the collapsed sorcerer, smiling bitterly.

18 (Aug.31_PM00:57)

Mikoto Misaka held the wrapped hamburger to her chest and listened to their conversation with her back to a wall around the street corner.

She hadn't heard everything they'd said, though. There were two Mitsuki Unabaras, and one of them started a fight with Kamijou. Then, when she hurried to catch up, Unabara's face was cracked apart like some kind of special makeup, and someone else's face was inside. And on top of it all, the unfinished building had suddenly collapsed. A whole lot of things she didn't understand had happened. And because she was keeping her distance, she only caught bits and pieces of their conversation. In fact, after scrambling out of the path of the falling girders, she was the one least able to keep her calm.

But she still got the gist of it.

She knew why they had been fighting each other.

Who they were fighting over.

Who they were fighting for.

She shook her head violently from side to side.

I-I've got it all wrong! Of course, I must be misunderstanding this! He says that sort of thing unconsciously all the time! It doesn't mean I'm special or anything!

But still, she stopped shaking her head to deny it.

She knew all that, and yet she stopped.

Ugh...

She knocked the back of her head against the wall she was leaning on with a *thunk*. It really was the worst, she thought. How was she supposed to go and face him after hearing a line like that?

Especially that last thing Kamijou had said.

...Man, even though I know I'm mistaken...why does that idiot have to be so confusing about it?!

She sighed. She couldn't even predict when her red face would go back to normal.

Aug.31_PM01:04 End

CHAPTER 3

A Certain Misaka's Last Order

Tender_or_Sugary.

1 (Aug.31_PM05:20)

The laboratory Accelerator had come to was immense.

It consisted of a line of three giant buildings that looked like field warehouses—they were the cultivation facilities made to provide the twenty thousand Sisters for the experiment. Inside them, metal shelves would be hung up all the way to the ceiling, each packed with cylindrical capsules like books in a library bookcase.

The building with the actual laboratory in it was next to these three buildings.

Made from reinforced concrete, the rectangular two-story building looked tiny next to the three cultivation facilities. It certainly didn't look like it would be the main building in the complex.

Accelerator stood before the door of the laboratory.

There was a retinal scanner on it, but he ignored it. He doubted his ID would still work anyway. Instead, he rapped lightly on the door. He focused the impact of his knock at the lock, precisely and accurately destroying its metal fitting.

The old, mansion-like door opened with a *creak*.

The interior looked more like an IT room than a laboratory. What looked like industrial refrigerators lining each of the walls were apparently the latest and greatest in quantum computer technology, but it seemed to him that they were just older models—all that they could get their hands on for the experiment, basically. At the very least, he didn't consider them appropriate substitutes for the Tree Diagram. The windowless room was illuminated by the eerie glow from dozens of monitors. The floor was all but invisible underneath the piles of data paper the machines had spat out. The only sound to be heard was the low, heavy whirring of cooling fans.

The room might not have seemed like a laboratory at first, but the devil was in the details. This kind of setup was commonplace for labs that focused mainly on simulations, like evolution experiments based on artificial life or modeling aerodynamic resistance on aerospace models.

One woman stood there, alone, in the middle of the room.

During the experiment, there had always been at least twenty researchers packed in like sardines doing their work, but there was no sign of them now. The woman was well aware of that, too. Instead of reclining on a chair, she was sitting on a table. She held sheets of data snaking across the floor, marking them up with a red pen. She didn't seem to care much about manners at the moment.

"Hm? Oh, welcome back, Accelerator. You didn't have to break the door. Your ID will still be valid for another ninety days," she said, as if she hadn't so much realized Accelerator entered as she had just looked up from the data sheets when her focus waned and happened to see him standing there.

This was Kikyou Yoshikawa.

She was in her late twenties but wore no makeup at all. She had on a pair of washed-out old jeans along with a T-shirt that had been worn thin by countless trips through the washing machine. Atop that was a white, long-sleeved sports shirt—the only thing she had on that sparkled like new.

Accelerator looked at the terribly long sheet of data Yoshikawa was holding and followed it down. There was a ton of dead trees scattered about below them, nearly covering the floor up entirely.

At present, the experiment was frozen. Its plan had been con-

ceived in the supercomputer Tree Diagram's simulations, but the results of those calculations had been judged to be erroneous.

But the experiment was only suspended, not canceled. All they needed to do was to locate the error and fix it, and then they could restart it at any time.

Accelerator didn't think that would be possible, though. It wasn't as if the Tree Diagram was performing overly complex calculations. However, the quantity of calculations it needed to make was enormous. For example, a human could easily calculate that one times ten equals ten, but a machine would end up doing one plus one ten times. This method was probably easier on the machine, but he pitied whoever had to confirm all of it. How many tens of years could it take just to skim through the entire code base?

"Jeez. Good work, I guess. Is starin' at data all day actually fun for you?"

"No, not at all. I'm having so little fun that I'd actually want you to help out if you were able. Your calculation and problem-solving skills are fairly widely known, after all."

"Wouldn't it be a problem if I read what was behind the scenarios?"

The main part of the experiment only required him to complete twenty thousand scripted combat scenarios. Its ultimate goal was to initiate Accelerator's shift from Level Five to Level Six by improving his skills as an esper through battle and controlling the direction they grew in.

In other words, if he knew more than he needed to, it became possible that he wouldn't act in accordance with these predetermined scenarios. So they'd been careful not to let him see too much of the experiment's data...

However, Kikyou Yoshikawa looked up once more from the data sheets and said, "Don't worry, I'm actually not looking at the Tree Diagram data at the moment."

"Eh? Leaving that goddamned mountain of data for later? Man, you sure have a lot of free time or somethin'. Or didja already give up?"

"Well, I think you'd probably be almost dead by the time we

finished analyzing all of that. And in answer to your question, yes. As far as I'm concerned, at least, these data have more relative importance."

She spoke with a tone implying that she didn't actually have much free time, but Accelerator didn't particularly care. All he needed right now was an incubator to adjust Last Order's incomplete body, the necessary facilities to do so, and the knowledge and skill to actually use them.

He looked around, but all the files, notes, discs, and paper were strewn about the floor like a storm had gone through. He couldn't tell what was what.

"Hey. Where's the Sisters' specimen-tuning manual? I need it for the hardware and software side—so I need both an incubator and a Testament. Also, I'm borrowing one of the tuning facilities. Don't ask why. Just consider it my contract price for this whole experiment going under."

Yoshikawa was a bit surprised at this.

"Hold on a second. Why do you know all this? I only found out about it three hours ago."

"Eh?"

"I'm talking about this," she said, waving the data paper she was holding.

It was the code for Testament.

The Sisters were clones of Mikoto Misaka that were created in approximately fourteen days thanks to a special cultivation device. Their personalities couldn't be constructed via normal learning, though—it wasn't enough time.

So their personalities and intelligence were electronically input via Testament, a so-called "learning device," but more realistically, it was a brainwashing machine. Essentially it did the same thing as when a computer overwrites information on a hard drive.

In other words, Yoshikawa was looking at a blueprint of the Sisters' minds.

"So what're you doing with that?"

"Can't you tell by looking? I'm searching for mistakes," she came back, marking up the data sheet with her red pen. "Of course, I only noticed it three hours ago, so I'm still not finished."

Accelerator frowned.

Then, Yoshikawa's pen stopped.

"I'm in the middle of cleaning out the bugs in her personality data. Well, actually, they're man-made commands…so maybe I should call them viruses."

"…Wait. What did you just say?"

"Well, that's not to say that all the Sisters' personality data have been destroyed. It'll still be an issue if the one goes berserk and ends up infecting the other Sisters, though." Yoshikawa gave a little shake of her head. "I hadn't explained it to you, had I? There's a unique specimen called Last Order."

Last Order.

Sparks ran up and across the back of Accelerator's neck like electric impulses.

"You mean…her?"

"Her, huh? Do you already know her?…That must mean she's still in the city," she mused, twirling her pen. "Well, that's all right. I'm sure you know some parts, but I'll go over Last Order's current situation again for you. This is important, so listen carefully," she said, bringing herself down from the table and into a chair. She motioned to the chair next to her, urging Accelerator to take a seat as well, but he didn't go for it.

He hated this side of Yoshikawa. She was acting like a mediocre teacher.

"First of all, she wasn't created for the purposes of the experiment. Did you know that?"

"What's that supposed to mean? They're all dumbed-down clones of Railgun, so they were all made to be killed, weren't they?"

"That's correct, but how many of those battles needed to be done before it ended?"

"Whaddaya mean? Twenty thousand, right? I did think that was a nice, round number, but—"

Accelerator broke off, realizing something.

"Right. **Her serial number is 20001.** It seems like you knew that already. She is a specimen not required for the experiment's scripted battles. She's more like a safety measure."

Yoshikawa sighed, then continued. "Try imagining this. What would happen if the Sisters revolted after we had already made twenty thousand of them? There were only around twenty of us—we wouldn't have been able to handle it."

"So that brat was your trump card? The hell? Is she a man-made Level Five or somethin'?"

"We can't make something like that, and there wouldn't be any point. Why add an artificial Level Five to the revolt? We created her as a safety measure, so she needed to have a more trustworthy system. She needed to be someone who even weak researchers like us could have complete control over."

"?"

"Have you heard the term *Misaka network*?"

Accelerator scowled. If he recalled correctly, that was the name of the brain-wave link thing that connected all the Sisters. The network itself had a giant will of its own, and it also had a way to control each Misaka.

"You see, Last Order is the opposite. By sending a certain signal pulse into her brain, she can instead control the Misaka network. That would make it possible to send a halt signal to all twenty thousand other Misakas if we needed to. This way, the Sisters would never be able to betray us."

Yoshikawa exhaled before continuing.

"Last Order is the command center for all of the Sisters. She cannot be allowed to go free. That's why we kept her in that incomplete state. We really wanted her to be in a vegetative state, but we had to give her a certain amount of self-awareness to allow her to connect to the Misaka network in the first place."

"So she's basically…a breathing keyboard?"

It was a graphic way of putting it, but Accelerator wouldn't put it past the staff here. And the other Sisters were basically just disposable walking targets to begin with.

Of course Last Order seemed different than the Sisters. Her body and mind had both purposely been kept in an immature state.

"And whaddaya mean 'bug'? Or virus or whatever."

"We were going to secretly keep her here in the cultivation devices even after the experiment ended, but about one week ago, we suddenly detected some odd brain waves from her. When we rushed over to the device, it had already been destroyed from the inside and she'd made her escape."

Yoshikawa ran a finger over the data.

"We don't know what exactly happened. The cause of her going out of control is still unknown, so for now, we're having the staff look into that."

"Eh? Why not just call up Anti-Skills or Judgment or somethin'?"

"We can't. Our superiors have ordered us not to say a word about the experiment. I mean, it's obviously not something you want going public."

"So you never caught her. Wait, a freakin' week?! That's ridiculous. And dangerous. Isn't she in control of all ten thousand Sisters?!"

"Our confidence in how well we made the system led to our mistake. We never considered she could run away. She shouldn't be able to live outside the cultivation device in the first place, so I suppose we underestimated her capabilities...Goodness, the fact that she's still alive after seven days is already against all logic. She wasn't made to be very strong, was she?...I wonder if she got attached to you, hm?"

Accelerator gave a bitter, sarcastic smile at that one.

She didn't notice it.

"Thinking on it now, that might have been one of her defense reactions. Somebody wrote some bad programming into her head, and she fled the laboratory to try and prevent it. She probably doesn't realize herself why she ended up running away from the laboratory, though..."

And Yoshikawa had only caught on to this three hours ago.

She wanted to get together all of the research staff and have an emergency meeting about it, but she couldn't get in touch with any of them. It seemed like they had already covered up the fact that they ever worked here in the first place.

"But, y'know, she wasn't tryin' to run away or nothin'. She came to me asking if I could get in touch with any of you scientists."

"What? Wait, when and where was the last time you saw her? And—why were you even in contact with her?"

"Like I said, she just started followin' me around. Besides, I don't care how troubled they are or if they're cryin' or what, could you really imagine me goin' over and talkin' to them?"

"…I wonder what it means."

Yoshikawa rested her face on her hand and began to think. She froze as still as a statue, like the thoughts flying about in her head were dizzying.

"So that bad programming—well, I guess it was nothin' good. Like you said, that brat was supposed to be in charge of all of the other Sisters."

He thought back to their conversation at the restaurant.

"———*The brain-wave link and each individual Misaka are like synapses and brain cells.*"

"That's right. I got myself an output of her personality data in order to find the root cause of her flight and pinpoint her current location, but upon closer inspection, there's odd code everywhere, like graffiti. I've picked up on some of it, but it's literally all over the place—including dummy data—so I don't even know if I'll be able to completely remove it. And as for what the bad code is doing…"

"What? What's it doin'?"

"Well, I can't say anything for sure, since I haven't totally analyzed the code yet, but if I'm to assume the outcome from the general direction these statements are headed in…it looks like something that will make a command to indiscriminately attack humans." Yoshikawa broke off for a moment before continuing. "I've figured out how long there is until this virus activates. It's set to go on September 1 at exactly midnight. At that time, the virus will begin to activate, and it will finish ten minutes after that. It will infect all of the live Sisters through the Misaka network, and they will begin to run wild. Once that happens, they'll be unstoppable. They may not be on your level, but if ten thousand of them all start swinging around Metal-eaters, then they will be a force to be reckoned with."

"...Wait, that means..."

"That's right. What happens after that is exactly what you're thinking," said Yoshikawa in a hard voice—not calmly, but rather one that felt like her thoughts had all hardened around this point.

Accelerator thought about what she meant.

At the moment, nearly all of the ten thousand remaining Sisters were spread throughout the world, having their bodies readjusted. That meant that it was impossible both in terms of time and distance to have an anti-esper force stationed in Academy City, such as Anti-Skills or Judgment, quietly take care of the problem.

The Sisters that went berserk and attacked people would probably be dealt with by outsiders. And if it happened to nearly ten thousand of them outside the city all at once, there would be no way to keep it secret. Plus, if they discovered that all of the espers responsible for the situation had been artificially created, secondary problems would spread like wildfire. Even if by some miracle there were some Sisters who were excluded from the command, they'd be eliminated as soon as someone decided they were dangerous.

The corporations and agencies throughout the world cooperating with Academy City on the readjustments would see this, and it would flip their opinion of the city upside down. After all, it was an insurrection of ten thousand clones. If all of those institutions dropped support for Academy City after that, the city itself wouldn't survive.

And he could scarcely imagine what would happen after that.

Academy City would likely be dismantled entirely, and the various scientists would probably be pulled into military laboratories across the planet because of their strange skills. Or maybe Academy City, held back by the fear of destruction, would resort to more forceful measures and begin a world invasion using next-gen weaponry and supernatural abilities.

Either way, it would completely shake up the world's power balance. Panic the world over would ensue. In the worst case, there was a danger of all-out war. And not on the simple level of the inside of "Academy City vs. the outside." The huge political and social tremors would tear subtle but profound fissures across every government, people, religion, and ideal. It would scatter pieces of the world map right and left like a once-complete jigsaw puzzle thrown to the floor.

It would be the end of the world.

Accelerator understood what those words meant. He could imagine it more realistically than anyone else, since he held the power to destroy in the palm of his hand.

No matter how the world was destroyed, Accelerator would almost certainly live through it. He would stand there, alone and unharmed, in a city ruined so badly he wouldn't even be able to tell up from down.

But there wouldn't be anything left there. Convenience stores wouldn't be open, the power wouldn't be working, and he wouldn't be able to get his hands on even one can of coffee. The only thing that would be left for him would be a primitive lifestyle, subsisting on animals and berries cooked over a fire. Actually, if the nuclear option ended up being the one to do it, there wouldn't even be anything left alive. If that happened, he'd just have to live by eating mud or something. And if it came to that, he'd end up cursing his powers for not letting him die. He had searched for strength, and yet what awaited him was a position at the lowest end of the food chain. The weakest. People create civilization, so if there were no people, there would be no civilization.

That was what it meant for there to be nothing.

"Hah, that's interestin'. Totally interestin'. So that's it, then, huh? End of the world? And here I always thought that was my job, heh." Accelerator grinned savagely. "Can't you just call Anti-Skills or Judgment or somethin' to help? The city may be big, but it's got freakin' walls around it. Just send 'em out in human waves to attack, and they'll catch Last Order in no time. Besides, she was just walkin' around and eatin'. No caution at all, I'm tellin' ya."

"I can't report it to them. Like I said, when you think about what we were doing...The upper echelons are keeping silent, certainly, but this is way too big for us to go public with. Besides..."

"Besides what?"

"We wouldn't save the Sisters that way. If Last Order gets picked up by outsiders and studied, they'd discover that the ten thousand Sisters could have gone berserk. That's reason enough to get rid of any artificial object, isn't it?"

"So if you don't catch this one brat, it won't help."

"I don't have any way to respond to that. She may not know she's running away, but I think she's using the protocols regarding destruction of evidence, which are up in the Misaka network. She does basically seem to be living on the streets, after all. She won't use any money, nor will she use an ID. She doesn't leave a paper trail. There are areas where the satellite can't quite see, and if she avoids the police robot patrol routes, she won't even show up on those videos. Ahh...How long has it been since you left her? There isn't another organization who has caught on to this, right? If she gets kidnapped, I'll have a serious problem."

At first, her tone made it sound like she was only thinking about herself, but he noticed just a hint of actual worry for Last Order.

When he saw that, he clicked his tongue angrily.

This particular researcher was more naïve than most. She'd desperately try to remember the faces of each of the genetically identical Sisters. She'd also try and give them human names instead of serial numbers.

But that was just naïveté, not kindness. It was her being soft. If she had truly been kind, she would have stood up against the whole experiment in the first place—like that boy and that girl had.

Yoshikawa didn't notice his annoyance and continued.

"But the flee command only applies to us, the researchers. She's not showing any sense of caution toward you, after all...Yes, if we take advantage of that, we may actually be able to do something..."

She trailed off like she was talking to herself, but Accelerator was listening to her carefully. He scowled. There was no way these people were going to use him as a pawn. He immediately changed the subject.

"You said virus, right? Not a bug, but a virus. Some warmonger agent tryin' to start somethin'? Or is some bankrupt military business tryin' to get back in the game?"

"Ao Amai," replied Yoshikawa briefly to Accelerator's banter.

He frowned. He was pretty sure he saw the guy while he was eating lunch with Last Order at the restaurant. But if he really was the culprit, then why on earth was he still wasting time in Academy City? If there was a week until the thing actually went off, then he should have just escaped the city…

Yoshikawa read his thoughts and explained.

"Only one of the researchers disappeared right before this happened. Though he did send me a text saying he was going to use some paid vacation time."

"That's it?"

Accelerator looked around the deserted room.

Only eccentric people took on jobs for no money. He wouldn't think it strange if the guy were to sell out to some other lab or become a convenience store clerk. The rest of the researchers had probably done just that.

Yoshikawa, on the receiving end of his doubtful stare, went on.

"He was one of the original researchers on the deadlocked Radio Noise project. When the Sisters were substituted in for the experiment, he transferred here as staff. His specialty was the creation of personality data using Testament. Basically, he was the most knowledgeable about the Sisters' software—their minds."

"Wait, it's like he wanted you to know or somethin'! And the way he did it, too! Why the hell did he decide to have it wait till today? If he wanted to destroy the world, he shoulda just ended it all as soon as he put the virus in. Why wait a week?"

"That would be a question for him, not me. Though if I had to make a logical guess"—she sighed—"he was waiting for the Sisters to become accustomed to the outside establishments where they're awaiting treatment. He wanted to create a situation where they were perfectly safe until now, and then they suddenly go crazy. Perhaps he had to plant a sense of trustworthiness toward the Sisters in them first?"

Accelerator paused for a moment.

He thought about what should be done.

"So what the heck were you doing? How're you gonna stop the virus in the brat's head?"

"That's what I'm trying to figure out now."

Her words were tinged with a hint of confusion. Accelerator curled his lips. She could use Testament to mess around in Last Order's head all she wanted, but she had to write a vaccine program, find her, and inject it. The chances honestly seemed around fifty-fifty, if not lower.

What to do, then?

Of course, he knew the answer to that full well. If they didn't find a way to deal with it, they would dispose of the infected specimen to prevent the virus from being transmitted. That way, the 9,969 remaining Sisters outside the walls of the city would be protected from the infection and be able to go about their normal lives.

By sacrificing just one person.

By disposing of her, by throwing her in a trash can, just because a little problem came up.

"…I'm working as hard as I can to keep that from happening. Of course, there's something you can do, too," she suggested, as if she had noticed something from Accelerator's reticence.

"Did you forget who you were talkin' to or what? I'm the guy who killed ten thousand of 'em. You're telling me to save someone? I can kill, but I sure as hell can't save."

"Allow me to respond that we were the ones who urged you to do that. You did take out more than ten thousand of the Sisters. But if we had found a way for you to shift to Level Six without using them, you wouldn't have had to kill anyone."

"And you're telling me to believe you just because you said that?"

"There's no helping it if you don't want to. I'm not strong enough to detain you. Go spend the rest of this time doing whatever you want. And pray—pray that her body will reach its limit and die before the virus activates."

" . . "

Accelerator looked right into Yoshikawa's eyes.

There she sat, same as always.

She just sat there, expression unchanging, and spoke.

"I can't catch her. Her trait of unconsciously running away if she sees a researcher relies heavily on the magnetic field patterns emitted by our bodies. Even if I kept myself out of sight, she would detect my magnetic field and flee. On the other hand, if I could just figure that out, it would give me a chance to get closer to her...but I don't think I'd be able to pursue her while analyzing the virus code at the same time. But if you're here, it's different. If we work together, we could be able to do something about it."

"...What a damn pain."

Accelerator fell silent, narrowing his eyes. This was why he hated this woman. She was just so naïve. If she wasn't strong enough to shoulder something herself, then no matter how far she went with it, it would never become kindness.

It wasn't so much about the ten thousand Sisters going berserk— the notion was too vast to seem real. Instead she used the idea of Last Order's death, which was much easier for him to grasp. *That's some psychological manipulation, right there,* he thought, speechless. Even if she were doing it because she wanted peace, a person couldn't call it kind.

Yoshikawa took a pair of large envelopes, which looked like they had project proposals in them.

"Right now, you can do one of two things. The first is to subdue the culprit, Ao Amai, who is in hiding somewhere in the city, and force him to tell you how the virus works. The second is to secure Last Order before the virus activates. Pick whichever you like. Of course, you seem more suited to killing than protecting."

She slid the envelopes across the table, and they came to a stop before Accelerator. Some of the documents from the two open envelopes peeked out.

————There were a number of photographs in the one on the left. They were shaky pictures, like from cameras used to detect speed violations on the highway. They depicted a low-riding sports car from above, and in the driver's seat was Ao Amai. There were also maps that had been marked with a red ballpoint pen.

Yoshikawa had probably hacked into all sorts of police and crime-fighting systems to investigate where Ao Amai would be predicted to hide and in what area he was moving. The fact that he still hadn't been caught probably amounted to the simple fact that there weren't enough people or that he was switching hiding places in rapid succession.

————What looked like a data stick and a superthin electronic book came out of the one on the right. The data stick had a label on which was written "Serial Number 20001 Personality Outline (Before Infection)." It might have been too much to output on paper.

It must have been Last Order's personality data. It was probably telling him to predict her path based on her likes, dislikes, principles, thoughts, intellect, motions, biases, etc., and use that to chase her down or anticipate her movements. Of course, the last time he saw her in the restaurant, she didn't look like she'd be moving anywhere by herself.

"Hey. None of you can catch Last Order, right?"

"Yes, since she appears to be using the experiment cover-up protocols subconsciously. And besides, the only piece I have to move around the board is me."

"But Amai's the guy who made all those data? He's a personality data specialist, isn't he? So wouldn't he know about that cover-up protocol or whatever?"

"Knowledge and skill are two different things. He is actually putting in a lot of effort, though. It's just that he slacks off, so he hides his head but leaves his tail sticking out. On the other hand, any knowledge input into the Sisters instantly becomes skill. That's why we can't catch Last Order. And we can look at the money flow, too. He leaves traces of where he's been when he uses a store, but she lives on the streets. She can conceal herself completely. It goes without saying which would be easier to follow."

"..."

It also went without saying which one Accelerator was more suited to.

His power was good at breaking things, not protecting people. No, actually, there was a more fundamental problem than theory and practical skill.

"Ah, she's here she's here finally! says Misaka says Misaka, pointing to the waitress. Yay! Misaka's food came first!"

He'd never protected someone before. He didn't know how he would do it, either. He couldn't even imagine using his power to help somebody.

"Wow, this is the first time I've had a hot meal, like, ever! exclaims Misaka exclaims Misaka. Some really hot steam is coming off the plate and stuff, says Misaka says Misaka, eyeing the food carefully."

It was already a more fundamental problem than theory. His power couldn't save anyone, and that's just how his world was. People in his world never got saved. If someone did, that would be stranger—that was the first statement of the common sense within him.

"But this is also the first time I'm eating with somebody else, answers Misaka answers Misaka. I've heard that people give thanks for their food before eating it, recalls Misaka recalls Misaka. I wanna do that! says Misaka says Misaka, ever hopeful."

If, hypothetically, he were to try and save somebody with that power, then all the common sense he'd surrounded himself with would come tumbling down. He wouldn't be Accelerator anymore.

An Accelerator who helps others was not Accelerator. He would, in essence, have been replaced with an entirely different person.

"Heh, guess so. Anyone would understand which one I should take, huh?" murmured Accelerator to himself almost mockingly.

He wasn't that boy or that girl. There were plenty of other people far more suited to saving others than him. Unfortunately, every seat was taken. There was absolutely no room for him to come in at this point.

If his power wasn't suited to saving people...

If his power was suited to killing people...

Accelerator recalled someone's face, just for a moment.

"Hah, hate me all you want, you freakin' brat. This was my only choice."

Then he chose. He selected his option by removing one of the big envelopes. As though giving up on something, he took one of them in his hand.

The envelope on the right.

The envelope containing the data stick loaded with personality data and the electronic book.

So that he could go secure one man-made girl named Last Order.

At that moment, Accelerator ceased to be Accelerator.

He rose to protect. He acted to help. He wielded his power to save another. It wasn't at all about whether it was unlike him. Far from it. If someone who knew him well had seen what he had just done, they'd think there must have been something wrong with their eyes. Perhaps they would shout that this Accelerator was a fake.

That's how much impact his decision held.

You could say that he lost his entire identity as Accelerator.

The boy, who was now no one, without power, spoke as if sneering at himself.

"Smile already. Looks like I still somehow want salvation, eh?"

"Yes, I will indeed smile wide for that." Yoshikawa fixed her gaze on him. "If you still have those sorts of emotions within you, then that is something to celebrate. So relax, and prove that your power can protect somebody important to you."

Accelerator took the envelope with the data stick in it without replying, turned on his heel, and headed for the exit. *That's exactly why I hate her and how damn soft she is,* he said to himself.

"I'm gonna be workin' for you researchers, got it? You'd better have a hefty reward for me when I get back."

"Yes. You can leave her physical adjustments to me," answered Yoshikawa to the boy's silent back as he left the laboratory.

2 (Aug.31_PM06:00)

Kikyou Yoshikawa sighed, now alone in the room.

Accelerator coming here at the last moment was nothing short of a miraculous stroke of luck. If he hadn't, she really wouldn't have been able to do anything, and Academy City would have been destroyed.

Now that he was going looking for Last Order, Yoshikawa's job was to catch Amai and make him explain the virus code, but she lingered here—making sense of the code herself seemed the simpler option when compared to getting herself involved in a running fight, which she'd never done before.

Nevertheless...

Weeding out every last bit of the virus code from the enormous personality data when she didn't even know how much of it existed was an arduous task in and of itself. She couldn't mess up and delete needed code, either. If she got rid of memory-related programming, Last Order would simply lose some memories, but if she damaged the code governing her autonomic nervous system, the girl would die.

She sighed again.

She looked up from the data sheet. Readjusting Last Order's body was no simple task, despite her easy reply to Accelerator previously. It was less of an issue of technical skill and more one of her current position.

The laboratory had only frozen the experiment, not terminated it entirely. That meant they had to make sure the experiment could be restarted at any time. Of course, they could never allow Last Order, the core of controlling all the Sisters, to run amok because of a single researcher's own scheming. If she took independent action, she would doubtlessly be on the receiving end of the responsibility.

Yoshikawa was just soft. She was not a kind person.

For example, when that experiment was on the brink of ending, when just short of ten thousand Sisters conspired to control the wind-generating propellers in Academy City to hamper Accelerator's attack, she could have stopped them by sending a halt signal through the Misaka network with Last Order, but she didn't.

The fact that she didn't, however, was not out of any sort of kindness because she didn't want them to die. It was only because she was too soft to risk causing irreparable damage to the whole experiment by interfering with the Sisters during their work.

"Still, though..."

Kikyou Yoshikawa made up her mind.

Accelerator was trying so hard to save someone that he had thrown aside his own identity. That reality was probably enough to drive a heavy shock into his heart. It was a pretty simple, fundamental point that he could help people with his power—but he had given up. He purposely deprecated himself, *saying that he couldn't do anything but kill, to give himself a way out of his own life, in which he would never be saved.*

If Accelerator, in that condition, were to realize that he was able to protect someone with his own hands...

...he would definitely have regrets.

About what those people who had fallen before him meant to him.

About why he didn't lend a hand more quickly.

However, he still set his mind on facing that reality so that he could save just one girl. Yoshikawa didn't want to walk all over his feelings. Even if he had realized it far too late, and even if he had reached a point from which there was no return, she didn't want to trample that.

"In the end, I'm just soft. I'm not kind at all."

Dry words, spoken to herself. Yes—Yoshikawa was not a kind person. A truly kind person wouldn't have begged for Accelerator's help and made him bear such suffering. A truly kind person wouldn't have relied on him and instead chosen to settle the score by herself, even at a huge disadvantage.

Yoshikawa hated herself for being so soft.

She wanted to try being kind just once in her life.

"Well, then, I suppose the time has come for me, too—to destroy myself."

She sighed again, then got to work preparing for Last Order's physical adjustments with the data sheet in one hand. Being prepared to take a risk to do something for somebody else didn't seem like an action she, soft but not kind, would ever take. If it were the normal her, if she ran across an abandoned cat on the street while it was raining, she would only think that she felt sorry for it. She wouldn't actually take it back home and raise it.

But she hated that side of herself.

Just once, she wanted to try doing something unlike her.

3 (Aug.31_PM06:15)

He remembered something that happened a long time ago.

The person who came to be known as Accelerator once had a human name. His last name was two syllables, and his first name was three. It was a very Japanese name and not at all an uncommon one.

It wasn't as if he'd reigned as Academy City's strongest since the beginning.

At the beginning, he only knew his skills were a bit above average.

And, as they say, the nail that sticks out gets pounded down.

The disaster probably came because he was more talented than he'd realized.

Boys in his class attacked him, and their bones broke just from touching him.

The teacher who tried to stop it ended up having bones broken, too.

Then, a group of adults surrounded him, but he dispatched them all, too. In the end, Anti-Skills and Judgment rushed to the scene like he was some bank robber, attempting to attack him using all sorts of abilities and next-generation weaponry, but he wiped them all out, too.

He was just scared.

He was scared of having a fist raised against him and just waved around his arms frantically.

For the ten-year-old him, that was the most natural response.

But that's all it took for him to turn out like this.

Unmanned, windowless attack helicopters flitted around in the air, while robot-like Anti-Skill reinforcements wearing powered suits stood between him and wounded comrades. He was like the giant *kaiju* monsters he'd seen on television. A fearsome creature feared by all.

Then he realized it. Despite his age, he figured it out. He could hurt people just by touching them with a fingertip. People could die if he so much as thought *grr* to himself. If this madness escalated, eventually all of Academy City, then all of the world, would become his enemy, and he might really have to destroy everything.

In order to avoid such destruction, he had to prevent himself from displaying any emotion to anyone. That went for malice as well as goodwill, since even the latter could turn into aggression via jealousy.

He had to become an immovable rock, so that no matter what anyone did to him, he wouldn't hurt them. If the slightest bit of annoyance could cause someone's death, then he couldn't let himself even feel a little bit of emotion. If he became like ice, then he could protect people from his rampant powers.

But his younger self had already made a mistake at this point.

He would become like ice, so that he wouldn't think about anything anyone did to him and that was exactly the problem. Somebody who didn't complain about anything others did to him was actually somebody who had no interest in the lives of others.

And so he set himself upon this path, never realizing this.

He had just barely managed to avoid destruction.

He surrendered himself right then and there, having lost all interest in others. He was stuffed into a coffin that others insisted was a "special class." But the cogs in his mind would not be so easily stopped. His awareness floated along aimlessly like a jellyfish until it guided him to another solution.

If he didn't want to war with others carelessly, then he could just create a situation in which that conflict wouldn't occur.

If he could acquire such power that even beginning a conflict with him would seem insane...

If he could move past being the strongest and become absolute...

Then he wouldn't have to hurt anyone else, nor would anyone else threaten him anymore. His rust-covered heart wondered if people would then be able to acknowledge his existence.

He just didn't realize his idea would harm so many people afterward.

"What a pain..."

Accelerator left the laboratory and, ignoring the memory stick with the personality data on it for now, ran through the city and toward the restaurant where he had left Last Order. Hours had passed since then, but he didn't think she could move around on her own strength given the state she was in.

He ran through the city.

He bared his teeth against the fragments of memories that clung to his mind and ran.

Someone had acknowledged him.

Not as someone absolute, nor as the strongest.

That one girl had done it.

Maybe it was too late. Maybe it was far too late to change anything at this point. But she'd acknowledged him. With an equal gaze, with no fear, as a fellow person.

He had embraced something that he didn't want to lose.

And somewhere in his mind, he reveled in the fact that he felt like he didn't want to lose it.

Something was about to change.

He was finally able to think that he might be able to change something.

Even though he knew he was too late.

4 (Aug.31_PM06:32)

Accelerator ran through the city.

It took a few hours to walk from the laboratory to the restaurant. His conversation with Kikyou Yoshikawa had taken a while, so the sun had already set.

As he ran, he picked up on nearby sounds. There seemed to be a lot of Anti-Skills in the area. Listening in revealed that there was apparently a foreign invader who had broken through Academy City's security.

Someone with Ao Amai? That would mean that he put the virus together for someone outside, eh? Damn. Does he want to get out of here?

He thought further, running with a speed that could overtake an average bicycle.

Nah, if the other guy came in to let Amai escape, they wouldn't have busted their way in and tipped off the police. So it must be something else entirely…but I guess I can't just ignore it.

Either way, Last Order came before Ao Amai right now. He didn't know whether or not the intruder had anything to do with this. It could wait.

While he was deciding as much, the restaurant he'd left Last Order in came into sight.

What a damn pain. If I knew this was gonna happen, I'd'a just brought her to the lab with me.

He hadn't, though, because he didn't know what kind of position Last Order would find herself in once they got there—he was concerned that they'd just up and dispose of her, but his decision to leave her had totally backfired. Too late to curse his luck now. Was Last Order still in there, or had they kicked her out? He darted toward the restaurant...

...when *crash!!*

All of a sudden, the restaurant window in front of him shattered to pieces.

"Eh?"

Accelerator paused in spite of himself.

The window was facing the road, and on the road, a man almost two meters tall and big enough to be a pro wrestler was standing. He was wearing a jet-black suit and was currently leaping in through the broken window.

He heard a retort from inside the building—angry words.

After a moment, he heard somebody's footsteps coming out through the smashed window and into the road. But it was only footsteps. He didn't see anyone. It was like an invisible man; he heard glass breaking as a transparent distortion in the shape of a foot crunched one of the window shards underneath it.

The invisible man ran off in the opposite direction from Accelerator. He collided with a strange girl with black hair and shrine maiden clothing as he went. Everything the girl was carrying flew all over the place. It looked like cat food. The box's lid must have been open, because the invisible man got covered in the cat food from head to toe.

As Accelerator was trying to think of what to do, wondering who that guy was, a single boy leaped out of the smashed window into the road.

He knew that one.

"It's…that bastard!!"

Accelerator glared at him. It was that Level Zero kid who'd punched the hell out of him and gotten the experiment frozen in order to save the Sisters.

The boy also ran off, going after the invisible man. Though from an outsider's perspective, it looked more like he was running away. There was a man and a waitress chasing him around for some reason.

What the shit is going on in that restaurant?…Does it have anything to do with the brat? I can't even think about it. Guess there's always a chance that moron would stick his nose into this.

He wondered for a moment whether or not to chase after him, but decided to go into the restaurant. He didn't have the luxury of moving around in the dark. Besides, once he got some information, he could easily catch up to him with his legs.

He went in.

It was like a whole different world from how it had been earlier that day. The front-facing window had been broken, and one of the tables was on the floor, ripped apart like a laser had cut it in half. The other patrons still hadn't regained their calm after whatever had happened and were all staring at the busted table from afar, talking among themselves as if they were watching a small fire.

Accelerator looked around.

The inside of the restaurant wasn't very big at all…but he couldn't find the now-familiar Last Order anywhere.

Hey, wait, did they seriously kick her out? I don't think that brat could've even walked by herself.

He cast his gaze around again and locked eyes with one of the waitresses. She was short in stature and looked easily mistakable for a middle school student. At first, she returned Accelerator's stare vacantly. She seemed to have been caught up in everything and forgotten that she was on duty. After about three seconds had gone by, she finally snapped back to reality and came over to Accelerator. She gave him her business smile, though her face was pale.

"W-welcome. Um, is it just you today? Also, we don't allow smoking here—"

"I'm not a customer. I'm looking for someone. She should've been here."

"Huh?"

"It was this naked kid like ten years old wearing a light blue blanket as a cloak. She was with me at about three. You remember?"

There was no real way Last Order wouldn't have stuck out in people's minds, so Accelerator didn't go into details. He thought it would be enough.

Unfortunately, the short waitress gave him a troubled stare.

"Um, well, I'm sorry, I don't remember. Do you know which table you were sitting at?"

"…You're kiddin', right? You don't remember? She was in here today and wearing that."

"I'm sorry."

The waitress bowed her head politely, but her facial expression made it evident that she was about to cry. She really didn't seem to remember.

Damn. Is it because of all this nonsense that just happened?

Accelerator clicked his tongue. It had been a few hours already since Last Order was looking for food, after all, and some incident had occurred here just minutes before. It was somewhat natural that would make someone forget about a guest who came in dressed oddly.

He'd suddenly lost her. His expression turned to one of irritation, and the small waitress, scared, disappeared into the back of the restaurant.

What do I do? Check the security cameras?

Normally, this sort of video recording would be transmitted through a direct line to a security firm. The master copy wouldn't be kept here. If one were skilled enough, they could use hacking to steal a peek at those recordings from the outside, but…

…but I can't do that. Where do you think we are right now?

Accelerator shook his head.

He didn't have those skills, and there was no way that Academy City, with all its research institutions and confidential information, would leave its safety to a common security firm. As a matter of fact, he didn't think there was even a path into it in the first place. The only ones who would be able to do that would be a seriously abnormal genius who was able to find a back door without the system's developer himself realizing.

Then, as he stood there thinking, two or three employees came up to him from the back of the store. The short waitress from before was there, too, hiding behind one of them.

Maybe they think I'm obstructing their business or whatever, he predicted. Of course, he didn't have time to give them any more than a brief explanation about his circumstances. A sharp, dangerous light glittered in his eyes.

But actually, a male employee in his thirties gave him a relatively friendly smile and asked, "Are you that blanket girl's family?"

"Huh?"

"Well, the girl who came in at three. We wondered if she had some sort of chronic disease."

Accelerator mulled over the man's words in his head. Last Order had fever-like symptoms as a side effect of her unadjusted physical body. She couldn't get up and walk around by herself.

"I think it was past four? She was still laying on the table, so I thought it strange. I had my daughter try and talk to her, and that's when we realized she had passed out. We called an ambulance, thinking it was an emergency."

"Wait, so is that brat in the hospital right now?"

"Actually, before the ambulance arrived, a man in white clothes came in. He said he was a relative and that her symptoms visited her from time to time but didn't pose a threat to her life, and then brought her away."

A man in white clothes.

Accelerator pulled his lips back. It was too soon to judge from just that, but…

"If you're looking for the girl, then why don't you ask him? You know who, right?"

"…Yeah. I know him far too well," he spat in response.

It could only be one person—Ao Amai. He'd witnessed Accelerator hanging around here during lunch. Besides, Last Order didn't have any relatives.

5 (Aug.31_PM07:02)

Accelerator left the restaurant and decided to contact Yoshikawa with his cell phone.

"What? Amai took Last Order away?"

"I heard it from someone else, so I dunno for sure. What do you think? The virus would start up by itself, so he could just leave it alone, right? Why's he messing with her now?"

The fact that Ao Amai was still present in Academy City was weird from the start. He had disappeared, fearing that he'd be suspected. Wouldn't the obvious thing to do be to get out as soon as possible? Even the powerful Anti-Skills and Judgment wouldn't be able to bring much force to bear on the outside—their peacekeeping abilities could only be used on the inside.

"If we just look at his skills, the guy's a top-class scientist. There's probably a ton of places outside that'd be happy to shelter him despite the risks."

"You're right, and I don't know, either. The answer could end up being simpler than we think, though."

They both paused for a moment.

On the other end of the phone, he could hear the sound of keys clacking.

Finally, Accelerator said, "He apparently took her away at around four. Think he's still in the city?"

"It's already after seven…so it's been a little less than three hours. I'd normally say that we're in trouble, but it seems that for once our luck is turning around."

"Eh?"

Accelerator became attentive to the sounds on the other end—Yoshikawa was typing on a keyboard, hard at work on something.

"Somebody has broken through the security net from the outside and forced their way in to the city. On top of that, a large-scale battle occurred near a fast-food restaurant in the Seventh School District since a bit after noon. Earlier today, the security code was orange, but it's gone red. Code orange...you know what that means, right?"

Orange meant that there was the possibility a terrorist had invaded, and red meant that it was completely certain. If either of them had been issued, it would mean that entrance to and exit from Academy City was entirely restricted. Convenience store managers were probably worried about their products not being delivered even.

If code orange had been in effect since noon, then Amai wouldn't have been able to take Last Order outside the city, even if he had captured her. He didn't know what idiot caused all this, but he was thankful for it for the moment.

"He's still in the city. Then do you know where he is?"

Yoshikawa answered his question, still typing. "It's tough to search for him, but he'd probably avoid crowded places. If a proper adult were walking around with a naked girl in just a blanket, he'd stand out far too much. I don't think he'd want that, fugitive that he is."

It sounded logical, but it also sounded like a pain in the ass. Today was August 31. Most of the students were shut up in their homes grappling with their homework, so the entire city was like a ghost town.

"Can't you hack into the police bots, or the satellite's observation data, or something? There were data in the one folder on where Ao Amai was that you got from hacking into the security systems, wasn't there?"

"Mechanized security isn't really that secure. I mean, we did conduct that experiment despite being under alert, didn't we?"

"..."

"I don't think security is any more than pursuit support. I've been tailing him mostly by targeting the movement of money. Did you know that there is an IC chip embedded in your wallet right now?"

"Huh? Yeah, you mean, you can make all the fake bills you want. It's to stop that, right?"

"It actually has another use. It collects detailed information on money distribution by recording personal information on the holder," she explained, still typing. "I mean, we live in an age where if you buy more than one thousand yen's worth of stuff using a credit card, the information will get stolen...But on the other hand, if you don't use any money and live on the streets like she is, then we have no real way of following her."

"Okay, fine, different question. How has he been getting away so far?"

"Mainly by car. He seems to be stopping at parks and abandoned buildings to sleep. He does have to clean himself and acquire gasoline, though, so he is using money. He couldn't seem to completely cover his tracks."

As the sound of keys being pressed came through the phone again, he replied plainly, "So he's not using any hotels or inns or anything. Has he gone to visit people he knows?"

"I'm not sure he even knows anyone well enough for that."

"...Heh. He's trash, then, just like me."

"He has quite a bit of debt resulting from the lab's closure of the Radio Noise project. This was a private institution. It was emotionally like he was the president of a company that had just gone under. Love lasts only as long as money endures, right?"

Accelerator clicked his tongue, uninterested, and thought about it.

"He can't get out of the city at the moment, right?"

"If he's worried about being inspected, then he probably can't even flee the school district."

"Hmm. All right, then."

Accelerator told her the name of a certain building.

Kikyou Yoshikawa, upon hearing it, raised her voice in surprise.

"Hold on a second...That's strange. It's true that he hasn't gone near that place yet. I'd have thought he wouldn't hesitate to go straight there, but..."

"He'd normally avoid the place you'd think of first, right? But when humans lose their cool, their movements get easier and easier to predict."

Grinning, Accelerator walked out onto a big road.

His destination was the former site of a certain laboratory.

It was the facility where the mass-produced Level Five Railgun "Radio Noise" development had been carried out.

6 (Aug.31_PM07:27)

A sports car was parked next to a certain former laboratory.

The air-conditioning was up way too high in this cramped car, but his palms were still drenched in sweat.

In pain, he desperately held his stomach with his sweat-soaked hands.

He had originally wanted to go into the actual building. There were plenty of places to hide a car, as long as everything was how he remembered it. He'd even be able to escape the eyes of the satellite. Unfortunately, the front gate was locked up with thick chains and padlocks, and he couldn't get them off.

But he also couldn't leave. He might be stopped for inspection as soon as he started moving. And he'd be stopped for sure if he left the car behind and carried Last Order, who was essentially naked, around the city.

"Damn it…"

This was the wrong choice, he thought in regret. He had initially prepared to flee Academy City as soon as he'd injected the virus into Last Order's head. Members of an anti–Academy City faction were waiting for him on the outside. Then, he'd follow them out of the country and go to whatever institution he liked in whatever country he wished, bringing his supernatural ability–related skills as a souvenir.

And yet, Last Order ran away as soon as he injected the virus.

His grand schemes began to unwind at that moment.

Last Order's body was incomplete and unadjusted, so she couldn't live for very long outside her incubator. If he was careless, she could die before the virus activated.

If that happened, the virus wouldn't infect the Sisters throughout the world. His plans of destruction would come to naught. The enemy faction wouldn't forgive that. Not only would they refuse to assist his escape—he wouldn't be surprised if they just killed him on the spot.

Strangely enough, Amai needed to capture Last Order—to save her life.

Now that he couldn't prepare an incubator for her, though, the goal seemed unattainable.

He'd been frantically running around all week looking for Last Order. And when he'd finally acquired his target, having evaded the vicious Accelerator, with whom she had been for some reason, he'd finally ended up in this sorry situation.

"..."

He turned his glare to the passenger seat.

The incomplete physical body of Last Order was sunk into the seat, wrapped in the blanket. She was sweating all over, and her breathing was so shallow he had to pay attention to even hear it.

A handful of electrodes were attached to her face. The cords coming from them connected to the notebook on her lap.

The screen displayed various vital signs, such as her pulse, body temperature, blood pressure, and respiration. The numbers and graphs would have been undecipherable to the untrained eye...but those who could read it would be dumbstruck. It was bad enough that she could stop breathing at any moment.

This can't be happening. Not here, not now...

Ao Amai had a reason he needed to get away.

He was responsible for the Radio Noise project to create mass-production espers based on Tokiwadai's Railgun. Unfortunately, the mass-produced versions were low spec—he'd been unable to recreate Railgun perfectly. The project was deadlocked and the labs were shut down. Deep in debt, he had barely managed to pick up Accelerator's Level Six project.

Unfortunately, that project, too, was essentially frozen for good.

He couldn't pay back his debts like this.

He had no place to return to in Academy City. All he had left was an enormous debt—enough that he could buy a submarine with the money. The fact that the Level Six laboratory was a private institution, unlike the Radio Noise one, hurt him all the more. If he still wanted to go on living, he had to skip out on his debt and flee.

So he'd joined forces with an enigmatic group. If he broke with them now, hell surely awaited him. He wasn't optimistic enough to think he could make an escape while caught between both Academy City and the opposition faction.

Damn it, damn it! Why is this happening?!

He punched the steering wheel of his small sports car.

He had finally managed to capture the runaway Last Order today. Unfortunately for him, the security code had been set to orange and soon changed over to red, making it impossible for him to leave the city. On top of that, Last Order's physical state was worse than he had anticipated. At this rate, she really might just take her last breath before the virus activated.

Please, please! Just a little longer! Just hold out until the virus activates!

He had plenty of other options when it came to places where he could regulate Last Order's body, but now that the security code had moved to red, everywhere in the city was to be inspected. He couldn't bring a naked girl wearing a blue blanket through an inspection, especially since she was an artificial, mass-produced specimen without an ID.

Ao Amai couldn't get out of this one city block, much less the city. And so there he sat trembling in the cramped vehicle, staking everything he had on a virus he wasn't sure would activate.

Suddenly, something flew past his front windshield.

"?!"

His lowered gaze reflexively shot back in front of him. However, it wasn't anything related to Anti-Skills or other researchers. It was a crow. A black crow had simply flown past the car, from right to left.

"Ah—"

But his eyes opened wide.

There was nobody in front of him. There was an unoccupied road before him, plain and simple. Nothing that was any danger to him. It would have seemed like he had lost his calm and was freaking out at an impossible hallucination.

"Aahh…"

However, Amai wasn't looking in front of him at all.

He was staring into his rearview mirror.

What he saw in it made his blood curl. His irises vacillated. Sweat broke out over his whole body like a thin film. His fingers tensed and trembled.

There was a lone boy in the mirror.

He was walking slowly up behind the yellow sports car Amai was in.

It was a white-faced, white-hot, bright white Level Five.

"…Eh…hee!"

A strange voice leaked out of Amai's throat.

From his point of view, he didn't know why Accelerator had come here. However, the fact that he was trying to do anything made things dangerous.

Accelerator unhesitatingly made his way toward the car.

Amai glanced at Last Order in the passenger seat.

She was someone he had to treat more delicately than snow crystals. He didn't know what Accelerator was about to do, but if he gave her over, she wouldn't last a second before being destroyed.

He could not let him have Last Order.

He needed to intercept him.

But how?!

He had a pistol tucked in a pocket of his white coat, but that wouldn't help much against Accelerator. Taking him on physically would be as reckless as racing on foot against a Lamborghini Gallardo, as foolish as engaging a Type 90 tank in a game of tug-of-war.

Then he had to run.

Amai grabbed the car key.

His quivering hands had trouble locating the ignition. He tried over and over again to get it in, about to cry the whole time, until *clack*, it went in.

He feverishly twisted the key.

The engine roared to life. In his tension, he mistook it for a manual and went for the nonexistent clutch. The car kicked up and leaped forward.

7 (Aug.31_PM07:39)

Accelerator watched Amai's car with a grin as it violently shot forward, betraying the man's panic.

Let's see, that brat is...in there, is she? Here I thought he'd just throw her into the trunk or something, but I s'pose Amai can't afford for her to die, he figured to himself, slightly dropping his stance.

Bang! He kicked off the ground.

Accelerator flew nearly ten meters into the air, overtaking Amai's sports car, and touched down in front of it. He could see the man's face pull back in surprise and terror. He threw the wheel to one side, but it was too late. The accelerator of the cheap domestic sports car had been jammed right down to the floor, and it crashed into Accelerator with the force of a cannonball.

Then roared the sound of crushing metal, a thousand times stronger than the noise an empty soda can makes when stepped on.

Accelerator stood there, without budging an inch. Not a single hair on his head even moved. The car was what had been crushed. He had redirected the car's force vector straight down. All four of its tires went flat, and the wheels got squashed into an egg shape. The ground clearance of the car went to perfect zero, and it sunk into the asphalt a few centimeters. The glass windows on all sides shattered to pieces, too, as if the car's body itself had been twisted out of shape.

The face of the driver, Amai, was a contorted smile.

He must not have been able to believe he was unharmed, even

though his car had been completely wrecked. The air bags weren't working, either. His mercy directly showed the sheer difference in strength between the two of them.

"Ek...gh...d-damn it!"

Face nearly in tears, Amai slammed on the accelerator over and over, but the front wheels had already been so deformed that they were eating into the bumper. The car wasn't moving any time soon. It took him more than ten seconds to finally realize this, and then he threw open the door, maybe deciding to flee even if he had to abandon Last Order.

"Calm the hell down, old man. You look disgraceful."

Accelerator lightly kicked the car's front bumper with a *bam*. However he'd controlled the impact, the open driver's seat door slammed shut again. It was less a normal door opening and closing than it was a steel trap clapping shut. The fleeing Amai got caught in the door, which knocked the wind out of him. He slid down to the ground, motionless.

"Yeah, sorry about treating you so roughly. Hey, at least you're not dead, right?"

He received no response, but he wasn't expecting one anyway. He looked at the passenger seat. Unlike the sunken driver's seat, it was gently cradling the girl.

"Stupid brat. You sure are a pain in the ass," muttered Accelerator, as if venting the pent-up pressure within him. Then, he took out his cell phone.

"Yoshikawa? Yeah, I've got her."

There were more than four hours left until the virus's activation.

8 (Aug.31_PM08:03)

Accelerator opened the passenger door. Last Order, wrapped in her blanket, didn't react. Her splayed limbs were soaked with a sickening sweat.

He was about to carry her out of the seat when suddenly he realized something.

"Hey, there's electrodes or somethin' stuck to the brat's head. Should I leave 'em on?"

"Hm? Could you give me a little more detail?"

Yoshikawa listened to what Accelerator had to say about it for a few moments, then said, "That's probably the Sisters' system scan kit that our staff has. It just displays her physical state, like her breathing, pulse, blood pressure, and body temperature, as well as the healthiness of her mental state, including her personality data. You can remove the electrodes if you need to."

There was a laptop connected to the electrodes' cords. A handful of graphs were being displayed on its screen. Aside from them, there was a percentage value of some sort, which said "BC Rate."

When he asked what it was, she responded, "Oh, that's the operation rate of Last Order's brain cells. BC stands for brain cells."

Accelerator was taken aback. It was no small order, keeping the movements of every single one of a person's brain cells under observation. Such a small device didn't even seem able to handle something like that. The Sisters were electric users, though, so maybe they assisted.

Either way, the technology was all foreign to him.

"Hey, can't you use this thing to get rid of the virus? It's gonna take me some time to actually get back with her."

"That wouldn't work. It's just a terminal to display those data. You need a special incubator and Testament to write to her."

Accelerator mulled on that for a moment...then noticed something.

All sorts of noises were coming from the other end of the phone.

"Wait, aren't you at the lab?"

"You just realized now? I'm driving over there as we speak. I've got an incubator and a Testament in the back. I figured this would take less time than you returning to the lab. She might try and run if she sees me, but with your athletic abilities, I don't think there's anything to worry about," she said. "So you just wait there. I obviously couldn't manage to pack one of our giant quantum computers in here, but the DNA computer was just the right size, so I'm bringing that, too. It doesn't have as much power, but it should be more than enough for this job."

"...You know, if you can just analyze this with a machine, then what were you doing with that pen before? Doesn't seem like you needed to do anything by hand."

"Leaving it up to a machine would be inflexible, too polite...Anyway, it has its own problems. Are you familiar with video games? Debuggers have to physically hold a controller and brute force it. They run the data through a machine, then fix them by hand, and then run the data through again to make sure they're not wrong... They just repeat that process over and over."

Accelerator reached out a hand for the electrodes stuck to Last Order's face, but then suddenly asked, "So did you finish analyzing the virus code?"

"I'm about eighty percent of the way through. I need to write a vaccine to get rid of it after I'm done, so we're still in a race against time here," she explained. Then, she added, "Of course, I'll make sure we succeed."

Accelerator frowned, thinking that something about her was different from usual, but he relaxed his shoulders a little. He could feel things marching toward their resolution.

Sheesh, what a pain. How much trouble does this stupid brat think she can put me through?

It was the first time he'd ever had to wait for somebody. It felt like time was stretching out, each second going by meaninglessly. It didn't feel very good. He tapped the asphalt with his foot, anxious, but even that motion caused odd fissures to erupt in the road.

"Mi...sa..."

Suddenly, her mouth moved.

Her lips trembled like those of a human with a terrible thirst for water.

"Mi...saka...is...Misa...Misaka...is..."

Eyes still closed, her mouth was the only thing moving— desperately, earnestly, as if to complain. Accelerator thought about whether or not to ask about it. Either way, until Yoshikawa the specialist arrived on the scene, he had no way to ease her pain—

"Mi...sa...ka, misa. Ka misa, ka misa! Ka misaka misaka misaka misaka misaka misa misa misa misa misa misa misa misa misa misa misa misa misa misa misa misa misa m<iju0058@Misagr misa qw0014codeLLG misaKA misaka ieuvbeydla9((jkeryup@[iiG:**ui% %ebvauqansicdaiasbna:!!"

"Eh?" muttered Accelerator at Last Order's sudden shout.

She didn't look right at all. The girl before him with her delicate body was tossing and turning like a fish out of water. She was bending quite a bit backward. Was the creaking noise her bones? Her muscles? Still there was no hint of pain on her face. He even sensed delight, like she was about to start singing a hymn or something.

But there was just one thing.

He could see tears coming from beneath her closed eyelids.

That was the only thing that wasn't delighted.

They were tears of pain.

The laptop screen started going crazy. Dozens of warning boxes popped up one after another like raindrops hitting a window, burying most of the screen underneath. The only sounds to be heard were the warbling tones trying to warn him of something.

"Shit! Yoshikawa, what the hell is this? Is this one of the symptoms or somethin'?!"

"Calm down, and explain everything to me in order! I can't know anything just with that. Right, does your cell phone have a camera? If you can sent a video text, that would be bes—"

Yoshikawa's voice suddenly cut off as he heard a surprised, quick intake of breath. Their call hadn't been dropped. He could hear her saying things to herself—and it sounded like the usual "No way," "It can't be," "This shouldn't be happening."

"What the fuck is wrong?! Can't I do some kinda first aid for this?!"

"Be quiet for a moment. Can you let me listen to what she's saying?"

"I said, give me an expl—"

"There's no time!!"

Yoshikawa sounded like she was at her wit's end. Accelerator could feel something was wrong. But he couldn't do anything but put the phone up to the screaming Last Order.

"aweuvll;**0012uui%%0025$#gui'&=//nsyulljwidnl'jwucla:@] aucneisdkaudj!!"

Her shouts were no longer even a language.

He heard Yoshikawa gasp again when she heard it.

"I see…so it's true."

"What is? What the hell's goin' on?"

Yoshikawa replied in simple tones to the aggravated Accelerator.

"It's the virus code. Though it seems to be encrypted. The virus is already starting up."

Accelerator froze.

The virus wasn't supposed to start until midnight that night. It was only just past eight. They should still have a little less than four hours…

He could only think of one possibility.

Dummy information.

The enemy, Ao Amai, had intentionally falsified the time limit. There was no way all the information from the enemy would be the truth. Accelerator said it himself, too—telling them what time the virus would go off from the start made the game far too easy.

It was a simple, cruel, playful trap.

Even Amai himself probably didn't think it would actually come in handy. It seemed more like something he'd thrown into it in his spare time than him trying to defend his interests.

Accelerator thought back to what would happen once the virus began.

"At that time, the virus will begin to get itself moving, and it will finish ten minutes after that. It will infect all of the live Sisters through the Misaka network and they will begin to run wild."

He remembered what would happen…

…to the girl in his arms.

"I haven't finished analyzing the code yet, so I can't be sure, but the symptoms will likely involve indiscriminate attacks against humans."

Accelerator found himself unable to move.

Last Order repeated her indecipherable screams. Hundreds of warning windows flooded the laptop's screen. Between the windows, he could just barely make out the BC Rate—the operation rate of her brain cells.

The number was rapidly increasing. Seventy percent, 83 percent, 95 percent…and then it exceeded 100 percent and continued rising.

Last Order's small body jolted and writhed like it had been struck with electricity.

Finally, another warning window completely covered up even that BC Rate value.

Just like the strange virus data were overwriting the personality data that originally belonged to Last Order.

Yoshikawa said something to him over his phone, but he wasn't listening anymore.

They wouldn't make it.

Yoshikawa hadn't finished looking at the virus code yet, and she hadn't put together a vaccine. On top of that, there were dummy data in the code she had analyzed, so there was no guarantee she could write a safe one anyway. And they couldn't even bring her back to the lab, where all the equipment was.

Amai, who had created the virus, would understand its code. But there was no time to interrogate him and then make a vaccine after that was done.

An odd sensation tingled at the back of Accelerator's head. Before he could figure out what it was, Yoshikawa's calm words carved themselves into his thoughts.

"Listen to me, Accelerator. It's too soon to despair. You need to seal the deal."

"…What deal? We can still do something?"

"Before the virus is uploaded to the Misaka network, the current code has to take time to gain administrator privileges so that the

Sisters won't be able to resist it. If it had privileges from the start, the virus code would be easy to detect within the actual personality data, so that's being prevented. You only have ten minutes. You understand, right? You can only do one thing—deal with her. Killing her will protect the world."

Yoshikawa had never considered saving Last Order in the first place.

That's what she meant by "seal the deal."

Protect the world.

In order to stop the Sisters, scattered to every corner of the world, from going insane, he had to...

This girl was writhing in pain, unable to even cry out for help, and he had to...

Accelerator sneered. Of all the things, she was telling him to use his power, which could only be used for killing people, for this outrageous reason. To consent to the smallest harm. To kill this one girl.

Given time, the commands written into Last Order's head would tear apart her mind. The only way to stop that from happening was to take her life before that mind fell apart.

"Fuckin'..."

Yoshikawa was saying that if nothing he chose could save her...

...then at least kill her with a smile.

"That's fucking bullshit!!"

Accelerator's teeth grated. A knife drove deep into his chest. It was the same kind of pain as when that Level Zero punched him in the switchyard. There was nothing like it. It was the pain of loss. He had figured it out. And he realized how heavy, how important, the girl in his arms really was. Ten thousand times this. He finally realized that he had caused ten thousand times this pain to someone.

It was too late at this point.

It was far too late for him to do anything.

Accelerator howled. He had no solution.

His power couldn't get rid of the virus inscribed in Last Order's mind. It wasn't that convenient. It may have been the strongest power, but it was only the ability to alter kinetic, heat, and electric force vectors. And the way to use them always ended in killing. He had so much power, but all he could think of was blowing people up by touching their skin and reversing their blood flow or bioelectric field—

...?

He suddenly stopped, caught up on something, after having thought that far.

He closely examined his own words.

Reversing bioelectric fields?

Wait. What am I hung up on?

Scraps of words began to float into his mind, one after another.

Then, all of a sudden, *whoosh*, time seemed to slow down for him.

Time's up in less than ten minutes. Can't call for help. Things I have here—memory stick and electronic book. They contain her personality data before infection. Level Five, Accelerator. The ability to alter any vectors, whether kinetic, heat, or electric. Doesn't matter. What I need now—Testament. A device for manipulating brain information via electrical means. Control of electrical impulses. The vaccine program. Data to find and delete the virus code from the enormous personality data. Solution for if we can't erase the virus quickly enough—killing Last Order.

Accelerator's thoughts reached breakneck speeds.

He eliminated all unneeded words, reducing his sentences to pure meaning.

Just a few seconds felt like an eternity as he immersed himself in his thoughts.

To not kill her. Need to destroy virus. Two options. One—find just the virus code in her enormous personality data. Two—manipulate electrical impulses within her brain and destroy only the virus code that I find.

In Academy City, which loaded its classes with supernatural Ability Development, the strongest esper in the city equated to the smartest esper in the city. Accelerator had once perfectly calculated and predicted the winds blowing through the city down to each and every particle. He used all of his neural pathways to search for a way out.

Data stick. Contains preinfection personality data. Find differences between it and current infected personality data...Wait. What am I so hung up on? This is masochistic abuse. Remember. What I'm good at. The thing that most easily comes to mind.

Finally, Accelerator's shoulders shook like he'd been hit by lightning.

Reversing bioelectric fields.

If Accelerator's ability really could control any and all vectors, regardless of what kind of force it was...

If he could reverse the direction of somebody's blood flow and bioelectric field just by touching their skin...

He looked up. Not even ten seconds had passed since he began thinking.

"Hey. If I can just control her brain's electrical impulses, I can mess with her personality data without having to use a Testament, right?"

"What are—" Yoshikawa began, then stopped and realized something.

A Testament was a device for installing a personality and knowledge base into a person by controlling their brain's electricity.

"...You want to be a replacement for a Testament? That's impossible! You can freely control any vectors with your ability, but manipulating someone's brain signals is...Wait!"

"There's nothing I can't do. I killed people by reversing their blood flow and electric fields just by touching their skin during that experiment, yeah? I can reflect stuff already, so it's not strange that I can go beyond and control it."

Of course, he'd never actually messed with someone's brain signals before. He wasn't absolutely confident in this plan.

But he had to go for it. It would have been better to use a Testament. It would have been perfect to write a vaccine program to beat the virus, but the situation wouldn't allow for it. Nevertheless, he didn't want to give up, so the only thing left was for him to do something.

With his own hands.

Even if it was a makeshift plan, he had to help her.

"There's no way you can do something like that. Even if you were able to control Last Order's brain with your ability, I don't have a complete vaccine program for the virus. It's impossible for you to remove the entire virus!"

"..."

Yoshikawa was right—she hadn't finished analyzing it yet. But considering she hadn't noticed dummy code, he couldn't be sure there weren't errors in the already-analyzed data.

"Do you hear me? I said to kill her. I know her body a hundred times better than you, and I say there is no other way. Do you understand me?" Yoshikawa's voice was like ice. "You cannot hope to eliminate her virus by yourself. If you fail, you'll be sacrificing ten thousand sisters, and when the problem escalates, Academy City will be an enemy to the world. You need to give up on Last Order to prevent that!"

She wielded her remonstrating voice like a sword, trying to stab it into him.

"Of course, maybe you can write a vaccine yourself. Can you do it in this situation? The virus is going to be finished working in minutes!"

"Sure thing," he answered immediately. Kikyou Yoshikawa caught her breath.

He lowered his gaze to Last Order, lying in the passenger's seat, and looked at the envelope's contents again. There was a label on the memory stick that read "Serial Number 20001 Personality Outline (Before Infection)" on it.

Her pre-virus personality data were in there. That meant he would match up Last Order's current brain with these data, find the extra parts, and root out the virus code. If he could do that, then he just had to overwrite it with the proper data to fix it, just like flattening a bumpy steel plate with a hammer.

The corrected data he'd stick back in after fishing out the virus could loosely be called a vaccine.

"Bullshit…Of course I can do it. Who the hell do you think I am?"

She said something back to him, but he was no longer listening. He was about to hang up, but the phone slipped out of his hands onto the ground. It was out of his mind already. He gave a crooked grin.

He already knew the weak point in his plan. The personality data he held were from before infection. So if he overwrote everything extra in her personality data, any memories she had would all be wiped away along with the virus. It was the same as smearing the ink all over a paint canvas, covering up the old picture with a new one.

Their meeting.

Their conversations.

Her smile.

All of that would be lost, and he'd have to bear the pain.

"…And so what? Her forgetting all that is for her own good."

It seemed pretty obvious. He just had to think back to that alley last night and to the state of his dorm room. If she stayed with Accelerator, she was liable to be attacked just for that reason.

Last Order had accepted Accelerator without fear. A person like that, however, couldn't be part of this world.

She needed to go back.

Not to this blood-soaked monster of a world, but to a kinder world of light.

He laughed weakly to himself, then inserted the memory stick into the electronic book. He read through the insane amount of text on the screen, scrolling past with the speed of a waterfall. It took him fifty-two seconds to read the whole thing and forty-eight to ruminate with his eyes closed. He opened his eyes again and spent sixty-five seconds comparing what he remembered to what was on the screen.

He was ready.

Ready to put an end to all of this.

His hands crushed the electronic book in them with a squash. Fragments of the machine containing the blueprint for a certain girl's mind fell from his hands to the ground.

"..."

He turned the reflection off on his hands, and his fingers touched the girl's forehead. Her skin was hot like she had caught a fever. He then found a bioelectric field and made contact with its vector, like it was an antenna leading to her insides. He started to calculate the vectors of the fields around it using the one he touched as a base.

Finally, the entire construction of the girl's brain revealed itself to him.

The thought circuits that came to him were very warm.

They were so warm it almost made him not want to lose them.

But...

Still...

"Seriously, you fucking brat. Do you not see me helping you? Don't you dare start saying I didn't do anything, got it?" he demanded, grinning.

If he had a mirror, he would have been surprised at how gentle his smile looked.

His hands trembled.

He would use this power that could do nothing but kill in order to save someone. It was a stunt as ridiculous as feeding a baby food using a spoon taped to a tank cannon.

"...That's pretty funny. I'll give you something to be scared of, sure," he declared to himself.

He applied his power. He changed a vector. The battle began.

The virus would activate at 8:13. There were fifty-two seconds left until time ran out.

9 (Aug.31_PM08:12:08)

"89aepd'das::-qwdnmaiosdgt98qhe9qxsxw9dja8hderfba8waop code9jpnasidj resist9w:aea from route A w'waveform red from code08 to code seventy-two subroutine to point A8 via route C sealing area D diverting code fifty-six to route S casting blue waveform to yellow"

Last Order's indecipherable words began to change into Japanese.

Sweat dripped from Accelerator. He felt like something hot was burning the back of his head. He could see his vision tunneling. As a result of him focusing all his calculation abilities to one place, his reflection didn't work, so his sweat clung to him unpleasantly.

He matched up Last Order's personality data now that she was infected with the virus with the preinfection personality data on the memory stick.

Any differences between the two would be due to infected code. Included in that were memories of Accelerator from after the virus, but he couldn't at all tell which parts were the virus and which were memory.

The number of lines of code he needed to rewrite came to him.

In all, 357,081.

The only thing to do was to delete all the code to get rid of the virus.

The monitor showing Last Order's vital signs continued displaying warning windows at a terrifying pace.

10 (Aug.31_PM08:12:14)

"after casting code twenty-one ~~from waveform red to orange~~ proceeding through route D branching to ~~points A7,~~ C6, F10 lifting sealed area D and ~~inserting code thirty-two~~ adding additional limitation to area F focusing ~~route A toward code 112~~ from code eighty-nine and so on with code 113 possessing point D4 ~~via route C~~"

As soon as he understood the alien code flowing through Last Order's brain, Accelerator issued a command to all of it—a single write command.

Whoosh...

He sensed the huge signal moving like a wave.

Last Order's body squirmed.

Her fingers began to dance madly, as if controlled by invisible threads.

He couldn't distinguish between virus and memory. For now, as if pasting Wite-out over letters written by a black ballpoint pen, he painted over every single piece of code that he deemed dangerous; 173,542 lines of code remained.

The speed at which the caution windows appeared on the monitor slowed, slowed, slowed...until finally, they stopped being shown. This time, they began to disappear one by one, like a video being rewound.

11 (Aug.31_PM08:12:34)

~~"casting every code from route K to waveform yellow dividing to points V2, H5, Y0 dividing code 201 changing to code 205 from code 202 registering waveform pattern to red constructing route G connecting to areas C, D, H, J branching to points F7, R2, Z0."~~

I got this, thought Accelerator, confirming. He'd already fully caught up to the part of the virus that had gotten ahead of them. He would wipe out the entire virus code just in time at this rate.

Some 59,802 lines of code remained. He thought of the code he was madly painting over and grinned with a bit of loneliness at what he was erasing along with the virus.

Electric signals danced in his hand.

The memories being erased were writhing in their final moments.

Warning windows were disappearing from the monitor. The speed at which he was overwriting data increased. Gaps appeared between the vanishing windows.

Sweat flew from the fearfully flailing Last Order's forehead, but those movements, too, steadily lessened and lessened, as if her body was restabilizing.

12 (Aug.31_PM08:12:45)

Then, all of a sudden...

Accelerator heard a rustle. He directed his eyes toward the noise as he overwrote and fixed the virus code to see that Ao Amai, who should have been out cold, caught in the driver's seat door, had approached his side.

This in itself wasn't at all a problem.

However, his hand gripped a handgun shining black.

"Don't...get in...my..."

Amai groaned, his eyes bloodshot.

Now 23,891 lines of code remained. He still couldn't remove his hand. If he caused a malfunction in the fragmented code, it could possibly destroy Last Order's brain.

The number of warnings on the screen was now numerable, but Accelerator saw that as representative of the state Last Order was in. He couldn't allow a single warning message to exist.

13 (Aug.31_PM08:12:51)

There were less than four meters between them. He couldn't miss at this range if he tried.

"Kuh...?!"

Accelerator was using all of his strength to control Last Order's brain signals, so he couldn't divide it to reflect anything. If he did, he'd introduce an error in the precise electrical signals on the scale of an electron microscope. That would mean frying Last Order's brain to a crisp.

Only 7,001 lines of code remained.

Only nine warning windows were left.

His work wasn't over. Time slowed to a crawl.

Amai probably had no idea what Accelerator was doing, but from his point of view, just the thought of him touching Last Order, whom he absolutely couldn't let die, was probably close to driving him insane.

"Don't...get in my way..."

Froth formed in Ao Amai's mouth. His eyes were red with blood.

He seemed to have even forgotten just how reckless it was to point a gun at Accelerator.

But Accelerator couldn't divide his power in order to reflect anything at the moment. There was nothing he could do in this situation.

If that one insignificant lead bullet hit him, he'd die from it.

His survival instincts implored him to take his hand from Last Order. They screamed to take back his reflection. He knew that if he did, he'd be saved. He wouldn't take damage from a rain of nuclear missiles, much less a handgun.

14 (Aug.31_PM08:12:58)

However, he still didn't take his hand from Last Order.

There was no way in hell.

Only 102 lines of code remained. Just one warning window was left.

"Don't...get...goaahhhh!!"

The trembling hand of the shouting Ao Amai, the handgun he held, its muzzle—all stared Accelerator down.

There was nothing he could do to avoid it.

He could only stare vacantly at his fingers moving to pull the trigger.

A dry gunshot.

Before the sound reached his ears, it struck Accelerator right between the eyes with a shock that felt like being walloped with a hammer. The impact to his head bent his entire body backward. He heard an unpleasant noise from somewhere around his neck. His feet, unable to withstand the blow, jolted up into the air.

But he still didn't let go.

He would never let go.

"Error. Break_code_No000001_to_No357081. Administrative command canceled due to improper usage. Reawakening serial number 20001 in accordance with descriptions."

With a light, electronic *blip*, the final warning window vanished. As soon as he heard the girl's familiar voice, he understood.

He'd finished overwriting the dangerous code all by himself.

Strength left his hand. His body had been blown into the air by the bullet impact. Slowly, slowly, he fell away from the warm girl.

Accelerator, now airborne, reached his hand out.

But his fingers couldn't reach her anymore.

He'd wanted something, but none of that would be fulfilled.

He'd desperately picked something up, but it all fell from the palms of his hands.

Lord, how naïve can I be? After all I've done—

His vision quickly blurred and then went black. He slammed into the ground below as if falling into the depths of hell. His muddy awareness crumbled, and his thoughts rapidly tumbled into the darkness.

—did I really think saving somebody would give me a chance to do things over?

15 (Aug.31_PM08:13)

"…I did it? Ha-ha…why? Why…why am I alive?"

Ao Amai, holding onto the automatic pistol with white smoke swaying upward out of it, was dumbfounded.

It had hit him right in the center of the forehead. Accelerator had taken a direct hit from the bullet, flown back close to a meter, and fallen to the ground faceup. His forehead was split open, and bright red blood oozed from it.

He had no idea why, but Accelerator hadn't used his reflection. That meant there was no way for him to live if he took a .09mm military round to the forehead. And Amai hadn't just used any bullet—he'd used a special-order trial product.

The Shock Lancer.

By carving special grooves in the bullet, it would deliver a shock-wave spear by controlling its own air-resistance properties. The spear would follow after the passing bullet to strike the target. On top of increasing a bullet's killing potential by five to ten times just by putting grooves on it, because the grooves were melted into the bullet's surface owing to the extreme air friction heat, it also couldn't be analyzed by an enemy, even if they had gotten their hands on it. The special bullet was currently being advanced by anti-berserk esper development teams.

The wound in Accelerator's head would have been struck two or three times over by both the bullet and the spear made of air.

"He's…dead…Hah! What about Last Order? And the virus code?!"

Ao Amai pried his gaze from the corpse on the road and looked at the unconscious girl in the passenger seat. If the virus didn't activate, he was finished. He'd end up on the run from both Academy City and the opposition faction.

The girl, with exhausted limbs stretched, moved her lips.

Her tiny mouth formed quiet words.

"Code 000001 to code 357081 have been suspended due to illegal operation. Reawakening based on current normal descriptions. Repeat—code 000001 to—"

All of the moisture in Amai's body burst onto his skin as sweat.

If the virus had activated properly, then Last Order would have sent the order through the Misaka network for all of the ten thousand Sisters to freely use weapons and their abilities to kill humans completely at random. Then, her heart would stop itself and she would die—which he'd engineered so that a cancellation order couldn't be issued.

But despite all that, Last Order was still alive.

The virus hadn't started. He knew well what that meant.

He realized he couldn't do a single thing anymore.

Wobbling, he took two steps back, then a third.

"Ha-ha-ha. Oh, ah, gah, uwwoaaaaaaaaaaaaaaaaaaaaaahhhhhhhhh-hhhhhhhhhhhhh?!"

Ao Amai screamed, then aimed his gun at the one person who had smashed his life to pieces.

At the one girl, asleep in the passenger seat.

He stabbed the gun toward her chest, rising and falling with her shallow breathing. He placed his finger on the trigger. Just by moving his finger a bit, his special bullet, the Shock Lancer, would tear her delicate body apart completely. He wasn't thinking about where he'd shoot, nor how many rounds. He pulled the trigger, content to keep on firing until the gun was empty.

The sound of the gunshot rang out in the night.

But that round didn't pierce the girl's body.

*　　*　　*

"—Not gonna happen, you pile of shit!!"

The corpse had risen.

The boy, blood steadily flowing from his torn forehead, had reached out with his hand to block Amai's gun. The bullet had been cleanly reflected back into the muzzle, and the handgun exploded from within. It ripped through the wrist holding on to the gun.

"Uhg, ghu…aaaahhhhhh?!"

He grabbed his left hand onto his right, which had been cut up like a pomegranate, and stepped away from Accelerator.

Shit! That special round went into his forehead. How the hell is he still alive?! It makes no sense!

The Shock Lancer was a next-generation weapon that reversed air resistance through special grooves cut into the bullet and created a spear of force behind it. There was absolutely no way anyone could survive a direct hit to the brain.

But Amai had been mistaken.

The specialized warhead created a spear-shaped shock wave using the bullet's air resistance. Because of that, a lot of the bullet's speed is taken away by the air resistance. It was like a bullet flying with an opened parachute behind it.

The shock wave would lag behind the bullet and follow its trajectory. The lag time wasn't even one fourth of a second. But in that time, Accelerator had finished healing Last Order, and at the last moment, he regained his reflection.

In result, the slow-flying bullet cracked open his skull, but he fended off the fatal shock wave.

But to Ao Amai, who didn't know these specifics, the scene he was currently witnessing was like a nightmare.

Amai pulled a second handgun out with his left hand, now the only usable one. He hadn't, however, had any training with his non-dominant left hand. It trembled under the weight of the gun. There was no way he could aim it properly. And Accelerator took one of

the special rounds to the forehead and still got up. His left hand's unnatural quivering made perfect sense.

Accelerator stood before him.

As if to shield the young Last Order behind him. As if not giving a thought to the blood flowing from his forehead. Despite his feet shaking badly, despite his focus beginning to waver, he stared down the muzzle of Amai's gun.

The scientist in white saw this and grinned.

It was a half-desperate smile, even though he was aware of his absolute disadvantage.

"Hah. What're you gonna do at this point? You're too far gone."

"…You know it, old man. I'm human trash. Even the thought of saving someone at this point is completely ridiculous. I'm so damn naïve my skin is crawling with disgust."

If he saved someone else, then he might be saved as well.

The words sounded pretty, but in actuality they were ugly and self-serving. Calculating the worth of someone's life against your own is not what a decent person does. Someone like that could never be saved.

And in the first place, every single person who lived on this planet was beyond salvation. The soft, yet never kindhearted Kikyou Yoshikawa. The one who blasted a lead bullet into a man without hesitation in order to protect someone, Ao Amai. The one who killed more than ten thousand people and just now began to talk about how precious life is, Accelerator.

Everyone in the world was rotten. Searching for salvation after all that was wrong. Granting salvation to man? The concept was beyond ridiculous.

He knew all that.

He was painfully aware of it—he was a member of this world, too.

"But"—he said, as if cutting himself off from something—"the kid has nothing to do with it."

Accelerator was grinning.

He was talking while smiling, despite blood gushing fervently from the hole in his forehead.

"No matter how rotten we may be. Even if I'm a helpless piece of human trash and it's ridiculous for me to even mention helping another person..."

The blood flowing from his wound slid into his left eye.

His vision was tinted with red.

But even now, he desperately retained the strength in his feet, which seemed like they would collapse beneath him at any moment.

"There's no fucking reason it would be okay to watch this kid die. No way it would ever be right for trash like us to trample all over what she has!" shouted Accelerator, his eyesight red with his own blood.

He understood his actions were unbecoming. He knew they were beyond his means. He felt his own words flying back to stab his chest.

He still shouted.

If he didn't have the right to save somebody, then would he not be allowed to save anyone?

Would it be natural to bat away the small hand that had reached out to him?

What had she done?

Had she done anything to deserve him shaking away her desperately outstretched hand?

"You piece of shit. How much more obvious...can it get?" he murmured, as if letting himself hear it.

Last Order needed to be saved by somebody. She still had that opportunity, unlike Accelerator and Ao Amai.

It didn't matter who it was that saved her.

That wasn't the meat of his reasoning. It didn't matter who it was—if somebody hadn't reached out to her, Last Order really would have died.

One way or another, he realized what that Level Zero who had arrived at the switchyard to stop the experiment must have felt like. He stood up to save the Sisters without any reason or objective. Accelerator had always thought the Level Zero had seemed like a hero who had lived in a different world than him all his life, but he'd been wrong about that.

There was no main character in this world. Superheroes wouldn't just conveniently appear. If a person stayed silent, nobody would help, and if one cried out, they still weren't guaranteed anything.

But if a person still didn't want to lose something important to them...If help didn't come even after someone waited such a long time, and they lost them because of such a stupid reason, then he would just have to become that savior.

Even if it was pointless, or meaningless, or beyond his means.

To become somebody who would defend what was precious to him with his own hands.

There was no salvation in this world. People could never become superheroes.

That's why whoever happened to be present there needed to do something.

They needed to act like the main character.

"Yeah, I killed ten thousand of those Sisters. But that's no reason to let the other ten thousand die. Ah, jeez, I know that sounds whitewashed. I know the words coming out of my mouth right now! But you're wrong! We may be the epitome of human trash, but no matter what your reason is, there's no fucking way it's okay to kill that kid!!"

Accelerator's feet lost their power with a *snap*.

Fresh blood spilled from the wound on his forehead as if it had been blocked before.

But he couldn't go down yet.

No way.

"...Ugh...gaaahhhh!!"

Accelerator dropped his body low, then leaped toward Ao Amai with the speed of a bullet. Though he looked to be in the stronger position, Accelerator was the cornered one. He couldn't endure a long fight. He needed to settle things with this one hit, or he'd pass out. And even though he understood that, he didn't have the luxury of using a big attack. So his only option was the simple one—to charge at him at close range.

Amai devoted himself to running away, perhaps because he understood that fact. Compared to the bullet speed of the jumping Accelerator, if he ran backward, he'd get caught. So instead, he lurched his body to the side to get out of the way of the incoming Accelerator. The nails of the devil ripped through where he had just been.

Accelerator moved his mouth silently and looked to his left.

He saw Ao Amai. He must have put all his strength into his sideways jump, because he fell to the ground quite pathetically. He wouldn't be able to repeat that leap in that state. Was he trying to stall for time? He pointed the gun that his left hand, the only safe one, was holding.

Accelerator turned his body around.

Or rather, he tried to. Unfortunately, his feet got twisted up, ruining his balance. He tried to stop himself, but his feet were no longer moving. Immediately after the wound on his forehead suddenly stung with great pain, the sensation disappeared. He heard a *thump* and finally realized he'd fallen to the ground.

In his sideways vision, he saw the girl he needed to protect.

A particular thought came to mind, but his awareness quickly slipped into the darkness.

16 (Aug.31_PM08:38)

Ao Amai, for a while, didn't feel like he had lived.

He stared at the fallen Accelerator vacantly, then finally wiped the sweat from his brow.

I'm...alive. Ha-ha...somehow...I survived somehow?

He smiled, drained of strength, and scratched Accelerator's forehead with his nails.

His reflection...gone. *I didn't want to bring something like this out if I could help it, but there's always the million-to-one chance he gets up again. He won't be able to dodge the next one.*

He pointed the muzzle at Accelerator's forehead.

If he didn't have his ability, Accelerator should be nothing more than an exercise-deprived student. He figured he would die normally if he hit him in the head with ten .09mm rounds. Of course, now that he'd failed to activate the virus and was caught between Academy City and the opposition faction, he had no time to be doing this. He had to run—as soon as possible, to get even another millimeter away—but he should pluck the seeds of disaster now.

"Hah. After all that, you weren't hero enough to settle things. It's only natural—we're all like that. Everyone is like that."

He put strength into his trigger finger.

Bang! came the sound of a dry gunshot. The murderous noise sounded like a firecracker.

"…"

Ao Amai's face distorted.

The shot hadn't come from the gun he was holding.

A hole opened in Amai's back, around his waist, and he felt a scorching heat burn into him as if melted lead had been poured into it. He turned around slowly—his body wouldn't move any faster.

Away from him was a parked, used station wagon, so old that one might begin to doubt the driver's car sense. Its door was open. A woman in white came out. In her hand was a toylike self-defense gun that only held two shots.

White smoke curled upward from the gun in her hand.

"…Kikyou…Yoshikawa…," he said, as if squeezing the words out of his throat. The woman in white didn't reply.

17 (Aug.31_PM08:43)

Amai was lying on the ground.

He shook his head at his flickering vision. Finally, his consciousness cleared up. He must have passed out, but he didn't know if it had been ten seconds or ten minutes.

He could see the woman wearing white.

Kikyou Yoshikawa.

With her back turned to him, she opened the back door of the station wagon and manipulated something inside. He knew what the equipment back there was—an incubator.

Geh...

He moved his shaking head around to look at his own car. Last Order, who had been sitting in the passenger seat, was nowhere to be found. The specimen was probably in that cylindrical glass incubator, though Yoshikawa's movements were blocking it.

He tried to stand up, but his body was barely moving. He just barely managed to get his upper half up and, with quivering hands, took his Italian-made military handgun.

Suddenly, Yoshikawa turned around.

Her work had long since finished, but after she closed the back door, she pointed her self-defense gun at Amai. It almost looked like she was smiling. She slowly walked over to him, gun at the ready.

"I apologize. I'm always so soft when it comes to things like this. Not kind or gentle, but soft. I didn't have the guts to go for your vitals, but I see I can't just let you leave. My choice to pointlessly prolong your pain may have been so soft it was cruel."

"How did you...find...?"

"Cell phones have had GPS for some years now, you know. Didn't you realize that the kid's phone was stuck in the middle of a call?"

Yoshikawa looked down at Accelerator with motherly eyes.

"I only know what was going on here from the sounds I picked up from the phone, but at the very least, there doesn't seem to be anything going on outside."

The shivering of Amai's hands grew more severe. Feeling steadily left his fingertips, like they were stuck in the snow for an extended period of time. The finger he had on the trigger trembled in violation of his own will. He heard the clinking of metal parts hitting together inside the gun.

"Oh, you don't have to worry about him. I know a pretty amazing doctor. His face looks like a frog's and he lacks dignity, but people do call him the Heaven Canceler and say that he can bring people back from the dead. I'm sure he'll be able to work something out."

He heard ambulance sirens drawing near from somewhere far away. She'd probably notified them before she even shot him. Perhaps she even designated which hospital to carry him to.

Yoshikawa looked down the muzzle. He could fire it at any time, but she didn't stop walking.

She didn't seem at all concerned about her own well-being.

She was here to defend the children. She forgot all about protecting herself by running away from the responsibility of the experiment's failure, which everyone was trying to push onto someone else. She didn't fear standing before a loaded gun about to fire. She did all this in order to return the children, who had been unfortunate enough to be wrapped up in this experiment, to their proper worlds.

And she said she was being soft? That she wasn't at all a kind person?

"...Why?" Amai squeezed out. "I don't understand. This doesn't follow your thought patterns. You could only ever put risk and reward on a scale. Your decision is impossible, given your personality. Or are you saying you have enough of a reward to justify this action?"

"If I had to answer that, it would probably be yes. I hate my own thought patterns. I didn't want to watch myself see more and more success by doing that. I've thought about it ever since I was born—that I wanted to do something kind rather than something soft, just once in my life."

Kikyou Yoshikawa smiled with loneliness and continued to walk.

Not three meters were between them anymore.

"You see, I never wanted to turn into this kind of scientist," she said, adding with a hint of scorn directed at herself, "though you may not be able to believe it."

Ao Amai was astonished at those words—he knew of her talents well.

"I wanted to be a schoolteacher. A teacher, or a professor, or whatever. Not some rigid job. I wanted to be a nice, kind teacher. I wanted to remember each and every one of my students' faces. I wanted to give them counsel whenever they had trouble. I wanted to engage myself, so that I could give a reassuring smile to just one student without expecting anything in return. I wanted to be a kind teacher, the sort that would be made fun of at graduation ceremonies when they saw me crying. Of course, I abandoned the idea myself, thinking that somebody as soft as me and not at all kind should never be in a position to teach others.

"But even still…" She smiled.

One meter between them. Yoshikawa slowly bent down onto one knee to meet the sitting Amai's gaze, like she was trying to talk to a small child.

"I probably still had regrets about it. Just once, I wanted to try doing something nice, instead of defaulting to being soft. I wanted to display the same kind of actions as a teacher who would do everything she could for just one student.

"That's all," she finished.

Their guns each pointed into the other's chest.

She herself should have understood how difficult it would be to bring Accelerator back into everyday life. There was no doubting the fact that he had murdered ten thousand of the Sisters. And that didn't mean it would end here. He may have had vast power, but the one controlling it was an unstable mind in the first place. If left alone, he could even cause more damage than before.

But still, she wished in her heart.

The strongest esper, whose real name nobody knew anymore, had tried to protect a single girl, even with a bullet in his head. Even if he couldn't walk alongside her, even though he could never meet her again as she walked the path of light, he never gave up. He never abandoned her. So instead of choosing the softer option of protecting himself, he was able to choose the kinder option of saving another.

He may have been far, far too late, but he had finally realized that he was capable of making that choice.

He now knew the meaning of defending someone with one's own hands.

Yoshikawa wanted to protect the kindness he showed.

She couldn't allow the cruel ending that came at the end of that kindness.

"It's over, Ao Amai."

Each placed their finger on the trigger of the gun pointing at the other's chest.

"You're probably scared to die alone. I'd be honored if you chose me to go with you. I will absolutely never allow you to lay a hand on those children. I will bet what little kindness I have within me on that."

"Hmph." Amai gave a half smile.

Either way, though he was caught between Academy City and the opposition faction, there wouldn't be a tomorrow for him.

"Kindness really doesn't suit you," he intoned, placing strength in his trigger finger.

"What you have is already what they call strength."

Two shots rang out.

Amai and Yoshikawa, their bodies both pierced by bullets, were each launched backward.

Aug.31_PM08:57 End

CHAPTER 4

A Certain Freeloading Index

Arrow_Made_of_AZUSA.

1 (Aug.31_PM03:15)

Academy City.

A city for the fostering of espers, created by reclaiming a large swath of land in west Tokyo. It occupied one-third of Tokyo itself and had a total population of just under 2.3 million. Eighty percent of those were students who had awakened some sort of ability, rated on a six-step scale, ranging from Level Zero "Impotents" to Level Five "Superpowers."

In this city, these abilities were not occult concepts—it was no more than a scientific idea, which anyone could awaken within themselves by completing a standard Curriculum.

And in one corner of the slightly dubious city, an entirely average male student named Touma Kamijou was up to his eyeballs in homework. He buried his face in his hands.

"Come on, damn it! What is this factorization thing supposed to be?! Screw you, math! You're supposed to only ever have one answer, not two!!" Kamijou cried out and fell onto his back, as if to flee from the math problems spread out on his glass table. He was an amusing person—the type who would deliver a monologue whenever something bad happened. Even when he finished with math, there was a modern history book report and an English homework packet patiently waiting in the wings for him. He felt his nerves about to reach their limit.

Urgh...

He gave a look to his right hand as he lay on the floor.

The Imagine Breaker—the power in his right hand. Whether it was a million-volt spear of lightning or a ball of flame more than three thousand degrees, if it was some kind of preternatural power, he could nullify it just by touching it. It was a wonderful ability...but not terribly effective against his summer homework.

The current date and time was August 31, 3:15:00 PM.

What am I gonna do? he wondered, half seriously about to break down and cry on the spot.

And of course today, they were sold out of the coffee at the convenience store, he was accosted by Aogami and Tsuchimikado, Mikoto demanded that they pretend they were dating, and he was chased around by an Aztec sorcerer who had transformed into Mitsuki Unabara. It was terrible. He still had a substantial amount of homework left to finish.

To add insult to injury, his upside-down view of his room revealed a girl watching TV and a stupid cat with its face shoved into the bag of potato chips next to her, currently fulfilling all its wildest dreams.

The girl's name was Index.

Apparently it was a shortened version of some ridiculous name like "Index Librorum Prohibitorum."

She had the body of a foreigner, with white skin, silvery hair, and green eyes. Furthermore, she wore this ostentatious, teacup-like habit made of pure white silk with golden embroidery, and that was enough to give her a somewhat nineteenth-century Victorian feel. Actually, Touma didn't really know what Victorian things looked like. It was just a bluff.

Her appearance told the story—she wasn't a resident of the happy, fun science land that was Academy City.

In fact, she came from the exact opposite kind of world—the "viva magic" one. She wasn't a witch, per se, but her own wickedness perhaps put her on a level above that. After all, through the use of a certain means, she was the only person in the world who knew everything about all types of the world's sorcery.

And this real-life magical girl was nodding along, her eyes glued to the TV.

Incidentally, the current program was an anime—meaning fictional—account of a magical girl's adventures, being rebroadcast for summer break.

"I see! This 'Magical Powered Kanamin' girl is fooling the eyes of the Roman Catholic Church's famed Albigensian crusaders by blending right in as a normal student. But what on earth is that rainbow-shining staff—oh! They reproduced the elemental Ether Part, the Lotus Staff, didn't they?! I should have expected no less from the mythical land of Japan. Its oriental style is simply beautiful!"

No, that's just Japanimation—military provisions for Japan's famed legions of otaku. Kamijou considered shooting back the retort at the real magical girl, so seriously absorbed in what was on TV, but he decided against it. He needed to focus on his homework.

"Hey, I'm not gonna tell you to not watch TV or shut up, but could you please turn down the volume and lower your voice! Any minor lapse in focus could spell doom over here!"

"Huh?" Index turned around unhappily. "I'm only watching TV because you won't play with me. Besides, where did you go this afternoon? What was that call about? Were you secretly fighting a sorcerer? Have you not learned your lesson yet?"

"Uh...I'm telling you, it was nothing. I'm fine, see? I wasn't fighting or anything this time. We talked everything out peacefully. You know, Aztecs sure are gentlemen."

"So which ill-fated girl were you standing up for this time?"

"Listen to me! Did they already make it official that whenever I fight, that's what happens?!" shouted Kamijou, but Index sighed in resignation, tired.

"I guess there's no use in going on about something after it's over. By the way, Touma, I've been doing that whole escapism thing into the world of TV since this morning when you left me here."

"Then let's play pretend homework. I'll do the math, and you can do the English."

"...I don't wanna do something that boring," she sighed again. "Oh, Touma, thank you for the manga. I put the books I borrowed over there, okay?"

"Over there—hey!!"

Kamijou had no words. All the manga volumes he had put away in his bookshelf were now in a huge jumbled pile on the floor, like an earthquake had come through.

"Why...why?! Why do you do so much more when I don't have the time?! Wait, you made the mess, so you put them back on the shelves properly!"

"Okay, I know where everything went, so it's no problemo!" she declared calmly, still watching TV.

Kamijou's shoulders drooped, and he breathed a sigh of his own. The whole point of keeping things tidy was to put things where they would be easy to remember. A person who could remember exactly where things went wouldn't even have to do the work of putting the manga into the bookcase in order.

Index was essentially a library of grimoires. She'd memorized every last letter of 103,000 grimoires from around the world, like *The Golden Bough*, the *Book M*, the *Hermetica*, *The Secret Doctrine*, and the *Tetrabiblos*. She probably memorized the positions of every one of the books in this mess as soon as she took them out.

"Man, is that how you treat somebody who lets you borrow his stuff?"

"But that way is easier to remember," she said, seeming wholly unhappy. "Besides, if you clean your room without thinking about it, you end up losing pens and stuff. See, Touma, where did your Classical Japanese homework go?"

Huh? Kamijou picked himself up and looked on the glass table.

It wasn't there.

He'd finally finished the whole thing and stapled the entire mountain of papers together, but it was nowhere.

"What? Hey, wait! Where did it go? It was just here!"

"Whenever this sort of thing happens, it always ends up being in some silly, unexpected place, huh?"

"Don't give me that peaceful smile! Please, just help me look for it!! Gyaah!"

His shout echoed through the midsummer dormitory.

Common sense told him there was no way it could have gotten out of the room…but for some reason, Kamijou got the distinct feeling he wouldn't be seeing his Classical Japanese homework ever again.

2 (Aug.31_PM04:00)

The city streets on August 31 were almost empty.

Eighty percent of its residents were students. Just for today, most of them were spending their last hours of summer vacation struggling to complete their homework. The lonely, clattering sounds of the many wind-generating propellers that replaced electrical poles were the only noise around.

A man walked through the deserted streets, heat mirages swaying to and fro.

The man in the empty city was a sight to behold.

The scorching sun was glaring down. The lingering heat of summer at the end of August was relentless. And yet he was covered neck to toe in a black suit, topped off with a black necktie. It was easy to imagine the large man having these big, boorish muscles underneath his clothing. His eyes were closed, and despite the heat, he did not have a single bead of sweat on him.

He looked like either a mafia member or someone going to a mafia funeral. That was all he possibly could have been.

However, he wore one thing on his right arm that didn't follow along the lines of mafia funeral attire—a Japanese bracer. And attached to this bracer was a Japanese bow painted in black that looked like an arbalest. It was a complex mechanism, set up so that he could draw back the string and loose an arrow with a mere flick of his hand.

The strange man's name was Ouma Yamisaka.

He was one unbound by scientific ideas—he was a sorcerer.

"Index Librorum Prohibitorum...the archive of forbidden books."

The unrefined man's lips, however, spoke the foreign Latin language smoothly. Everyone knew that name. She was the girl who possessed 103,000 grimoires in her brain. And with that much knowledge, one could grant any wish they had, bending the world and its laws to their will.

Therefore, there were, of course, many sorcerers who had their sights set on her.

"Hmm. Still far away," Yamisaka said to himself, his stride unfaltering.

He had fought a battle to get inside the city. Academy City was surrounded by a great wall, and there was a police force dedicated to preventing entrance by invaders.

Yamisaka hadn't killed them, but some of them might need to worry about aftereffects later. He thought about it but didn't stop. Giving up now would be the same as spitting in the faces of those whom he had sacrificed for this. If he was to do this, he needed to go all the way.

Ouma Yamisaka walked through the mirage-filled streets.

He had but one destination—a room in a certain student dormitory.

3 (Aug.31_PM05:05)

It soon became time to prepare dinner, and the lost Classical Japanese homework was finally found.

Index, who had found it, had a big grin plastered on her face.

"Wow, I never thought it would be under those big piles of manga! So, Touma, did I do good? Huh? Come on, don't you have something to say?"

"You were the one who made the mess in the first place! It's abuse, that's what it is! Go put all the manga back into the bookcase this instant, got it?! And apologize to me!!"

"The manga has nothing to do with it. Sphinx was the one who had your homework in his mouth."

Sphinx was the name of the calico Kamijou was raising—not, of course, the legendary creature that would kill people if they couldn't answer riddles.

The perpetrator seemed quite enthralled by the three-minute cooking show on TV. He kept batting at the screen with a paw.

Kamijou heaved a serious sigh.

The current time was just after five PM. A little less than seven hours remained until the date tomorrow. If he risked everything on a complete all-nighter, there were still only fifteen hours until school started. Would he be able to finish his math questions, his English packet, and his book report in that time?

*And I lost so much time just searching for my Classical Japanese homework, too...*thought Kamijou, dejected.

On the other hand, Index seemed annoyed that he wasn't showering her in praise.

"Touma, Touma! I did my job, so I want a suitable reward...I want to eat something. That thing they're doing on the TV looks good, I think."

"..."

Kamijou's head silently turned with a *crick-crick-crick* to look at the television.

The three-minute cooking program seemed to be catering to children during summer vacation, so it was showing how to make a tofu hamburger.

Kamijou's head creaked back around to look at Index.

The corners of his lips turned up suddenly in an unearthly smile.

"...I'm going to kill you."

"Why are you so irritated? Touma, you're angry because you're so hungry. You want to eat that, too, right?"

"Well, I mean, if given the choice, then yes. But like I've been saying this entire time, I don't have the time to make—...!"

"If you **keep going at this**, your head's gonna explode. You should rest a bit."

"Argh! That's the nicest thing I didn't want you to say right now!!"

"Come on, Touma, don't grab your head like that. Huh? Where did the math homework you were just doing go?"

"Eh?"

Kamijou looked at the glass table.

It wasn't there.

4 (Aug.31_PM05:30)

Before said student dormitory, Ouma Yamisaka looked overhead to the seventh floor. Though, as both of his eyes were normally shut, there wasn't really a meaning behind his gesture.

"Here it is," he said to himself, manipulating the bracer on his right hand. The attached bowstring pulled back automatically due to the mechanisms inside. However, there was no arrow in the black bow.

"Tempest Bowstring."

Yamisaka fired it anyway. *Bsshhh!* came the sharp sound of the bowstring piercing the air. It echoed through the silent city streets, resounding surprisingly clear.

Roar! howled a gust of wind from near his feet.

He couldn't see it because it was transparent, but there was a clump of air about the size of a beach ball right there.

He aligned his feet and jumped slightly, landing on the top of the invisible ball of air.

Gsshh came the noise as his feet easily squashed it down.

Then there was the *pop* of the air springing back, and Yamisaka's body hurtled straight up into the air.

He flew straight along up the wall of the dormitory for several meters.

When he reached his destination—Touma Kamijou's room on the seventh floor—he grabbed the balcony railing to stop his ascent, then brought his feet down onto the railing. At the same time, he drew the bowstring back.

"Impact Bowstring."

Slam!!

The bow let loose an invisible shock wave at the same time the bowstring made a noise. It completely destroyed the thin window-pane like an invisible wrecking ball.

The shrill cry of glass breaking echoed throughout the entire area.

A rain of thousands of pieces of glass flew into the room. He didn't particularly care what would happen to somebody standing in front of it. He stepped into the room to secure Index.

However...

"...They're gone?"

Yamisaka looked confused. There was no one in the room. He checked the bathroom just to be sure, but no one was in there, either. They seemed to be out.

Still perplexed, he returned to the balcony, now crestfallen. The window glass was still smashed to smithereens, but he was not the type of sorcerer to mind it.

Hmm. He scratched at his head stupidly.

"Sweeper Bowstring."

He made the bowstring resound like a sonar. Its small sound reverberated incredibly vividly. It ran its tongue over the city in less than an instant, telling him of Index's current location.

5 (Aug.31_PM06:00)

"...I've got this bad feeling...," said Touma Kamijou to himself. He was now sitting in an air-conditioned family restaurant. *Why am I getting this chill?* he wondered, confused. He had locked all the doors behind him, so he shouldn't have to worry about burglars, but...

Despite it being August 31, there were people out and about at meal times. The warriors were calling a temporary truce and restoring their energy at various convenience stores, restaurants, and beef bowl places. Then it was off again to the battlefield, where their confrontation with the homework on their desks awaited them. After all, there were only six hours left until the end of summer break.

"Touma, Touma, what should I choose? Can I pick anything on here I want?"

There in the seat across from him was Index, peering at the stupidly large menu, eyes glittering like a kid waiting for Santa Claus. Also, this restaurant was completely fine with pets—a revolutionary policy if there ever was one—so the stupid cat was curled up on Index's lap.

He sighed.

He had moved to the restaurant for a change of atmosphere (and because he had no time to cook dinner). His plan was to get serious and immerse himself in the merciless hunt for the survivors of his summer assignments…but it seemed she hadn't quite understood that.

Kamijou shook his head without tearing his eyes from the composition paper he bought at the convenience store. He wanted to get his book report done in one fell swoop. Unfortunately, he had a gut feeling that his current situation had some other ideas in store for him.

"Hey, Touma. Hey, Touma. Can I get whatever I want?"

"What do you want already? Just order something!"

"Okay, then here I go. The most expensive thing on the menu!"

"…" He smiled sweetly. "Okay, then two thousand yen's worth of raw eggs."

He could hear the roar of her very soul howling his name in anger.

Kamijou ended up getting coffee, Index the set lunch meal A, and the stupid cat got something called "cat lunch C." As a restaurant that allowed pets, it had this amazing—yet also somehow terrifying—menu prepared specifically for them. There were others on there, too, like lunches for dogs and lunches for turtles.

It would take some time before their orders arrived. Kamijou took out his composition paper and a mechanical pencil, deciding to get started on the report immediately.

…Unfortunately…

"Touma, Touma, what are you gonna write a report about anyway?"

"This year's theme is Momotaro."

"…Wow."

"Hey, wait, you foreigner, do you even really understand the true meaning of Momotaro, I mean, it's a famous Japanese children's story known throughout the world, and see, it makes perfect sense for a summer book report!"

"Boy, Touma, you sure do hate reading books."

"Well, I don't think memorizing every letter of a hundred thousand books is anything like normal, either."

Index's temples twitched.

Her smile could melt cheese.

"Touma, Touma!"

"What is it now?"

"...Did you know it's actually a really scary Japanese fable?"

"Stop! I'm going to write a totally normal report on Momotaro! If you add any information now, it will derail my entire essay! And besides, why the heck can someone from England even do the whole dark side of the Momotaro spiel, anyway?!"

"Mgh. What are you saying anyway? Momotaro is a magnificent example of an occult book. In fact, I have its original copy stored neatly within my 103,000 grimoires."

"Huh?"

"It happens especially often in Japanese culture—a story will seem like a lullaby or a fable, but it's actually a cleverly camouflaged occult manual. Momotaro was born from the peaches, right? Well, that person didn't even exist in the original version."

*Uhhh...*Kamijou's thoughts stopped there. *This is bad. Index is really starting to love explaining things to me. And I can't waste another second! I need to get this massive amount of homework done!*

"Since ancient times, the river has been depicted as a border separating *shigan*, or this world, to *higan*, or the netherworld. When they mention people on the river and crossing the river, they're talking about just that—transcendents who can control life and death, Touma. It might be easier to imagine dead people being ferried across the Sanzu River."

"I'm sorry, stop, stop!"

"The correct way to think about the peach that floated down from the river is as a forbidden fruit that has transcended life and death. And if we're talking about fruits that grant immortality in eastern cultures, you have to think of the sentou, or hermit peach, which protects the holy queen mother. The original version of the story didn't have a Momotaro born from peaches, but instead featured an old man and woman who ate a peach and regained their youth. As you can tell from that, the story is actually describing secrets of Taoist alchemical arts, and—"

"Stop it, stop it, stop it! Enough with the off-topic occult discussion! Viewers, please look forward to Miss Index's next work! I mean, jeez, just let me do my homework already!!"

Index gave a dissatisfied whine. He ignored her and wrote on the composition paper with his mechanical pencil. He wasn't going as fast as he thought he was. *Great, now I'm basically just having to write a letter of apology,* he thought, eventually somehow filling up three pages.

Kamijou sighed in relief as he finished his work.

And then the waitress came over, as if she had timed it that way.

"Sorry for the long wait! You ordered the coffee, the set meal lunch A, and the cat lunch C, right?"

Oh, finally here! He began to put away the composition paper all over the table…

…when suddenly, without any reason or prior warning, the waitress fell over magnificently.

"What?!"

He watched dumbstruck as everything on the tray fell onto the table with a clatter and a crash. When the dust settled, a veritable mountain made of dinner towered before his eyes.

The small, sizzling-hot iron pan used as a steak plate for what appeared to be today's specialty landed directly on Kamijou's lap. He leaped up, brushed the plate off, and looked at the perpetrator with at least half-serious tears in his eyes.

There was the waitress, flat on her face, making a pitiful "Owie…" noise.

Would you forgive a bust, klutzy waitress for this?

"No way in hell! You freaking cow! I'll overhead throw you straight to hell!!"

"Now, now, Touma…Huh? Touma, where's your essay?"

"…"

It wasn't there.

And he wasn't sure he wanted to find it underneath this piping-hot dinner mountain.

6 (Aug.31_PM06:32)

"Sweeper Bowstring."

He drew back the bowstring, again and again.

Its air-splitting noises informed Ouma Yamisaka that he was drawing near to his target.

"...In there?"

Before his closed eyes was a single-family-restaurant building.

On the other side of a street-facing window sat a boy and a girl.

"I now go to the battlefield."

Yamisaka manipulated the complex contraption and pulled back the bowstring with one hand.

"I will light the beacon marking the outbreak of war. Executioner Bowstring."

He thrust the bow toward the boy on the other side of the glass. The glass hadn't done anything wrong, but it was in the way.

7 (Aug.31_PM06:35)

Touma Kamijou was exhausted.

The essay he dug out from the mountain of dinner was soiled and soggy, and he could barely read the words written on it. He couldn't hand in something like this.

Kamijou felt like a marathon runner who had run out of energy in the beginning of the race. Index, of course, was giving him a sympathetic smile, though her lips were drawn.

"B-but Touma, you can still read the words, so you can just copy it onto a new piece of paper. At least you don't have to do all the thinking over again! ♪"

"I guess so," he answered lifelessly.

The problem was that filling up three pages again was already a strain on his body.

"Damn it...If only I could have just used a computer..."

Kamijou's gaze fell to the table, which was (for now) nice and clean. He was bad at writing words, too, but actually physically writing them with a pencil was the worst. He had no problem taking normal notes, but filling up page after page of essay papers really made his hands hurt.

He sighed in defeat and looked out the window.

He figured the window would reflect back an exhausted image of himself, but he was wrong. Instead, there was some big man in a black suit right at the window, looking at them.

Well, actually, his eyes were closed.

At first, Kamijou thought he was trying to fix his hair by using the window as a mirror. But there was no way he could be using a mirror with his eyes closed.

What on earth is he doing?

He stared absently at the man, and then, at that moment, the man said something from across the glass.

His movements were gentle, much like those of somebody who had just been reunited with an old friend he hadn't seen in decades.

However...

He pointed a bow-and-arrow-like thing mounted on his right hand straight at Kamijou.

"?!"

A moment after Kamijou rose from his seat, the bowstring snapped back. There was no arrow nocked to it. But another moment later, something invisible shattered the giant window separating them. Whatever it was, there wasn't only one—the glass pane ripped apart like wires had torn through it.

Blades of air, ripping through even sound itself.

They sliced through the table, dancing madly right past Index's nose. The fragments of the shattered window didn't fly inward, instead just sliding down to the floor. The storm of blades came straight for Kamijou before the stupid cat could even stand its hair on end.

Nearby patrons panicked, rose from their own seats, and tried to scream. Only the fact that this was a city of espers was responsible for the immediate reaction everyone had to something as ridiculous as invisible swords coming through the air.

But not one person was able to cry out.

Wham!
His right hand had already blown away all of the incoming blades.

The Imagine Breaker—the power in his right hand.

If it touched any kind of strange power, whether it was a supernatural ability or sorcery, it could entirely erase it. Such an unknown power before the eyes of those nearby was enough to take their breath away—they forgot to scream.

Numerous blades had come right for him, but he didn't even get scratched.

The wind blew. It seemed to have been what destroyed the blades of air. Apparently they weren't made of vacuum, but rather compressed air. He also wasn't firing them one at a time—he was actually creating a small tornado of them. His right hand making contact with it had nullified the entire tornado at once.

He bared his teeth and glared out the broken window, when...

"Spectral Bowstring. ———I'm over here."

Suddenly, the man who should have been outside was standing right behind him.

Kamijou froze.

The man, still with his eyes closed, exhaled slightly, as if satisfied with his response.

"I had not entirely predicted this, but I would much rather avoid needlessly taking lives. Surrender to me now, and I will not lay a hand on you. Once I acquire what I am after, I promise you that I will retreat with has—"

"Aaaggh!! Look what you've done, you bastard! My book report is nothing but confetti now!!"

Kamijou's shout had cut off the man's words.

A slightly confused expression crossed his face. He certainly

didn't seem to have expected this. From the man's point of view, he probably wanted Kamijou to accept the situation as more serious.

Kamijou, however, couldn't care less.

He looked at his composition paper, now sliced into pieces—or, more accurately, transformed into small paper trash—with tears in his eyes, and continued. "You! Yeah, you, the one standing there like an idiot! This is all your fault, so you're taking responsibility! Rewrite my book report this instant!! The theme is Momotaro, it needs to be at least three pages long, and you're aiming for the Ministry of Education Award for Fine Arts!"

"I do not care."

"...Okay, then. I hope you don't mind me getting a little bit violent, eh?"

The moment Kamijou gave a half smile and tried to grab the man, he suddenly vanished into thin air.

Wha...? He looked around.

The man was now, unbelievably, standing behind Index.

"I'm finishing this quickly. I haven't the time to fool around with children."

The man held Index's body to him.

It looked like a light touch, but Index's body suddenly lurched, as if his hand was lightning, and then stopped moving. The stupid cat rushed onto the floor and got away from the man.

Who is this guy? thought Kamijou.

He seemed to have something to do with Index. She was, of course, rather unique, what with the whole being a living treasure chest, her mind packed with 103,000 grimoires.

However, that should mean nothing to an esper living in the totally scientific Academy City.

So if this man was trying to get his hands on Index, then...

"...You're a sorcerer."

The other abnormal power standing at the opposite end of the spectrum from supernatural abilities.

A sorcerer.

"Indeed," the nameless man confirmed with one word.

"You seem pretty mild, though. All of a sudden you try to slice people open with invisible swords, and then right after that you start sexually harassing a girl from behind, eh? What the hell are you thinking? You know there's such a thing as protection for the lives of children, right, you lolicon?"

"What am I thinking?"

The man smiled coolly in contrast to Kamijou's heated attitude.

"You should understand, if you have acquired the knowledge, that this is the archive of 103,000 secret, forbidden books."

Then, without warning, the man disappeared into thin air again, holding Index.

Only the words "Spectral Bowstring" were left hanging in the space he'd once been.

Is this like…teleportation?

"Agh, damn it, you didn't even deny being a lolicon!! So this is your taste, isn't it?!"

Kamijou, as if grasping at straws, grabbed at where the man had just been standing.

His right hand hit dead air, but his left grasped something soft, something that shouldn't have been there.

"Uhyah?!"

From the empty space came a cry from Index. "T-T-T-T-T-Touma! Where do you think you're touching me?!"

"Eh?"

Kamijou tried squeezing the air with his left hand, where nothing should have been.

He got the feeling that there was, in fact, something in this empty space. The man was using some kind of trick to conceal them. Maybe he was manipulating light refraction or something.

He heard the man give an irritated *tsk*.

That was all he needed to know. Index and that man hadn't disappeared from any kind of teleportation. They were here; he just couldn't see them.

And that meant...

That both the man and Index would have been standing in this empty space, so...

So...

What was the soft thing Touma Kamijou was grabbing right now?

"..What?"

As if aiming precisely for the moment Kamijou's thoughts blanked out...

...the man's hand appeared by itself all of a sudden from the space right next to him. It was as if he were reaching through an invisible curtain.

The man's right hand had a bow mounted on it.

"Executioner Bowstring."

Kamijou reflexively brought his arm back from the empty space as soon as he heard the man's low murmur. A blade of air stabbed straight past where his arm had been, then cut into the floor with the weight of a guillotine.

"Damn! He got me!!"

He swung his arms around urgently, but he couldn't feel anything else there.

He was already gone.

"Gah!" Kamijou grabbed the stupid cat by its neck.

He was worried about Index. She was a walking library of grimoires, with 103,000 of them recorded in her brain. He was pretty sure that if a person used all of them, they could bend the entire world to their will.

If that's what the man was after, then he might cause her harm by getting the information out.

Bullshit...

He gritted his teeth.

...So what if she's got 103,000 books up there? That's a stupid freakin' reason to kidnap someone and get violent! It isn't worth it!!

He clicked his tongue, whipped himself around to face the exit...

...and there was the waitress, standing with a smile (except her eyes weren't smiling at all).

And she appeared to have class-changed from a klutzy, big-breasted waitress to a high-mobility-type combat girl.

"Could you please wait a moment, sir?"

"...Uh..."

Kamijou cast his gaze around the restaurant one more time.

The large window had been cleaved like butter, and the table was in big, circular pieces. He wasn't exactly sure what the value of business furniture was, but he got the feeling it was quite a bit higher than the regular kind you'd put in your own house.

".......Uhhh..."

Kamijou's lips drew back.

The manager was coming out from the back, also smiling, his bulging muscles looking about to burst.

8 (Aug.31_PM07:30)

"Shit! Damn it! I'm gonna kick your ass, you lolicon kidnapping demon!" shouted Kamijou, roaring through dark alleys holding the stupid cat.

He had run from the restaurant, of course. He'd been running from the brawny manager, the smiling waitress, and a few courageous, well-meaning patrons who happened to be there for a little less than an hour now. He weaved in and out through back roads and alleys, but he had no evidence he'd completely shaken them off yet.

Homework was the least of his problems at this point. If he made a wrong move, he could end up getting suspended.

"Uhu...uhuhu. Uhu-uhu-uhuhuhuhuhu!!"

Kamijou laughed a very dangerous laugh as he dashed through the unlit alleyways.

His rage had peaked. On top of not having any time, just when he'd finally been working so hard on his homework, an actual freaking lolicon threw cold water on that plan, then framed him for a weird crime that forced him to consider being suspended. Who wouldn't be angry?

*Man, I wonder if she's all right...*Kamijou sighed.

Index was a member of Necessarius, or the Church of Necessary Evils, an English Puritan combat group specializing in witch-hunting…but he doubted the shrimp had any actual ability to fight.

He wanted to go and take Index back from that pervert first, but he had no clues.

Okay, so seriously, what am I doing now?

As he racked his brains over the problem, the stupid cat slipped right out of his hands and onto the road. It didn't pay another glance to him and ran straight ahead.

"H-hey! Wait a minute!"

Kamijou was about to go into full-on panic mode, but suddenly he had a thought. *Don't cats have pretty sharp noses? Or was that dogs? Well, even cats probably have a better sense of smell than people do. But then I've never heard of a police cat. Which is it?* He ran after the cat, not very deep in thought. *Maybe it's searching for Index by using its sense of hearing, or smell, or whatever.*

The stupid cat ran fast.

He chased it at full speed lest he lose it. He ran, ran, ran, and ran some more.

And they finally arrived at…

"…What is this? Is this the back door to a hotel?"

It didn't look so much like a hotel as it did a multipurpose building that had everything one could think of packed inside, like department stores, restaurants, sleeping facilities, game rooms, and super resorts. Except a normal hotel corporation was the one managing it all.

He stared up the back wall of this "hotel" and felt a terribly bad feeling wash over him. *Did that lolicon seriously drag Index into a place like this?* He paled. *He's seriously stuck on this. Can I even do anything anymore?*

Then, out of the corner of his eye, he saw the stupid cat scavenging around at something.

"?"

He casually looked over and saw that it had skillfully opened up a bucket lid with its front legs and was poking its face inside.

Kamijou looked up again at the building.

It was a fairly large hotel. It was easy to think that in general, the cordoned-off Academy City had little need for sleeping facilities, but there were a handful of them for conferences and other academic events. And the building itself looked so extravagant that it seemed out of place—perhaps it was also trying to appeal to people who came from outside (of course, unless there was a conference, there would be zero guests. In a pathetic solution to this problem, they always had department stores, game rooms, etc. within the same building).

Which meant that the restaurants inside the building would also have good ratings, and the trash scraps of food would basically be a gourmet meal compared to normal animal food...

"Graaaaahhhhhhhhh! Don't you have any obligation toward your master?! Even if it was Index who picked you up!!"

Kamijou yelled at the dumb cat, but it just opened its mouth and made a meow noise.

What had he learned? That the stupid cat was, indeed, a stupid cat.

9 (Aug.31_PM08:15)

In actuality, Ouma Yamisaka was standing against the wall of the water tower on the roof of the hotel the stupid cat had stopped at. Index was laying a little ways off, tied up with rope.

He looked high and far up into the sky and clicked his tongue. From the information he had, Academy City kept a faithful eye on the entire city with a man-made satellite, but word was not spreading, nor had he been obstructed. However, he did not think those of Academy City were powerless. Perhaps they were letting him squirm for now.

...It matters not. I will simply get what I came here for, and furthermore, worm through their traps.

He had the will to do that from the start, so he did not fear the situation he was in.

He took a slow, deep breath and quietly opened both of his eyes.

If someone were to have seen him, they would have forgotten to breathe.

It wasn't that his eyes were terribly sharp or anything. Nor were they false, artificial ones.

He had a completely average pair of eyes.

He had pure eyes, utterly unfitting of one dressed in a jet-black suit, of a combat professional calling himself a sorcerer. They were the eyes of a young man who hadn't yet seen the world's darker side.

He took a photograph out of his suit pocket.

The woman in the picture was a complete stranger.

She was two, maybe three years older than Ouma—not a girl, but a woman. She had slight curves, a fair complexion, and looked like she would collapse if left out in the summer sun for even thirty minutes.

That impression was not mistaken. Her body had always been weak, ever since he saw her for the first time. And it was because of a curse—not something normal medicine could ever fix. From an eastern viewpoint, it was Jugondo voodoo magic using mirrors and swords. From a western perspective, it was a type of sympathetic magic, an imitative curse. It didn't matter what one called it. The only important thing was that she was on the verge of dying, beyond any help.

It wasn't as if the near-dead woman had asked him to save her.

All she could do anymore was give that exhausted smile.

Yamisaka had no connection to this woman. She was not family, nor was she a friend. They'd only exchanged words on occasion in the hospital courtyard, and she was unaware that he was a sorcerer in the first place. There was no need for him to take action for her sake. It wasn't a good enough reason for him to fight with his life on the line.

However, Yamisaka had always thought that if he became a sorcerer, he'd be able to do anything.

He never wanted to be discouraged again, so he vowed to become one.

Yamisaka didn't care about this woman. But he was supposed to be able to do anything. He was never supposed to be discouraged again. He couldn't let himself stumble over something so simple. He wouldn't give up on his dream over something so trivial.

That was all.

At least, it should have been.

"...Hmph."

He returned the picture to his pocket and closed his eyes once more, as if closing off his human heart, then looked up. Yamisaka's sense organs were all strengthened, so cutting off one or two posed no problem.

His gaze fell to Index. She was bound with rope all over her body, immobile and lying on the hard concrete surface...or at least, she should have been. At some point, she had gotten up, and now she was sitting cross-legged.

"This is surprising. You've managed to undo two of the knots in such a short time. Rope-binding techniques are not my specialty, but I did have confidence that I could at least bind low-class monsters."

The ropes tying Index's whole body up were as slender as electrical cables, but it made a fine *shimenawa*—the rope used in Shinto rituals. In simpler terms, she was currently imprisoned by an extremely small barrier.

Despite being cornered in an absolutely desperate situation, her expression held no fear.

"Ropes may be a method of torture unique to Japanese culture, but the sloppy job you've done won't make me talk."

Her words came out smoothly and easily.

Bindings. Despite their simple appearance, they were a gruesome form of torture that could potentially kill someone. For example, if a person tied somebody's wrists up and left them for three days, the stoppage of blood flow would allow them to be shown the sight of their own hands rotting away. The physical pain involved went without saying, but the mental anguish was immeasurable.

Index glared at Yamisaka.

In reality, **this sort of danger** was always present for the girl who protected the 103,000 grimoires. Therefore, she had developed a certain amount of endurance. She was purposely creating an ane-mic condition by regulating her breathing, thereby dulling the pain she felt.

But she had only a certain amount of it.

She wasn't confident that she would be able to maintain her own sanity even when her wrists, no longer receiving blood, began to rot away in front of her.

She actually had another layer of security that even she hadn't noticed, but it was currently disabled thanks to a certain boy's right hand.

Yamisaka exhaled slightly.

"I see. My rotten luck—you're still a member of the English Puri-tan Church, so you would have extensive knowledge of witch-hunting and trials."

"...Rotten? If that was a joke, then it was the worst one I've ever heard, I think."

"No, no. Such was not my intention. And by the way, I have no intention of torturing you, either."

"Then these ropes are far too tight. You can't just clench the arter-ies to my arms and feet or constrict my lungs like this! If you're still trying to let me live, then you could have just lightly tied my thumbs together and I wouldn't be able to move."

"I see. Your expertise is most welcome," responded Yamisaka in turn, undoing several of the knots as Index had suggested. This instead seemed to confuse her. He was acting far too honestly for an enemy.

He replied to the unspoken thought with a composed look. "As I have already said, torturing you is not my goal." He continued. "Of course, it is true that I want to get a certain grimoire out of you."

Index glared at him.

One hundred and three thousand grimoires all sealed away within her memories. Protecting them was her duty.

"Now, then..."

He coolly caught her stare.

"It will take a bit of time to prepare. First, I must draw an amplifi-cation barrier."

10 (Aug.31_PM09:21)

The stupid cat's odd diversion tactic wasted a lot of time.

Kamijou ran through the night streets, the cat's neck firmly in his grasp. It was way past dinnertime, and the students who had been out and about temporarily had all disappeared like a wave pulling back from the shore. The only noises floating through the near-empty streets now were the voices coming from televisions in shops and electronic stores. In one customer-less convenience store, he saw a lone man who looked like a part-timer (and who seemed quite bored), tending the register all alone.

I messed up. There may not be any time left.

Anxiety welled up inside him; he sighed to try and lessen it.

The man probably hadn't kidnapped Index to kill her...at least, he didn't think so. He also didn't think she'd come to harm very easily, either, but that obviously was not enough to bring him any peace of mind.

The most troubling part of all this was probably that he had no idea where to even start looking. He always got the feeling he was running directly away from where he needed to go. Everything he did caused him to get a little bit more impatient.

But I can't just stop at this point. Damn it! I'm at a huge disadvantage here. I need to get where I'm going and fast!

Kamijou swore under his breath, cursing that sister in white for causing him this much trouble, and was about to whip around a corner...

...when he nearly collided with a girl who had just come around it herself.

"Ack?! Wh-what do you think you're doing?!"

The one who screamed in such an extremely unfeminine manner had shoulder-length brown hair, a face that belied an unyielding spirit, and was wearing a gray pleated skirt, a short-sleeved blouse, and a summer sweater.

"I finally found you! You just left me there after that and ran away with the fake Unabara. Did something happen at lunchtime? I thought a whole building had collapsed on you, so I guess you're not hurt. Jeez, if you're safe, you should at least call me and say so!... Hm? Wait, you don't have my number, do you?"

Mikoto Misaka.

She was the ace of Tokiwadai Middle School, an elite institution for Ability Development, and an electric user, one of only seven Level Five espers in Academy City. The lightning spears she fired from her bangs reached more than one billion volts. Their relationship was more akin to that of sparring partners than friends, but Kamijou couldn't be bothered to care about any of this at the moment, so he ignored her and dashed around the bend.

Then, Mikoto, having been left behind, said, "Hey, wait! What? Wait a second! You're just gonna ignore me completely, huh?!"

She seems to be shouting at me, but it's not important.

Forward, forward!

"Hey! Don't you think you're being a little bit rude? Like, at all?!"

I said it before, and I'll say it again. It's not important.

You don't get to appear in the events of this episode.

"Don't...give me that...!! You do this every single time! Every single time, damn it!!"

He heard what he thought was the sound of sparks fizzling behind him.

Surprised, he turned around. Bluish-white sparks were flying off of Mikoto's bangs. As mentioned previously, Misaka's lightning spears were more than one billion volts. If the moniker *lightning spear* didn't spell it out for a person, then just try to think of a natural disaster flying straight at their face.

Kamijou put his right hand up.

It could nullify any abnormal powers just by touching them, whether they were supernatural abilities or magic. He understood that it could cancel out Mikoto's lightning spears, of course, but it didn't change the fact that this was terrifying. After all, he was thrusting his right hand straight toward a bolt of electricity.

Zap! The sparks leaped from her bangs.

Slam! The lightning attack shot through the air, a thunderclap trailing behind.

"?!"

But it hadn't been aimed at Kamijou. It struck a nearby cleaning robot that was currently busy trying to get a piece of gum off the pavement.

The robot's internal speaker exploded instantly. *Whump!!* The sound and force of the resulting shock wave ripped through the air and caused the glass doors of the department store next to them to shudder.

Of course, this caused intense damage to him, since the ear-splitting noise had gone off right next to him. The shock wave splashed into his ears and threw off his entire body's sense of balance and caused his feet to stagger. He stood there in place, head spinning. As for the stupid cat in his arms, its cute "Minyaa" cries had evolved into actual ones that sounded more like "Bgyaah!" and "Shaaaa!!"

On the other hand, Mikoto looked fairly pleased with herself that she'd stopped him.

"Hah, you finally stopped. I swear, you nearly smashed into me, and you didn't even say a word—um, hello? Why on earth do you look like you're about to cry?"

"I'm in a really, really big hurry here! Homework, kidnappings, there was a mess at the restaurant, I ran out without paying...!! Please, just try and figure the rest out by yourself!!"

Kamijou's more-than-half-desperate cries seemed to catch her off guard.

He didn't notice.

"Come on, what do you want?! What is it that you need?! If you have something to say, then please wait for the beep and explain in less than forty seconds! Okay, beep!!"

"Eh? Uh, huh? Well, I was just sort of mad that you weren't responding to me, but I didn't really have anything I needed from you...I didn't, but..."

"Sorry!"

He swiveled, turning his back to Mikoto, and dashed off again.

If he had calmly understood what she had just said, he would have heard what she had said as oddly friendly. Unfortunately, he didn't have enough time to analyze it.

"Wha…hey! Are you actually just gonna leave like that?! Hey!!"

She's shouting something behind me, but it's not important. Forward, forward!

11 (Aug.31_PM09:52)

Index couldn't quite get a grip on the situation she was in at the moment.

All that her presumed enemy, the sorcerer, had done was tie her up. He hadn't caused her any more harm. He appeared to be trying to draw a barrier around the area by using thin *shimenawa* ropes (it seemed his comment that he was not a specialist in rope-binding techniques had been a modest one). Evidently he'd pushed Index to the back of his mind for now.

The idea of him thinking, *Yeah, she's over there, tied up with rope* was certainly not proper manners to show a girl. Even so, she supposed she should be grateful for what was, in essence, a first-class treatment as a prisoner.

The torture employed in witch hunts could be thought of in terms of orange juice. One would just squeeze the orange—their body—until the juice—the information they had—came out. No one cared what happened to the squashed orange. If they had any thought as to the pain of a discarded orange, then they wouldn't be doing any capturing in the first place.

Even within the English Puritan Church, only a very few people could actually do **that**. Index didn't specialize in combat, so she couldn't hurt people anyway. And in reality, most of the Inquisitors sitting in on the trials would use suggestion and magic drugs on themselves in order to temporarily erase their sense of guilt toward what they were doing. One didn't come across the kind of person who could squeeze a person like an orange with a totally straight face.

Index watched the sorcerer as he created the barrier in front of her.

This person didn't seem to be able to make orange juice.

Was that because he was weak?

Or was it...?

12 (Aug.31_PM10:07)

"Hah! Hah!!"

Kamijou had been running around the city aimlessly, steadily throwing Mikoto Misaka off his trail, but he just couldn't find Index anywhere.

"Ah, forget this! There's less than two hours left in the day! What am I supposed to do about my homework?! If that lolicon makes it so that I can't finish it, I'm seriously gonna kill him!!"

He continued his maniac sprint through the night streets, spouting what would make him sound to a bystander like an extremely dangerous person.

But his voice also sounded like he was trying to force down some great anxiety. It had already been a few hours since Index had been taken away.

I can't do this myself. Should I just be honest and report this?

Academy City's peacekeeping system was not made up of a normal police department, but rather by Anti-Skills and Judgment. Anti-Skills was a corps of teachers armed with high-tech weaponry, while Judgment was a force made up of espers chosen from the student population.

Even if he had run and fled in order to evade pursuit, psychometers could read his destination from things left behind at the scene of the crime. It was probably safer to crush him with sheer numbers in this case, too.

But...

Kamijou bit back. Index was from the world of the occult, not

Academy City. She had essentially smuggled herself in. If he carelessly asked for help from the police, he ran the very real risk of causing a wholly different problem.

What do I do?

He stopped. There was a police box right nearby.

What do I do?!

As he debated the decision, a man standing in front of the police box came over to him. *Did I look so panicked?* He still wasn't sure he wanted to consult anyone, but the male Anti-Skills officer was rapidly approaching.

Before he could say anything, the Anti-Skill said this:

"Would you happen to be the one who broke the glass and caused an uproar at a restaurant in the Seventh School District?"

"Eh?"

"We had a psychometer read the mind of the manager who put in the damage report and draw a likeness…Wait, I feel like I've seen you before. Ah, right, we've had witnesses saying that they spotted you this afternoon, too, when the building in District Seven collapsed. That was what caused them to issue code orange…I don't think they could have gone to code red just from the one incident, but…"

"…………Huh?"

Kamijou smiled without emotion and made an about-face…

…and began to sprint away incredibly fast.

I left that sorcerer with Tsuchimikado, since he had nowhere else to go, but…is he actually looking after him like he's supposed to be? he thought, running away at a terrifying speed.

"H-hey! Just you wait a minute! Stop, I say!!"

He didn't stop, and he certainly didn't wait. He continued to speed down the road—if anyone from the track team had seen him, they'd be drooling at the prospect of recruiting him. *Can I shake him? Did I shake him? Aha-ha, you slow-ass tortoise!* he thought, bathing in victory, when suddenly he heard the *bang* of a gunshot ring out behind him.

He looked back to see white smoke billowing from the .22 the Anti-Skill had taken out.

It had been a beautiful horizontal shot. And the first one, too.

"Wait, the hell?! You tryin' to kill me or something, you punk officer?! You can't treat people like that!!"

"There is no need to fear. We know children's rights. These are rubber bullets."

"You mean that thing's loaded?! Wait, you can still break a few bones even with rubber bullets!" screamed Kamijou, fleeing into a back alley. This wasn't the time to be thinking about his homework or about what time it was. The only thing he thought was this: Was Index safe?

13 (Aug.31_PM10:52)

Innumerable ropes hung on the top of the building.

From afar, it might have looked like the flag display at an athletic meet. Ropes extended in every direction from the top of the water tank and were tied to the fences on the edge of the building. Dozens of talismans with symbols drawn in ink on Japanese paper hung from them at regular intervals.

Index looked quizzically at it, still sitting tied up.

"This is…a kagura stage?"

Kagura—a dance dedicated to the gods.

"It is nothing so outrageous. At present, it is more like a Bon Odori stage. The syncretizing of Shinto and Buddhism, if you will," responded Yamisaka.

Now that he mentioned it, the water tank did look like the *yagura*, or the raised platform on which people stood, and the ropes stretching from the *yagura* looked like the lines of lanterns that traditionally hung from them (though Index's information source on this was only made up of pictures from books—and it was only in recent history that *yagura* and lanterns began to be used in Bon Odori).

The normal Bon dance and the more religious kagura dances were two separate things, of course. However, when a person traced them back from an occult point of view, Bon Odori was a dance offered to the dead for the repose of their souls—so it was similar to kagura in that one would come into contact with spiritual entities.

Just like Bon Odori, one would create a ritual site and align it with specific rules, and then multiple people would spin around in a circle. That in itself implied some sort of spiritual contact. The Rochtein Circuit, a devil-worshipping ritual in the western world; the Cottage Square, a modern urban legend—those and others all expressed similar things in different forms across different cultures and time periods.

But why is he preparing something like this?...Is he going to try and make me tell him someth— Ow!

Her rear end came down on something. She squirmed to get out of the way and saw that it was a cell phone. It was an extremely slip-shod, zero-yen phone that Kamijou had given her, but Index didn't know how to use it. The screen was brightening up for some reason, but Index, still with her hands tied and knowing she mustn't incite Yamisaka, wormed her way in front of the cell phone to hide it. She pressed a few buttons on the way, but she didn't think about it.

Thankfully, Yamisaka didn't seem to notice.

As if boasting about the bow strapped to his right arm, he said, "What? My hidden intention for drawing this barrier was to strengthen this, even by a bit. This bow was originally meant for the one dancing, after all."

Index gave the barrier a brief glance and let the knowledge in her brain do the rest.

"An azusa bow?" she surmised, invoking the Japanese name for the catalpa tree.

"Excellent. I see that grimoire library of yours covers Japanese culture as well."

An azusa bow was a Shinto ritual tool. It was said to be not for firing arrows but for destroying demons using a shock wave made from the sound of pulling and releasing the bowstring. It was origi-nally a musical instrument used in kagura, by a shrine maiden dur-ing her dance; the sound would lead her into a trance and assist her in summoning a god.

"It normally only has the power to deliver a slight impact to the mind to correct imperfections." Yamisaka looked at the ropes above.

"However, with all the proper conditions fulfilled...I can read a person's mind in detail. Yes—I could even expose the 103,000 grimoires you're desperately concealing in your heart."

Index looked at him incredulously, and a moment later, the space around them began to glow faintly, the light seeming to come from the ropes hung every which way. Using the mechanisms in his right hand's azusa bow, Yamisaka pulled the bowstring.

"Y-you can't!" shouted Index like a young child. "What I have isn't what you're thinking it is! If a normal person even glances at one of them, they'll go insane. Even if you're a specialized sorcerer, you couldn't endure even thirty of them! You know what would happen if anyone but me reads the 103,000 grimoires, don't you?!"

Ouma Yamisaka smiled quietly, as if truly caring about what his enemy had said.

Then, he responded, "Of course. I am fully aware."

14 (Aug.31_PM11:10)

As Kamijou ran through the dark streets trying to throw off Anti-Skills, he listened.

He could hear the voices of Index and the pervert over the cell phone. All of a sudden, he'd gotten an incoming call from Index's zero-yen cell phone, which should have been turned off. Their voices were muffled somewhat, as if there was a piece of cloth over the microphone. And she wasn't trying to converse with Kamijou, either. It was like he was overhearing someone else's conversation.

Tiing.

With an odd noise, the roof of a far-off building began to glow faintly. It looked like a huge pillar of light going straight up into the clouds.

That's...Damn it, that's the hotel I was at before!! What the hell did I do all this work for?!

Of course, he didn't have any proof that Index was actually there. But he didn't have any other places to check. He decided, for now, to visit every likely location and plotted a course toward the building.

15 (Aug.31_PM11:20)

Something strange happened right after it began.

Wrapped in the light of the giant barrier, Yamisaka, having pulled the string, began to shake and shiver like he was sick with the flu. A disgusting sweat broke out all over him, and his eyes began to lose focus and waver.

What Yamisaka was doing was simply reading Index's mind. There was no spell or technique involved, so nothing could go wrong. This magic didn't have any dangerous side effects in the first place.

Nevertheless, he clearly felt his life draining away.

That was how utterly poisonous the 103,000 grimoires stowed away inside the girl's mind were.

"——, —————!!"

Merciless pain was trying to pound out of his skull. He found himself unable to speak.

Not even Yamisaka was considering getting all 103,000 of the grimoires. Copying that many of them into one's own head was impossible anyway.

He just needed one. It was called *Baopuzi*. It was a grimoire from Chinese culture meant for becoming an immortal, ageless hermit. Within it would be written the Chinese alchemy that could create an elixir, which would heal any illness or curse.

That one was all he needed to get.

Replicas with added nonsense information and copies with mistaken interpretations would not do—if he had the one grimoire that was the absolute closest to the original work, it should have been enough.

"—————, ——!!"

And yet just the one grimoire had this much force.

At this point, Yamisaka understood why those replicas and copies had been made impure and had tactless, thoughtless additions in them. It was because their poison was just too strong. So strong that unless they were messed up in some way, normal people couldn't even stand reading a few paragraphs.

Yamisaka looked at the girl. She was shouting at him to stop.

Just reading one page felt like the grimoire was gouging out his brain. This girl had gotten 103,000 whole volumes into her head.

That wasn't something a human could do.

And yet she had done so. There was no doubt at all that she was something profoundly abnormal.

"_____!!".

Page after page of the venomous grimoire was dragged into his brain at each sounding of his bowstring. Each toxic page mixed into his mind like milk into coffee, soiling it.

But Yamisaka kept on. He gritted his teeth and drew the bow again.

So far he had lived thinking that if he became a sorcerer he could do anything. He had vowed to become one, never wanting to be set back or frustrated again. He couldn't allow himself to stumble here. There was a woman on the verge of death. She no longer even had the willpower to cry out for help. She was powerless, able only to smile in the face of approaching death. If he couldn't save one insignificant woman, then he would be set back and he would be frustrated. He would never even think of harming the dream he held because of some insignificant woman like her.

And so he drew the bowstring back.

Even if blood were to pour from his eyes and ears, he would acquire the grimoire he was after with his own hands.

He wounded his body and drowned himself in sin for the sake of his ambitions.

It was not for the sake of such an insignificant woman.

And it was certainly not her fault!

16 (Aug.31_PM11:37)

Kamijou kicked in the back door of the building, rushed inside, and sprinted up the emergency stairwell.

"...You're wrong!"

As he ran, he heard Index's voice coming from the cell phone.

"I can tell. That azusa bow—you've strengthened it too much. It's flowing upstream, back into your mind. I can tell!"

Her voice was pained, as if she might break into tears.

As if steadily understanding a breaking heart.

"You loved her. That's all! That's why you wanted to save her life, even at the risk of your own. But to save her, you needed to hurt others and commit crimes. You didn't want her to have to bear that responsibility. You never wanted to tell her that it was her fault you committed them, or that you wouldn't have needed to if it wasn't for her!"

Index's shouts were trying to stop someone.

"No, that was all it was! So...so please, don't ruin yourself, even if it would undo the curse on that woman! If you're destroyed, then she'll have to live with the guilt for the rest of her life!"

Kamijou, still running, clenched his teeth.

"You want to save that woman, don't you? You wanted to reach out to her, even if you were the only one! You just couldn't ignore the fact that someone was cursed to death, that's all! So you mustn't... you mustn't resort to such unworthy methods!!"

So that's how it is, thought Kamijou, getting the picture.

He accelerated his mad dash to the top floor. He went straight for the door leading out onto the roof and, too impatient to turn the doorknob to open it, simply kicked it down.

17 (Aug.31_PM11:47)

As soon as he got onto the roof, Kamijou's right hand touched something.

It was the end of one of the ropes creating the barrier. As soon as his fingers came into contact with it, it crumbled and vanished, as if instantly fading with time. Like that, its speed was as fierce as the light on a fuse.

In no time at all, the destruction spread from that rope to the others, and finally, the dim glow surrounding them disappeared as well. The next thing he knew, it was just a normal hotel roof again.

The stupid cat slipped out of his arms and down to the floor.

It probably didn't understand what was going on at all. It left Kamijou's side and defenselessly walked over toward Index, who was sitting on the ground, tied up.

And Index was…Well, he didn't really understand, but she was tied up in a fairly complex manner with ropes. From where he stood, she didn't look injured or anything. Her clothes weren't even messed up.

Kamijou diverted his gaze.

He looked at the man standing one step to the side of her.

It was the pervert—er, rather, the sorcerer.

All of the large man's veins were standing out on his skin. He was drenched in so much sweat it looked like he'd been rained on, and a band of blood came out of the side of one of his closed eyes like a teardrop, coming down over his cheek.

The sorcerer, whose name Kamijou didn't know, quietly faced him.

"…Is it wrong?"

Click. Using the mechanism in his bow, he pulled the string and repeated, "Is it so wrong to want to protect someone, even at the cost of your own life?"

A silence descended upon the darkness.

The night breeze blowing between the two of them was a cold one, not at all gentle.

And Kamijou answered, "Of…course it is!

"You know the pain of losing someone important, don't you? You know the suffering of not being able to do a single thing for somebody who is suffering and hurting right in front of you, don't you?"

Kamijou knew it.

He was able to answer the man because it had been forced upon him in that white hospital room on that day.

"You were panicked. You were in pain. You were suffering. You were hurting. You were scared. You were trembling. You were shouting. You were crying…So don't do it. You can't go pushing that kind of massive shock onto somebody else!"

Instead of an answer, the sorcerer silently readied his bow.

He probably already knew what was right and what was wrong at this point.

But even still, he couldn't give up.

Because he was scared.

He was scared more than anything else in the world of losing the one person important to him.

"Executioner Bowstring."

That was the name of the magic that created the compressed blades of air. Kamijou began to run at the same time he announced it. He balled his right hand into a fist to stop this single magician, who was just too kind and too weak.

But his fist never reached.

Before the bowstring snapped, the sorcerer's body wavered and he fell to the ground.

He wasn't getting back up.

Red fluid oozed from his fallen body, staining the floor below.

Kamijou paled and he sprinted over to the sorcerer at full speed.

The sorcerer's mouth opened slowly, as if he had felt him coming near.

With a wet sigh filled with blood, his bloodstained lips formed words.

"What nonsense. I read just one book…and now I'm like this." His voice somehow sounded extremely sleepy. "My tiny vessel was far too small to obtain even one of the original copies in the first place. Ha-ha…what is this? My life is full of failures. I've already given up three times so far."

"…"

"There was something I could never give up on, though."

The sorcerer looked toward the moon hovering in the sky and managed a smile.

Tears began to fall from his closed eyelids, just too kind and too weak.

"Just one thing…that was all…but…"

His lips' movements slowed, then finally stopped.

Kamijou heard Index gasping.

He bit down onto his lip and then said one thing.

"Get him."

At his command, the stupid cat ran up to them and executed a full-strength combo attack on the sorcerer's face with its claws.

"Bgh?! Gbah?!"

"I didn't give you permission to wrap up the conversation like that, you asshole," murmured Kamijou with a sigh, relatively serious, looking down at the sorcerer.

"That was for my summer homework. Jeez! There's no hope left to finish it now, and it's all your fault. What I'm saying is, I'm prepared to help you out, even if it means I have to stand out in the hallway later, so you could at least let me get in a cat attack."

The sorcerer moved his mouth up and down, trying to say something, but Kamijou didn't think about it. He continued, asking, "So where is this important person of yours, anyway?"

"Gha, gheh...what?"

"What I mean is, we can do something without having to use the archive of forbidden books, got it?" Kamijou scratched his head lightly. "Like this right hand I have. It's called Imagine Breaker. It's a weird power that can cancel out any other weird powers, like magic and supernatural abilities. **Of course, a curse, or whatever the hell the problem is, is no exception**."

Kamijou waved his right hand toward him as if expecting a handshake.

The sorcerer's expression froze.

"Eh...?"

"I'm no sorcerer, so I don't have a clue what a curse is, **but if I use this, the curse will just disappear completely, won't it?**"

"Wh...a...impossible."

"Far from it. You just saw me do it! **I wiped out all your wind**

swords. Do you understand? I'll say it once. I don't need your stinking logic. **That's just how my right hand works**."

The sorcerer, whose name he did not know, listened to Kamijou, dumbstruck.

He didn't know how to react to such a sudden and unexpected development.

He had never dared to hope he'd even get a second chance.

Kamijou, for his part, scratched his head casually again.

"Anyway. It may be tough, but you're gonna take me there. Also, sorry, but I need to get back by tomorrow at seven to make it to my entrance ceremony...Wait, do trains run at this time? Oh, also, a curse, right? Isn't it the kind of evil magician sort of thing you read about in books? Does that mean I have to crush that guy, too? What a pain."

The sorcerer listened silently to Kamijou essentially talking to himself.

At last, he asked...

...slowly and fearfully, seeming uneasy that he wasn't letting go of his hand, "Uh...are...are you actually serious?"

"Of course I am. You totally wasted all my summer homework. It's all your fault! I'm not going home empty-handed at this point!" said Kamijou angrily. "So you're gonna take responsibility for this, got it? You're going to show me where this person is even if I have to drag you there. I don't give a damn whether we're on code red or what. We're gonna save that important person of yours. It's your job to come up with an excuse for me forgetting my homework, at least, got it?"

Time had stopped for the sorcerer. Kamijou smiled at him quite savagely.

"For that, I need your help. Not anyone else's—I need your help to do it. So you're gonna help out whether you like it or not. You want to save her with your own hands, right?"

The sorcerer groaned in confusion.

At Kamijou's words, his facial expression twisted and distorted.

Then, tears began to streak down his face, as though from melting ice.

Kamijou sighed. Then, he had a sudden thought.

"I guess that means I'm giving up on my homework...or, hmm, yeah, I'll...wait. Hey, can I go get my homework before we leave?"

Sep.01_AM00:00 End

EPILOGUE
The Night It Ended
Welcome_to_Tomorrow.

0 (Sep.01_AM00:00 timeover)

"Surgery complete. Right, that was some good work, everyone."

Kikyou Yoshikawa opened her eyes at the voice. She didn't know what time it was. She didn't know where she was. She seemed to have been sleeping somewhere. She could only see a blue tiled floor and walls. The ceiling was completely white, and there were glass windows lined up on the walls close to the ceiling. It was like a gallery.

She heard a metallic *click* sound from outside her vision. There was a guillotine-esque synthetic fiber curtain hanging near her neck, so she couldn't see anything going on farther down. The only part of her she could move was her head. The rest wasn't moving. She couldn't even feel any of it.

Then, someone peered into her face.

It was a middle-aged man, his hair wrapped in a green hat, his mouth covered by a large, similarly colored mask. His face looked like a frog's, and he was looking down at her like she was an old friend sleeping in the grass.

Yoshikawa finally realized where she was and immediately gave a *tsk*.

"Such bad taste. Heart surgery with local anesthesia?"

"Best to lighten the burden as much as possible, no?"

Local anesthesia was something one used on simple surgeries, like removing an appendix. The patient was conscious during the surgery, and some patients even got to see the process happening with a hand mirror.

But one wouldn't use local anesthesia for something as huge as heart surgery. It wasn't a matter of whether or not it had merits. A person just didn't do it. It would be like a street performance. The doctor may as well have been holding a scalpel between his toes.

And yet this doctor had done it and the surgery had succeeded.

She couldn't imagine why. Maybe they'd come out with a new method of surgery.

He was the Heaven Canceler.

He prevailed over any injury or disease. He would do whatever it took, making use of new technologies and theories not even approved for use by the Academy City General Board, much less by the medical world outside the city. He had only one belief: never to abandon a patient. He walked his own path with only that in his heart.

His skills were said to be able to bend even God's will and that he had once triumphed over even aging and life span by developing a special life-support device using untested theories. Nobody understood what he thought at that point, but she'd never heard of him continuing to do any life-span research after that. She only knew that there existed a single test model, safely installed in a certain windowless building.

"…So this means that I survived, then."

"Of course you did. Who do you think performed your operation?" he said in an easygoing way, never once showing any stress to his patients. "Though you were in a real bad state. Even I can't heal a dead person, after all. Perhaps you should thank that boy for it."

"That boy…Wait, what happened to him? But wait…I was shot straight through the heart with a military-grade handgun at point-blank range, wasn't I?"

"To be precise, it didn't go through your heart, but instead ruptured the coronary artery coming out of it. Well, either way, you probably would have died on the spot if left alone."

Her coronary artery—it was the largest artery in the body, connected to the heart. Its rupture meant certain death, of course. It was no different from severing the carotid artery with a knife.

"But then, that…"

"Hm? Well, that's probably because of the boy's ability to control blood flow. He was almost like an invisible hose—he passed the blood from your torn artery from one opening to the other, without letting a single drop go. Thanks to him, we could transport you here without you dying, and after I connected a hastily built bypass, we headed for the surgical room. You really should thank that boy. He was using his power all the way until you got to the surgical room, even though he was unconscious, you see."

"…" Yoshikawa listened, baffled.

"Three hours have passed since we brought you here, and it sure isn't smooth sailing over there, either. He's having to endure the removal of skull fragments from where his frontal lobe was pierced. I'm about to go over there to cheer them on—is there anything you want to tell him?"

"…You aren't using local anesthesia on him, too, I presume," she reflexively asked, though she knew the answer was of course not. "Will he be okay?"

"Hm? Well, his frontal lobe is injured, after all. It'll effect his speech and mathematical abilities, see?"

"His mathematical abilities…"

For Accelerator, that could be lethal. In order to alter vectors, he needed to calculate the vector before changing it and the vector afterward. His unconscious reflection was no more than him solving the simplest equations without thinking about them.

He might not be able to use his power anymore—not even his "simple" reflection.

"Well, I don't think there will be any problem, hm?" The doctor must have figured out what she was thinking from her expression. "It's my creed to do something about the impossible, see? I will restore his speech function and mathematical abilities."

His last sentence hadn't ended with the upward-rising rhetorical question that time.

Yoshikawa was about to catch her breath, but the doctor turned and said in a breezy voice, "Of course, I'll need his own understanding and consent. You seem to have made something quite troublesome as well, so I'm going to use that. Do you think ten thousand brain links would be enough to compensate for a single person's language and mathematical functions?"

Ten thousand. The Sisters. Last Order.

"! R-right! What about her?!"

"Oh, the girl in the glass vessel? There's no need to worry about her. Fortunately, I've come into the care of a similar child. I believe her serial number was 10032—Little Misaka, was it?"

"Wait...wait a minute. You have...incubators here?"

"I will procure anything my patients need, see? And I've heard all about this. It seems there's a parallel arithmetic network that created the ten thousand clones, too. I'm going to use that in order to restore the lost parts of the boy's brain. What? I'm not returning lost memories, I'm only substituting for his lost functions. It's not that difficult a thing to do, see?" declared the doctor in an easygoing voice, though for a moment, a cloud came over his expression.

Lost memories.

It was said that even this doctor could not return the memories of a certain hospitalized high school student back at the end of July. That was probably the first defeat he'd ever tasted.

"But that network can only be made up of people who have the same brain-wave wavelengths. Accelerator's are different, so if he forces himself to log in, the conflicting wavelengths will fry his brain."

"Then we just need to come up with a converter that can match the two wavelengths. Design-wise, perhaps it would be a choker with electrodes attached to the inside?"

He said it so simply, but the amount of skill and budget needed for such a venture would be staggering. He probably wouldn't hesitate even when he found out, though. And he wouldn't ask for the development funds from anyone else. That's the kind of person he was.

"Well, then, off I go for real this time. What are you going to do?"

"What am I...?"

"You seem to be suffering with extreme anxiety, but it looks like the higher-ups have been informed of this incident, see? The lab has been dissolved, and the experiment is now entirely stopped, not just frozen. In other words, you've been laid off. It wasn't a private establishment, so you won't have to shoulder any monetary debt, and the whole gun thing can probably be explained away as pure self-defense. But it is a rather large ignominy, an entire laboratory going under. I don't believe you can live as a scientist anymore, do you?"

"...Then I wonder...what other road is there for me?"

"Plenty, I would think?" he responded easily. "There are plenty of roads to choose from."

Yoshikawa's eyes glazed over at that as she remembered days long past.

One of a multitude of paths—perhaps one of them was as a schoolteacher. A teacher who was kind, not soft. Perhaps the path was to teach the important things to Accelerator and Last Order, who didn't have a scrap of common sense.

That was an attractive prospect.

So attractive that she gave a tiny smile in spite of herself.

"Hey...," she addressed the doctor, who had his back turned and was about to leave the room.

"What is it?"

"Please save that boy. If you can't, then I'll never forgive you."

"I wonder who you think you're talking to. That is my battlefield, all right? And I always come back alive from the battlefield—along with my patients, who had been fighting by themselves the whole time."

The doctor left the surgical room.

Yoshikawa closed her eyes. The people wearing operating gowns around her seemed to be finishing up, but she didn't pay attention to them. She directed her awareness inward, as if she would just go to sleep.

And then, she remembered the words of one boy.

And she recalled his words.

"You have any idea who you're askin' here? I'm the big bad guy. I killed ten thousand of 'em, you know? You're telling the villain to save someone? Are you serious? I can kill anything, but I can't save anyone."

"How about that." Yoshikawa gave the most minute of smiles. "He managed to do it anyway."

AFTERWORD

To everyone who has been reading since Volume 1: It's great to see you again.

To those courageous souls who purchased all five volumes at once: It's nice to meet you.

I'm Kazuma Kamachi.

This volume was more of a collection of short stories. It contains three parts, with stories printed on Dengeki Bunko's website (with plenty of revisions) and newly written material. The time in this series has always moved at a pretty gradual pace, but this one was far and away the slowest of them all. Looking back on the rest of them, it seems that I managed to stretch summer vacation out for five whole volumes.

Volume 5 was not constructed around an occult keyword or a particular heroine. Instead, the theme was August 31 in Academy City. This was a collection of short stories, so I needed to do things that couldn't otherwise be done in a full novel—so I put a certain character in the spotlight and created a variety of underlying themes shared by all the chapters (for example, the legendary Misaka-ignoring game). In short, I just did what I pleased.

There are plenty of other small topics that could probably go into short stories, like background on Index and Stiyl; background on

Kamijou, Aogami, and Miss Komoe; background on Mikoto and Kuroko Shirai…But this time, I wanted to do this sort of story. If I have a chance in the future, I would definitely like to build on those ideas as well.

My illustrator, Mr. Haimura, and my editor, Ms. Miki, have always been there through this entire process. I'd like to give another huge word of thanks to them and ask for their continued support going forward.

And for the readers, who so graciously picked up this book: There is no doubt in my mind that you're all the reason my inexperienced self was even able to publish five volumes. Thank you so much for all of your support.

Now, then, as I thank you for deigning to lay eyes on this book,

and as I wait eagerly for something to make it up to you,

today, at this moment, I lay down my pen.

By the way, Miss Komoe is the oldest heroine so far…What do you think, eh?

Kazuma Kamachi